Keegan contrived
to cancel her date

"How dare you!" Jancis snapped. "You lying, blackmailing, high-handed obnoxious...!" All her frustration poured out.

He acknowledged her description with a slight inclination of his dark head. "And you're bad tempered, pigheaded, rude... and now that we understand each other, shall we get on with some work?"

"You don't think you won that easily, do you?" she retorted scornfully.

His dark eyes showed his amusement. "What frustration will do for a woman!"

"Frustration?" She was puzzled.

"It showed in every line of your body when you kissed Mortimer," Keegan sneered.

"All right, so I enjoy kissing him. It's infinitely preferable to kissing you," she said recklessly.

Silence. Her last remark had almost amounted to a challenge and, judging from the gleam in Keegan's eyes, he was not going to ignore it.

ANNABEL MURRAY
is also the author of this

Harlequin Romance

2549—ROOTS OF HEAVEN

Keegan's Kingdom

Annabel Murray

Harlequin Books

TORONTO • NEW YORK • LOS ANGELES • LONDON
AMSTERDAM • PARIS • SYDNEY • HAMBURG
STOCKHOLM • ATHENS • TOKYO • MILAN

Original hardcover edition published in 1983
by Mills & Boon Limited

ISBN 0-373-02558-0

Harlequin Romance first edition July 1983

For my family—for their
encouragement

CHAPTER ONE

'KEEGAN LEROY! Why is *he* coming here?'

Jancis King's normally soft brown eyes hardened suspiciously, as she looked at her mother.

Mrs King swallowed nervously, anticipating the storm of protest which she knew would ensue once she answered her daughter's question.

'He . . . he's coming to look at the stables. He . . .'

'Mummy!' Jancis' heart-shaped face paled under the honey-tan. 'You wouldn't! You couldn't possibly consider selling The Kingdom to Keegan Leroy? Not him of all people!'

Mrs King's voice was pleading.

'But, darling, you knew we'd have to sell up. Neither you nor I is capable of running a large racing stables. It takes a man, and since . . . since Daddy . . .' She faltered into silence.

Jancis was instantly contrite. She flew to her mother's side, her strong young arms around Mrs King's slight, shaking shoulders.

'I know, I know, Mummy. I'm sorry. But why Keegan Leroy? Why him?' she repeated.

'Because,' Mrs King said drearily, 'he's the only person with both the money and the necessary expertise who's shown any interest. You know The Kingdom hasn't been too successful these last few years . . .'

'Primarily due to Keegan Leroy himself,' Jancis interrupted fiercely. 'Taking away several of our biggest and richest owners!'

'We must be fair, darling,' Mrs Kingdom pleaded. 'The owners hadn't been too satisfied with results. It wasn't Daddy's fault. He hadn't been really well for some time, you know . . . and I'm afraid he'd relied too heavily on his head lad, and of course Sam Roscoe, his jockey. When Sam left . . .'

7

'Also lured away by the disgustingly rich Mr Leroy,' Jancis commented.

'Yes ... well ...' Mrs King shrugged hopelessly. 'What's done is done. I don't like the idea any more than you. I knew you'd be cross with me, but what else *could* I do? We have to sell up ... and soon.'

'So you invited Keegan Leroy to look over the place ... without even telling me!' Jancis' brown eyes were reproachful.

Mrs King's expression was one of rueful guilt.

'I was afraid you wouldn't come home from college if I told you beforehand ... and I *do* want you to show him round.'

'*Me?*' Jancis said incredulously. 'Show *him* round?'

'I know, dear. I know how you feel about him. But you're more at home with horses than I am ... and so knowledgeable about the day-to-day running of the stable. And I thought, if we could impress him, we might get a better price.'

Jancis' first panic-stricken impulse was to refuse ... to escape before the hated Keegan Leroy could arrive, but the sight of her mother's pale, unhappy face tugged at her soft heart. Mary King was far too gentle a person to deal effectively with the self-made, arrogant man who for so long had been their near neighbour and her father's professional rival. Jancis wasn't even sure that she herself could deal with the threat he posed. But someone had to face him, and it had better be her. At least her detestation for the wretched man would provide her with a protective barrier against the bitter knowledge that the stables must be sold ... making her better able to withstand the ordeal than her mother, still utterly defenceless, crushed by her grief.

She sighed resignedly, combing a slim hand through tangled copper curls.

'What time is the horrible creature arriving?'

Mrs King was apologetic.

'I should think he'll be here in about fifteen minutes ... if he's punctual.'

'*What?*'

It was worse than Jancis had thought. Really, her mother might have given her more warning ... time to collect herself. Basically shy, Jancis hated the sensation of being, as it were, thrown into the deep end of a situation ... especially, she thought darkly, this particular situation. It would have been preferable almost to have to encounter a complete stranger, than Keegan Leroy. With a stranger, she could have been her natural, friendly self, even allowed herself the luxury of admitting their reluctance ... their sorrow at having to part with The Kingdom ... but never, *never* would her pride permit Keegan Leroy to witness any display of emotion on her part.

Her mother's soft, troubled voice interrupted her turbulent thoughts.

'Hadn't you better go and change, or something?'

Puzzled, Jancis looked down at the dainty turquoise summer dress, which made a striking foil for her glowing auburn curls. She was perfectly tidy ... apart from her hair. Enquiringly, she looked at her mother.

'I just thought, dear ...' Mary King said hesitantly, 'that you might look more ... more capable in jodhpurs, or at least a pair of slacks ...' Her voice became even more uncertain before Jancis' indignant gaze.

'Keegan Leroy can think what he jolly well likes about my appearance! It's the stables, the horses he's coming to look at, not me!'

Well aware that her daughter's temper could be as fiery as her hair, Mary King spoke soothingly.

'All right, dear, I'm sure you know best ... and you look very lovely. But Jancis,' she begged, 'you won't do ... or say ... anything to upset him, will you? He really is our only hope.'

'I'll be on my best behaviour,' Jancis promised grudgingly, 'though it goes against the grain to be polite to that monster.'

'And you won't let him get under your skin, dear?' Mary persisted. 'You know how arrogant and sarcastic he can be?'

Did she not! Jancis thought, remembering her very first encounter with Keegan Leroy. It had been at Doncaster, almost eighteen months ago, where both trainers had horses running in nearly all of the races. Keegan Leroy had only recently bought the neighbouring establishment, and Jancis and her father had been curious about the newcomer.

That fateful first meeting had taken place in the paddock, where Jancis, as capable as any of her father's lads, was leading their entry for the first race. The moment came for the jockeys to mount and their respective trainers were issuing last instructions. Sam Roscoe, the Kings' professional jockey, was late mounting and Purdey's Dad, a powerful brown gelding, was already sweating up badly. Seeing the other horses beginning to move away for the canter down to the start, the powerful animal plunged strongly, dragging the leading rein from Jancis' hands. Curvetting sideways, he jostled a tall man standing nearby, so that he almost fell beneath the horse's flailing hoofs.

Jancis would never forget the man's contemptuous, furious anger, his biting sarcasm, the totally unnecessary remarks he had made ... about allowing incompetent schoolgirls to handle valuable animals. Jancis knew that her slight build and wayward curls ... which no hairdresser had ever been able to train into a sophisticated style ... made her seem younger than her actual years. But at twenty-two, to be dubbed a schoolgirl! It still rankled after all this time ... nearly two years later.

So it had been mutual antipathy at first sight and when Keegan Leroy, for so the dark stranger proved to be, became so successful that owners transferred their horses to his care, Jancis hated him even more, for what he was doing to her father and to his establishment, registered as 'The Kingdom Stables', but always referred to in racing circles as 'The Kingdom'.

The doorbell rang ... a long, demanding peal. None of their friends ever kept their finger on the button for so long ... so strongly. Jancis looked at her mother, both faces registering apprehension. It could only be Keegan Leroy, predictably right on time.

Unconsciously squaring her slim shoulders, and making the most of her five foot three inches, Jancis walked to the front door, her pace deliberately slow. She refused to hurry for *him*.

Drawing a deep breath, she opened the door and looked up into the dark, impatient face of the man who stood there.

Keegan Leroy was not a handsome man. His features were

too harsh, too sharply incised for beauty. His black hair, which Jancis scornfully considered to be too long for a man of his age, curled over the neck of the bright yellow sweater, worn with impeccably tailored jodphurs and highly polished boots. Black, snapping eyes casuaoly appraised Jancis, as she stood in the doorway, and the surprisingly full, sensuous lips compressed impatiently.

'Well, are you going to ask me in, or am I expected to conduct my business here on the doorstep?'

Flushing, she stood aside, gesturing towards the drawing room.

'My mother is in there, Mr Leroy.'

He nodded and without waiting for her to precede him, strode towards the half-open door, which he then proceeded to close behind him.

Furiously Jancis flung it open again, stalking after him, her brown eyes smouldering.

Mrs King rose from the settee to greet the visitor.

'Welcome to The Kingdom,' Mr Leroy. I . . . I don't think you've been here before?'

'No,' he agreed shortly. 'Your husband and I were not on visiting terms.'

'How surprising!' Not for the life of her could Jancis have repressed the sarcastic words. Her father had been a good, decent man, but in Jancis' opinion, he would have needed to be a saint to make a friend of his rival trainer.

Keegan turned upon her immediately, the dark brows forming a V of intolerance.

'My business is with your mother, Miss King.'

'Oh no,' Jancis informed him coolly. 'That's where you're mistaken, Mr Leroy. My father left The Kingdom jointly to me and to my mother. Its sale is as much my concern . . . and my decision . . .' She paused to let her last words sink in. 'So you see, I'm afraid you will have to put up with my presence, despite your very obvious attempt to shut the door in my face.'

'Jancis!' Mrs King held out a hand that shook slightly. 'I'm sure Mr Leroy didn't intentionally . . .'

She stopped short, at the sight of the ironic expression on Keegan's swarthy face. It was all too obvious that he had intended to exclude her daughter from any discussion.

'Well, anyway, now that Mr Leroy understands . . .'

'Perhaps I could be shown around the property?'

He certainly didn't believe in wasting time, Jancis thought. She moved forward, her slender figure graceful in the blue dress, the soft material of which moulded to perfection her slim hips and tiny, tip-tilted breasts. Suddenly she was glad she hadn't changed. In sweater and slacks, she knew her slim figure was boyish and youthful. But in a dress which so obviously displayed her femininity, nobody, not even the sarcastic Keegan Leroy, could dub her schoolgirl.

'Certainly you may see the property, Mr Leroy,' she said coldly, 'If you'll come with me . . .'

He looked his surprise, turning from her to her mother with a questioning air.

Mrs King nodded.

'My daughter will show you round, Mr Leroy. I hope you'll excuse me, but I haven't been too well, since . . . since . . .' Hastily, she changed the subject . . . 'and in any case, Jancis is extremely knowledgeable . . . she's so good with horses.'

'Really?'

The implication in the word, accompanied by a sardonic lift of those black brows, set Jancis' teeth on edge. He hadn't forgotten their encounter at Doncaster, any more than she had. He still thought of her as careless, incompetent . . .

However, intercepting a worried glance from her mother, she steeled herself to remain impersonal and without further conversation, she led the way through the spacious hall and along the passageway which led to the back of the house.

Jancis could not help the surge of pride which she always felt whenever she returned to The Kingdom. The lofty, square rooms of the gracious old house were comfortably furnished, even though everything was beginning to look a little shabby.

They passed through her father's office, which had its own outside door, so that one could reach the stables without going through the rest of the house. The sight and smell of this room still had the power to bring a lump to Jancis' throat. Here, more than anywhere else in the house, her father's personality seemed to linger ... the smell of tweed, of tobacco smoke. It was a really horsey room ... the huge desk piled with papers, filing cabinets lining the walls, which were covered with photographs, paintings and sketches of horses, the shelves with crowded ranks of silver cups, now tarnished and neglected-looking.

Outside, mellow brickwork and weathered timbers blended restfully into the formal gardens which had survived from an earlier century. A belt of mature trees sheltered the garden, dividing it from the stableyard, with its range of looseboxes on two sides, the third comprising the hay barn and tack room.

She wondered what effect his surroundings were having on Keegan Leroy. She was uncomfortably aware that the gardens were not as well tended as in her father's more affluent days. The once pristine fresh paint on the looseboxes was beginning to chip and peel and moss was forming unchecked between the cobblestones. But perhaps, to someone who had not seen the property before, these small points would not be as obvious as they were to her.

In the sheltered, sun-filled yard, Jancis was gripped by a painful wave of nostalgia ... the bitter realisation that soon this familiar scene would be just a memory. No longer would she be able to come here at will, to chat with the stable lads, to experience the pleasurable odours of warm horses, clean straw and leather. But most of all, she knew she would miss the opportunity of riding these beautiful animals, a privilege her father had accorded her as soon as he had been satisfied with her competence as a rider.

She looked around her, almost as if she were viewing the stables for the first time, trying to see them from a newcomer's point of view ... from a buyer's angle. The few lads left to them were sweeping the yard and cleaning tack. Fred Higgins, her father's head lad for many years, an incredibly tiny man with a weatherbeaten skin and bowed legs, hissed cheerfully, as he groomed one of his charges; the heads of well-fed, contented horses hung over box doors, with dozing, drooping eyes, lower lips hung down and quivering, with the occasional flick of a lolling ear.

Slowly she led the way from box to box, very much aware

of the man following her, the keen, inquisitive eyes, which overlooked nothing.

'Do you want to see the gallops, and the schooling ground?' she asked him.

His darkling gaze swept downwards in insolent appraisal, taking in her dainty dress and strappy sandals.

'Yes, but you needn't accompany me. You're scarcely dressed for the occasion.'

Jancis bit her lip, cursing her own stubbornness. Her mother had been right: she *should* have changed. Her earlier satisfaction with her own chic appearance banished by Keegan's derisory words, she stood irresolute, watching the tall, muscular figure striding away from her.

She would wait here for him, she decided. She didn't feel ready to meet her mother's anxious, enquiring gaze. Mary King would be on tenterhooks, waiting for Keegan Leroy's decision, and as yet Jancis was unable to gauge his reaction to The Kingdom. Would he make an offer? If only there were some other way, she thought desperately. Although her mother had resigned herself to the fact that the stables must go, Jancis knew what a terrible wrench it would be for her, to leave the lovely old house to which she had come as a young bride.

'That the new gaffer?' The head lad, seeing her alone, approached, his brown, wizened face eager, curious. Of course, they would all be anxious about their jobs.

'I don't know yet,' she told him curtly, and turned away, to walk slowly back towards the house.

She regretted her abruptness with Fred. He was, after all, an old friend and ally and he was only concerned for his future. At his age, she supposed, it would be difficult for him to find another job. But she and her mother had more intangible values at stake. They were being forced to give up both the stables and their home ... the last links with her father.

At the thought of her father, Jancis' eyes pricked. How could she bear the thought of the arrogant Keegan, the man who had contributed towards her father's ruin, living here, striding through The Kingdom, adding it to his already vast list of possessions.

Half blinded by a sudden rush of tears, she stumbled on the uneven cobbles and was steadied by an iron-hard hand.

'You're liable to break an ankle, coming down here in those ridiculous sandals.'

She had not heard Keegan Leroy's silent approach and now she stared up at him belligerently, tears evaporating in the heat of anger. Resenting his intrusion on her grief, she pulled her arm away from the fingers which still enclosed it.

'Well, have you seen everything, pried into every nook and cranny?' she snapped, knowing she was being both rude and unfair. It was a prospective buyer's right to examine closely the property offered for his inspection.

To her surprise, he showed no sign of having taken offence. Instead, his speculative gaze swept her from head to foot, from the crown of auburn curls to the hopelessly inadequate sandals.

'I've seen everything that's on offer,' he drawled.

Jancis coloured, hoping she had misunderstood the implication in his words.

'And are you interested?'

'Oh, very!' He continued his insolent assessment, and this time there was no mistaking his meaning.

'I don't go with the property, Mr Leroy,' she snapped.

'No?' He raised satanic brows and Jancis felt strangely breathless. It was almost as if an unspoken challenge had been made and received.

'No!' she retorted, with a firmness she was far from feeling. Despite her twenty-four years, something about this man reduced her to the level of the unsophisticated schoolgirl he had once thought her to be.

'Which just goes to prove that you're not as knowledgeable as you claim to be.' Keegan Leroy sounded faintly amused.

'What do you mean?'

'That, obviously, your mother hasn't told you the full terms of my proposal.'

'Your . . . your proposal?' Jancis echoed faintly.

'Yes, Miss King. I want the stables, but there are certain conditions under which I am prepared to buy . . . and you form part of those conditions.'

He turned and marched away from her, leaving her paralysed with shock, her brown eyes wide with the effect of his words. Whatever did he mean by his cryptic utterance? What part had she to play in his plans for The Kingdom? On legs that had developed a decided tendency to tremble, Jancis followed Keegan Leroy back to the house.

Mrs King looked up anxiously, as they re-entered the drawing room, and what she saw in Jancis' stormy face did little to reassure her.

'Have . . . have you shown Mr Leroy everything?'

'I've seen enough, Mrs King,' Keegan interposed smoothly. 'Perhaps now we could get down to discussing terms?'

Nervously, Mrs King pleated a fold of her skirt.

'Would . . . would you like some coffee, Mr Leroy?'

Jancis sympathised with her mother's desire to postpone the irrevocable moment of decision.

Keegan shook his dark head, impatient of such social niceties.

'I should prefer to proceed to business.'

He swept back the sleeve of his pullover, revealing an exceedingly expensive-looking gold watch, and, incidentally, a tanned, muscular wrist, over which fanned a thick mat of hair, as black as that which framed his hawkish features.

'I have another appointment in precisely half an hour. So . . .?' He made a gesture towards the chintz-covered settee, indicating that both women should be seated.

Almost as if, Jancis thought resentfully, he already owned the place.

He turned to Mrs King.

'I gather you haven't retailed the full details of our preliminary discussion to your daughter?'

A quick, nervous nod confirmed his supposition and Mary King darted a guilty glance at her already seething daughter.

'Would you care to explain now, or would you prefer that *I* put her in the picture?' Keegan's tone was expressive of irritation; obviously he considered Mrs King's hesitant reluctance unnecessary.

Jancis, looking from one to the other, was torn between indignation and sympathy at her mother's obvious embarrassment. Impulsively, she intervened.

'Whatever it is, Mr Leroy, I should prefer to hear it from my mother.'

He shrugged his acceptance, leaning with indolent grace against the wide oak mantelpiece. It was evident that he intended to remain, to observe her reactions to his ultimatum ... for that it *was* an ultimatum, she had no doubt.

'I ... I don't really know where to begin,' Mrs King said, regarding her daughter helplessly.

'Mr Leroy said I formed part of the conditions ... the conditions under which he was prepared to purchase The Kingdom. Suppose you start there,' Jancis suggested.

'Very well, dear.' Once begun, Mrs King spoke rapidly, as though to have done with an unpleasant task, her fingers still restlessly mangling the hem of her skirt. 'You know, of course, that Mr Leroy already owns one racing stable?'

Jancis' answering grimace was a wry one. She was all too aware of that unpleasant fact.

'But the house which goes with it is a modern one ... very small. We ... we did anticipate that anyone buying The Kingdom would want the house as well?' Her voice was almost pleading.

Jancis nodded, a brief motion of the head, which expressed very clearly her distaste for the prospect.

'Mr Leroy has been very kind. He ... he realises what a blow it would be, for me particularly, to have to give up my home. So ...' Mary King paused, with another nervous glance at her daughter. 'So he's suggested that we continue to live here.' She gasped out the remaining words with breathless haste.

'What?'

Jancis stared at her mother. Surely she had misunderstood?

Mary swallowed convulsively.

'He ... Mr Leroy ... lives alone at the moment and ... and he would like me to remain here, as ... as his housekeeper.'

Jancis was incredulous.

'And you'd be prepared to do that, Mummy ... to live as an employee in your own home?'

'Well, it wouldn't *be* my own home, dear, would it?' Mrs King said reasonably. 'And it would mean I needn't go right away. It ... it would still *feel* like home ...' Her voice wobbled and her eyes misted over.

'And where would *I* fit into this charitable concern?'

Jancis asked icily, her mother's distress overlooked in a moment of cold, implacable anger. The idea of her mother at Keegan Leroy's beck and call was intolerable.

'Your place will certainly not be based on charity!'

Keegan Leroy, it seemed, had decided that his silence had lasted long enough. He wasn't a man, Jancis thought, who would be prepared to take a back seat for long in any situation.

'Like your mother's position, yours would be on a strictly business basis.'

'I see!' Jancis spoke from between compressed lips. 'And just what had you in mind for me . . . parlourmaid, perhaps?'

In any other man, the swift twist of the full lips might have been rapidly-concealed amusement.

'No,' he replied gravely. 'When I discussed this project with your mother, we decided that I should employ you to undertake the secretarial side of my business . . . race declarations, accounts, training fees, VAT returns, National Insurance. I'm sure you know the drill?'

Jancis gasped, small fists clenched. The utter gall of the man! How dared he attempt to dispose of her future in this way?

'Did it escape your notice that I already have a job, and a very well paid one?'

'No. I was given to understand by your mother that you're a lecturer in secretarial studies. I take it that does mean you're reasonably proficient in shorthand and typewriting?'

'And rather more besides,' she informed him grimly. Reasonably proficient indeed! she brooded. What a nerve!

'Exactly!' He nodded, as if, his assumption confirmed, the matter was now settled.

She'd like to show him just exactly how capable and efficient she was, she thought viciously. But as she wasn't going to take the job he had so high-handedly mapped out for her . . .

'I'm extremely satisfied with my present job,' she told him. 'And I have no intention of throwing up a very rewarding and interesting position to become your . . . your Girl Friday!'

If she expected a violent reaction, or protests, from Keegan Leroy, she was disappointed. He merely raised those

fiercely black brows and rose, once more consulting the gold
wristwatch.

'Very well, Miss King. It seems there's no more to be
said.' He turned to Mary King. 'I have two alternatives open
to me. Either I decide *not* to buy The Kingdom ... in which
case, you may find it difficult to obtain an equally
substantial offer ... or I can buy and install my own
housekeeper and office staff. It's quite immaterial to me.'

He moved towards the door.

'Goodbye, Mrs King. My solicitors will be in touch with
you, as soon as I've reached a decision.'

Mary King fluttered tremulous hands, her lower lip
trembling ominously, as she spoke.

'I ... I'm so sorry, Mr Leroy. I ...'

'Wait!' Jancis spoke curtly.

He paused impatiently in the doorway. He had the
irritating knack of being able to lift one eyebrow higher than
the other.

'How much were you thinking of paying us ... for the
stables, I mean?'

He named a sum which sent her own eyebrows flying.

'I see.'

He regarded her sardonically.

'Do you? I wonder?'

'And when would you expect me to start work? I'd have to
finish the term ...'

He inclined his dark head in an arrogant movement,
almost as if he had been certain of her capitulation.

'That would be quite suitable, Miss King.'

Jancis bit her lip. He made her feel like a school leaver,
applying for the position of junior clerk. Instead of which,
here she was, an extremely competent lecturer, being
blackmailed ... for that was what it amounted to ...
blackmailed into giving up a very rewarding career.

It would not be easy to reconcile herself to giving up all
that she had striven for ever since her own student days. She
enjoyed the mental stimulation of college life, the challenge
entailed in preparing the girls under her care for worthwhile
careers. Some of the more promising would almost certainly
go on to be personal assistants to top executives ... an end
result which would reflect favourably upon Jancis' own

capabilities as an instructor; and apart from the demands and satisfactions of her job, the college had provided a very full social life . . . pursuits both sporting and cultural, shared with like-minded colleagues, who had also become valued friends . . . the stimulus of other intelligent minds, the friendly banter of the staff room.

But, for her mother's sake, she had to renounce the rich, satisfying pattern of her life, just to pander to this man's insufferable vanity. For it would just suit Keegan Leroy to brag about this . . . that not only had he made a takeover bid for the only other local stables of any size or reputation, but he was forcing the late owner's wife and daughter to labour for him.

'All right, Mr Leroy. I won't pretend I like the idea, but for my mother's sake, I agree to your proposition.'

'Oh, darling!' Mary King breathed her gratitude.

'*Very* noble, Miss King,' was all the reply she received from Keegan Leroy, the acidity of his tone proclaiming his disbelief in her expressed motives.

'I mean what I say,' she told him furiously, goaded beyond all endurance by his manner. 'Although I love my home, the stables, the village . . . for my own part, I'd sooner move to the other side of the world than live here, to see you lording it around, riding my father's horses, giving orders in his house. But if it's what my mother wants, then I'll endure it . . . for as long as I can,' she qualified.

For a long moment, man and girl locked glances, fierce black eyes clashing with brown, made lustrous with angry, unshed tears.

'Is . . . is it settled, then?' Mary King asked anxiously, looking from one to the other.

For the first time, Keegan Leroy smiled, giving charm to an otherwise harshly featured face.

'It's settled,' he told her, his voice gentle by comparison with the tone he had used to her daughter. 'Shall we shake hands on it, Mrs King?'

He took Mary King's slightly tremulous hand, then turned to Jancis.

'Miss King?'

With a feeling of distaste, Jancis extended her hand, to find its slimness completely enveloped in hard, brown muscularity ... a warm, firm grip, which sent an inexplicable tremor through her, a sensation too fleeting to analyse, but which was certainly not one of revulsion.

CHAPTER TWO

JANCIS stared out of the staff room window, her soft brown eyes wistful. This was the last time she would look out over these smooth lime-green lawns, the tennis courts beyond ... hear the sound of girlish laughter, the regular, soothing pit-pat of the balls upon the hard surface. She had worked out her notice, so reluctantly given, and now, in a very few moments, she would be on her way home.

No, she corrected herself ... not home; not *her* home any more, but Keegan Leroy's home, where she and her mother would now be suffered to live as paid dependants. At the thought of this humiliation, the fierce pride rose in her gorge. It was intolerable, to be dependent on Keegan for both her livelihood and the very roof over her head. She wondered how her mother could bear it.

Keegan had been living at The Kingdom for just over two months now and already her mother seemed to have accepted the situation. Her regular letters were cheerful and full of Keegan's doings. She seemed almost to take a personal interest and pride in his rapid restoration of The Kingdom's reputation.

She wrote constantly of improvements ... redecorating, new horses, new staff, lads and jockeys. Jancis was dreading the moment when she must set foot in her old home, when she would have to witness the inevitable radical changes Keegan had made in the once homely, but comfortable, surroundings.

What would a man like Keegan know about interior decor? she thought scornfully. He was essentially an outdoor man, and by all accounts, he had not been born to wealth. He was just a jumped-up Johnny-come-lately. Moving into Jack King's former home was probably quite a step up for him. Deliberately, Jancis chose to ignore the self-assurance with which he had moved around the house, his quietly cultured manner.

Suppose the house was changed beyond all recognition? However would she manage to contain her indignation, hide her nostalgia for the dear old familiar colour schemes, so carefully chosen by her parents?

With a feeling akin to panic, Jancis saw the taxi turn across the gravelled sweep of the drive below. She had no excuse to delay the evil moment. Her luggage waited in the front hall, her final farewells had been made. With a dragging step, she left the staff room and descended the stairs.

She was in no mood to respond to the taxi-driver's loquacious humour and was relieved when they reached the railway station and she could be alone with her thoughts in the almost empty train.

Somehow, Jancis had always envisaged a future spent in the world of education, as a dedicated professional, among professionals. The vague possibility of marriage, some day, had of course crossed her mind, but had not caused her to swerve from her determination. These days marriage and a career could be successfully combined. Never for one moment had she foreseen leaving for any other reason . . . certainly not to work in any other field than that of her chosen profession.

Jancis had no doubt that she was both mentally and physically capable of the task that lay before her. She had often helped out in her father's office and had often surprised owners by her grasp of racing rules and regulations. She had ridden out on the early morning gallops and more than pulled her weight in the daily work of the stables . . . mucking out, rubbing down and feeding. One thing she had determined . . . as she had no choice but to work for Keegan Leroy, she was going to do so to the best of her ability. Resentment apart, and resentment would always be there, she was going to demonstrate just how efficient she could be. 'Reasonably proficient!' The words still rankled.

No, it was not the thought of the hard work that made her heart sink . . . the inevitable responsibilities, the need for care . . . there was no room for error in the racing world. It was the thought of the daily contact with Keegan Leroy, the need to work in such close conjunction with a man she detested and half feared for his unpredictable effect upon her. She was ashamed that, despite her dislike of Keegan, he could make her so aware of his undoubted masculinity.

She had disliked people before, but never with this fierce, almost physical violence, which in his presence threatened to overwhelm all self-control, all promptings of common sense.

Yet her mother seemed to like the man. Jancis, intensely loyal to her father's memory, could not understand Mary's apparent defection. Her mother's letters referred to Keegan admiringly, almost affectionately . . . Jancis thought indignantly . . . as though he were a son, someone to be proud of.

She sighed. She couldn't understand it, but as long as her mother was happy, for her own part, she must endure life as it would now be at The Kingdom.

The rail journey was not a long one, and all too soon Jancis was struggling from the train, a suitcase in either hand, her ticket clenched between her teeth.

At the barrier, the ticket collector, a local man who had known her all her life, greeted her cheerfully.

'Welcome home, Miss Jancis. The car's waiting for you, just back of the office.'

The car? Someone had come to meet her, then. It couldn't be her mother; Mary King had never learned to drive. Fred Higgins perhaps, or one of the other lads? Wistfully, she recalled how her father used to meet her . . . the delight of having him all to herself during the few moments it took to drive home, his absorbed interest in all her news, her own eager questions about the life of the stable, during her absence.

She did not recognise the car, its glossy, streamlined luxury, but she did recognise the craggy profile presented to her as she approached. She felt the faint stirring of hostility. Why on earth had *he* come to meet her? She might have been allowed a few more moments of tranquillity, moments in which she could have pretended everything was normal, just as it used to be . . . herself coming home for the holidays, to a warm, welcoming home.

As though sensing her presence, Keegan turned to look at her, then, with one swift, lithe movement, he opened his

door and uncoiled his long length from behind the wheel.
He opened the boot and indicated that she should place her
suitcases inside. The fact that he did not take them from her
seemed to her to subtly underline their employer–employee
relationship, and the first little curling sensation of the
familiar anger started inside her.

She did not wait to see if Keegan intended to hold open
the passenger door, but moved swiftly around the car,
seating herself before he had closed the boot.

He slid back into the driving seat and turned to study her
coldly averted profile, the determined rigidity of her slim
shoulders. The powerful figure of Keegan Leroy was
unnerving in its closeness, and determinedly she avoided
meeting his eyes. Staring obstinately straight ahead of her,
she vowed she would not thank him for coming to meet her
. . . she didn't feel the least bit grateful, so it would be
hypocrisy to pretend otherwise . . . or so she excused the
omission, which her conscience told her was extremely bad
manners.

Smoothly the big car moved away, travelling the familiar
route along lanes edged with verdant, luxuriant hedgerows,
their growth encouraged by the humidity of alternating rain
and sunshine.

'You had a pleasant journey?' Keegan enquired after a
while.

'Yes.'

Her reply was deliberately brief. If he thought she was in
the mood for pleasant small talk, he was mistaken.

'Everything satisfactorily concluded at the college?'

This time she was unable to confine herself to the
monosyllabic reply.

'Concluded, yes . . . satisfactorily, no! I was very sorry to
be leaving.' And sorry to be coming to work for you, she
added silently to herself.

To her relief, this brief exchange terminated his attempt at
conversation and the remainder of the short ride was made
in silence.

As the car swept up the broad driveway, Jancis gazed
anxiously about her, looking for signs of change. But the
grounds appeared much as usual, save that the lawns
fronting the property were now neatly trimmed, velvet-

smooth, the flowerbeds ablaze with brightly coloured annuals.

As they halted by the front door, Jancis jumped from the car, suddenly longing to see her mother, to reassure herself that all was well with her. One foot on the lower step, she halted, biting her lip, the hot blood of embarrassment rushing to her face. She no longer had the right to make her entrance this way. She was not Miss King of The Kingdom now, but a paid employee. If she judged Keegan Leroy aright, she would be expected to use the back door . . . the menials' entrance.

She had half turned away when a firm hand grasped her elbow, propelling her up the remainder of the steps and into the warm, welcoming aura of the hall. Just in time, she managed to restrain the gasp of delighted amazement which had almost escaped her.

The hall, when she had last seen it, had worn a faintly pathetic look, the timbers of the floor faded to lacklustre tones, while dust had formed a thin veil overall. For Mary King had been unable to afford servants, and without the incentive of a husband's comfort to care for, had lacked the energy or interest for more than the most basic chores.

Now the spacious area seemed to gleam, the floor shining like dark water, as restored, polished beauty reflected back the sheen of copper and brass, its twinkling greeting repeated too in the glint of leaded glass panes, in the full-length mirror, which reflected two figures . . . one a slender girl, her lips parted with the pleasure she refused to utter, the other the dark, saturnine man, his face slightly turned down to look at her, as if to witness her reaction.

At once, Jancis recollected herself, and the company she was in. She would not give Keegan the satisfaction of making the comments which he so obviously expected.

'Where will I find my mother?' she enquired, annoyed by the fact that she must look up so far to meet Keegan Leroy's glinting eyes. Her mother, she reflected, was probably in some corner of her old home, now designated as 'the housekeeper's quarters'.

He seemed surprised by the question.

'In the drawing room, of course . . . with my cousin.'

'Your cousin?'

About to open the door, Jancis paused, one hand resting
on a brass handle which, she noted, gleamed as brightly as
everything else. There had been no mention in her mother's
letters of a cousin.

Keegan reached out impatiently to open the door,
brushing her fingers with his own as he did so, causing
Jancis to draw back her hand as though it had been burnt.

Whatever was the matter with her? she wondered
irritably. Anyone would be justified in thinking her a naïve
girl, unaccustomed to the company of men ... which would
be far from the truth. An attractive girl, Jancis had not been
without boy-friends, though there had been no one for
whom she had felt more than a passing affection. But
certainly none of them had produced this embarrassingly ...
yes, *physical* effect upon her. It must be purely a chemical
reaction, she decided, born of her utter detestation of the
man.

'You are about to meet my cousin,' Keegan said, and with
one large hand between her shoulder blades, he propelled
her willy-nilly into the room.

'Jancis darling! You're home at last!' Mary King rose to
greet her daughter, quite unaware of Jancis' flinching
response to her words.

'Home, Mummy?' She could not resist the question.
'Hardly that, surely?'

But Mary King nodded happily.

'Mr Leroy ... Keegan, he says I must call him ... insists
that we continue to look upon this as our home.'

Jancis stared at her mother. Was this the wan, tremulous
woman she had left behind only two months ago? Mary
King's figure seemed to have filled out. She would never be
plump, but she had lost the gaunt, fragile appearance of the
weeks closely following Jack King's death. Her face was pale
no longer and her eyes were bright and alert, their former
apathy banished.

'Mary, won't you introduce me to your daughter?'

The voice was slightly plaintive, and with a guilty start,
Mary King turned towards the young woman who had
remained seated.

'I'm so sorry, Alyson. You must forgive me. It was the
excitement of having Jancis home again. Jancis, this is

Alyson, Keegan's cousin . . . Alyson, my daughter.'

Jancis looked curiously at the seated girl. So this was Keegan's cousin. Today was the first time she had heard of the relationship and there had been no opportunity to form any preconceived ideas, but nevertheless, Alyson was not at all as she would have imagined any connection of Keegan Leroy.

Jancis held out her hand and with a shock felt the lightness of the small-boned fingers laids in hers. Jancis herself was daintily built, but Alyson was as fragile as fine porcelain.

There was no warmth or pressure in the other girl's hand, and instinctively Jancis sensed hostility in Alyson's languid acceptance of her greeting.

Mary King was fussing around, clearing magazines from the coffee table, plumping cushions, amazingly energetic in contrast to her limp self of a few weeks ago.

'Sit down, Jancis love. I'll have some tea brought in—I'm sure you're ready for a cup.'

Keegan, it appeared, had gathered a small staff around him during Jancis' absence, for the tea was brought in by a young parlourmaid. This was the position she herself had jeeringly enquired if she should fill, she thought wryly. Involuntarily, at the recollection, she looked at Keegan and found him watching her. From the expression on his face, she knew that he too remembered her sarcastic words.

Sipping her tea, she was at leisure to look around her. The comfortable drawing room wore a new look of affluence and at first she was wholly unable to account for the change. Mary King had spoken of redecoration, of improvement . . . but this room looked just the same and yet, subtly, it was different. Then, with a sense of wonder, Jancis realised what had happened. Curtains, upholstery, cushion covers were all new, but they had been renewed in exactly the same colours and patterns. Everything had been rejuvenated, and yet the room still retained its essential character.

Jancis looked at Mary King and surprised a look of eager expectancy on her mother's face.

'Well?' said Mary. 'What do you think?' Without giving Jancis an opportunity to reply, she rattled on. 'It was Keegan's idea. He suggested that we keep everything just as it was. Wasn't it good of him?'

'Very,' Jancis muttered. This time she dared not look at Keegan. She was determined not to betray any reaction ... of pleasure, or otherwise ... not until she had fathomed his motives. This altruistic behaviour did not fit in at all with her conception of his character and she needed time to think. She had no intention of following her mother's example and giving unqualified admiration and approval to the usurper.

Keegan set down his cup and turned to his cousin.

'Aly, I'm sure Mrs King and her daughter would like an opportunity for private conversation. Suppose we leave them alone together for a while?'

Alyson's rather pinched face lit up.

'Are you going to take me somewhere? Somewhere nice?'

He laughed, and again Jancis wondered at the difference in his manner, the indulgent tone with which he addressed both her mother and his cousin ... a totally different inflection from that which he reserved for herself.

'I'm a busy man, chicken ... no time for gadding today. But I thought we might go down to the stables. There's a new horse arrived, and I want to see how he stood up to the journey.'

Alyson pouted.

'Oh, Keegan, you know I don't like your nasty smelly horses!'

He ignored her protest, however, and moved towards the settee, where, to Jancis' surprise, he bent over and swept Alyson up in strong, muscular arms, her meagre bones and flesh no burden to him. He walked towards the door, Alyson's fragile arm clasped around the strong column of his neck.

'Lunch at the usual time, Mrs King?'

Mary King nodded.

'Right, we'll see you later, then.' He turned briefly to Jancis. 'After lunch I'll show you the ropes in the office. The sooner you get started in there the better.'

Jancis glared after his departing figure.

'Show me the ropes!' she snorted, as the door closed behind him. 'I know more about Dad's office than he does!'

Mary King coughed diffidently.

'I ... I think you'll find he's made a few changes, dear. It

. . . it's not quite the same as it was in Dad's time.'

She might have known, Jancis thought bitterly. This room had probably been a sop to her mother's feelings. The rest of the place was probably changed out of all recognition. Just let her find out that he changed *her* bedroom . . .

'Would you like to come up and unpack?' Mary suggested. 'We could talk while you're doing that.' She consulted her wristwatch. 'I shall soon have to see about lunch.'

They took a suitcase each and mounted the wide, gracious staircase. Along the landing, most of the doors stood ajar and swift, surreptitious glances told a puzzled Jancis that in spite of the air of new prosperity, of freshly decorated rooms, like the drawing room, all was strictly as before. So what about her room?

She flung open her bedroom door, then breathed a sigh of relief.

Purple carpet, dusky pink curtains and counterpane made an unusual contrast with silky grey walls, still hung with her collection of old racing prints; and, in the alcoves on either side of the old-fashioned fireplace, her collection of horses . . . over a hundred of them, from the tiniest, barely half an inch long, to the smooth, gleaming, creamy beauty made of onyx, which required a whole shelf for itself. Here too were all her favourite books, the new and the dog-eared, some of them going right back to her childhood days, the majority of them about horses . . . familiar names . . . Pat Smythe . . . the Pullein-Thompsons, more recently Dick Francis . . . and biographies of many well-known jockeys and trainers.

Like the rest of the house, her room had been redecorated, but with strict observance of its former appearance.

Jancis sat down on the familiar bed.

'What's he up to, Mummy?' she asked bluntly.

Mary King looked at her daughter in genuine bewilderment.

'Up to? You mean Keegan? Why should he be up to anything?'

'Because I don't believe in all this big-hearted, charitable act he's been putting on for the last couple of months.'

Mary shook her head.

'I think you're misjudging him, Jancis. In fact, I know you are. He couldn't have been kinder or more considerate to me.' She sighed sentimentally. 'What a pity we didn't get to know him better while your father was alive. Things might have been so different.'

Jancis raised her eyebrows in exasperated disbelief. It was obvious that her mother had been completely won over by Keegan's charm ... and she had to admit that he could exude charm when he wished.

'Where does the cousin fit into his scheme of things?' she asked.

'Alyson?' Mary King's eyes became sentimental. 'Such a poor little slip of a thing. She lost her parents just recently ... about the same time as Keegan decided to buy The Kingdom. Apart from some cousins in Australia, he's her only living relative.'

'You mean, she's going to live here permanently?'

Somehow Jancis found the idea unappealing.

Mary nodded.

'She's never been very strong, but Keegan hopes the country air and good wholesome cooking will improve her health. That's another reason why he wanted a housekeeper, someone he could trust ... to look after Alyson.'

'So now you're acting unpaid nursemaid as well?'

Mary was shocked.

'Oh no, dear. Keegan pays me a very generous wage ... very generous indeed ... and when Alyson arrived, he insisted on giving me extra.'

Jancis threw up her hands in despair and started to unpack her suitcases. It was useless to expect any support from her mother, hopeless to try and understand just what motivated Keegan Leroy. She would just have to bide her time and wait for eventual enlightenment. He wouldn't be able to fool her for long.

It was another surprise to find that she and her mother were expected to join Keegan and Alyson at table. Keegan certainly didn't seem to be treating her mother as a servant, more like ... more like a favourite aunt, and she could not deny that her mother was blooming under his régime.

Nevertheless, it was an uncomfortable sensation, eating with the knowledge that those dark, probing eyes were constantly turned upon her. In Jack King's day, meals had been a pleasant, relaxed occasion, the food secondary to the day's gossip, the talk of horses, of owners and jockeys. Now Jancis ate in tense silence.

Not so her mother. Mary King did not seem at all inhibited. But then, Jancis reminded herself, her mother had had time to adjust.

Lunch over, Keegan rose.

'Shall we take our coffee into the office?' he suggested.

Jancis nodded, reluctant now that the moment had come to actually work with him, to see what he had made of her father's sanctum.

'Can I come too, Keegan?' Alyson looked up at him, exerting herself to make the most of her slight, sharp prettiness. 'I'll be as quiet as a mouse.'

Laughingly, he shook his head.

'No, my poppet. It's time for your afternoon rest . . . and besides, you'd be extremely bored. You know you're not interested in the details of horse racing.'

She pouted, but he ignored her protests and, as before, swept her up in his arms, carrying her effortlessly away up the stairs.

Over his shoulder, slightly protruding blue eyes looked back at Jancis with undisguised enmity. For some reason, Alyson was determined to dislike her, and Jancis wondered why. Was it merely the presence of another girl in the house . . . was she afraid that Jancis being there would divide the attention she had been receiving? Jancis couldn't believe that the rather self-centred Alyson had become that attached to Mary King in so short a time. Was it, then, the division of her cousin's favours she feared? If so, she was worrying unnecessarily, Jancis thought wryly. She had no desire for a half share in Keegan Leroy's good will . . . no more desire than his intention of bestowing it.

'Can't Alyson walk at all?' Jancis asked her mother curiously.

'Only with great effort,' said Mary, clearing the table as she spoke. 'And she loves Keegan to carry her. They're so fond of each other, sometimes I wonder . . .'

What Mary wondered was left unspoken, as, with Keegan's return, Jancis was summoned to her new duties.

It was a relief to find that the office was not too much

altered. True, the walls had been panelled in pine and new filing cabinets had been installed ... many more of them than her father had ever possessed ... and one corner was occupied by an unexpected innovation ... a telex machine. But the paintings and photographs had been returned to their original places and the cups now shone with the same efficient brilliance which seemed to emanate from everything that Keegan's influence had touched, during his short period of ownership.

Keegan indicated the desk Jancis was to use and an electric typewriter of the very latest design. Briefly he explained the contents of the filing cabinets.

'This section here relates to flat racers only, those on the other side of the office to hurdlers. Oh yes . . .' at her look of surprise, 'I know your father concentrated on flat racing, but my licence entitles me to have runners over obstacles too. To my way of thinking it makes good economic sense.'

Although she did not say so aloud, Jancis had to admit that this was so. Flat racing closed from early November to late March, and owners who also had horses which could turn out over hurdles in the winter had a better return for their investment.

'So, as a result, we have considerably more horses ... and I've taken on more stable lads,' Keegan continued.

'Naturally, since *you* can well afford to pay them,' Jancis retorted, not even trying to keep the resentment out of her voice, as she recalled her father's financial struggles. 'My father always said *he* preferred to do one job properly, instead of messing about with two.'

'The only drawback to that being that he didn't *do* the one properly,' Keegan remarked drily.

'My father had a very successful career,' Jancis retorted. 'He knew all there was to know about training horses. He wasn't inefficient, he ... he was a sick man.' She swallowed. 'And it didn't help, having a younger, richer man right next door, stealing all his best owners ... not to mention his professional jockey.'

She had expected an explosion of wrath in return, but Keegan's reply was almost mild; only the glinting eyes and a small nervous tic at the corner of his mouth betraying his rigid self-control.

'I've said this to your mother, Miss King, and I'll say it to you . . . *just once*. I'm sorry about your father's misfortunes, but I deny your implication that I was to blame for his eventual failure. Racing is a business like any other and it can't be run on charitable lines. Don't tell me your father wouldn't have done exactly the same, if he'd been able. Don't tell me he'd never accepted owners who'd become dissatisfied with their trainers.'

Jancis was silent. She couldn't deny the fact.

'With that settled, perhaps now we can get down to business.' He made the familiar gesture of consulting his wristwatch. 'I have an appointment with an owner in twenty minutes. I should like to leave you some paperwork to be getting on with.'

By the time Keegan had finished dictating, Jancis, despite the excellent speed of her shorthand, was dizzy with the magnitude of the task before her.

There were letters to aspiring apprentices to be answered . . . some an outright refusal, others offering a month's trial; bills for owners; telephone calls to owners about horses which had run the previous day, were going to run, or would be unable to run; and four-day declarations . . . this was the most daunting task.

Entries for forthcoming races were usually published in the Racing Calendar about two weeks before racing, but runners could still be declared four days before the event, and Jack King had usually made his declarations by telegram. To her dismay, Jancis found she had to master the unfamiliar telex machine . . . an unnecessary toy in her opinion . . . the innovation of a rich man, she thought resentfully.

The other tasks presented no problem. In the past, Jancis had handled them all for her father, though not in such vast numbers. By her reckoning, Keegan must have trebled the number of horses under training, and of course there was the same paperwork to be done for the other stable which he owned. He could really have used the services of two secretaries, but that was an unlikely eventuality. She judged Keegan Leroy to be a man who liked his money's worth. He had told her that her position in his household would not be based on charity, therefore it followed that he was going to demand the utmost from her of which she was capable. She gritted her teeth. Well, she *was* capable. Just let him suggest otherwise!

Keegan was watching her, with sardonic enquiry in his dark eyes.

'Think you'll be able to manage that lot?'

'This . . . this afternoon?' Jancis asked.

'Naturally!' His brows drew together, with the first signs of an impatient frown. 'I assumed you would be quite capable.'

'I am . . . of course I am,' she assured him hastily.

He removed the tweed hacking jacket from the back of his swivel chair, putting it on in one easy, fluid movement.

'Do the letters first. I'll be back in an hour to sign them, so that you can catch the post.'

With a swift movement around the desk Jancis intercepted his imminent departure.

'Do . . . do I get any time off?' she asked.

'Of course,' he said impatiently, 'but surely we can discuss that later.'

'And what about riding?' she insisted.

'Riding? I didn't know you had your own horse. But if so, there should be ample opportunity . . .'

'No,' she interrupted him. 'I meant going out with the racehorses, on the early morning gallops. I always used to.'

'That will not be necessary. You are employed as my secretary. We have sufficient lads to . . .'

'But I *like* riding. My father . . .'

'Your father is no longer the owner of these stables,' he reminded her unnecessarily. 'Personally, I don't approve of girls in stables. Apart from anything else, they're simply not strong enough, and not in the same class as riders.'

Jancis' brown eyes blazed an angry challenge.

'I can ride any horse you show me! I *am* strong enough and I've been told that I'm an excellent rider.'

'Not by me. You forget, I have had very dramatic, first-hand evidence of your skill with horses.'

The blood ran up under Jancis' lightly tanned skin. How many more times did he intend to remind her of that episode at Doncaster? She glared up at him, incensed by the satirical twist of his mouth. She would dearly have loved to hit him. How she wished Purdey's Dad had kicked him, trampled on him ... wiped that arrogant expression from his face.

Neatly he sidestepped her and turned in the open doorway.

'I hope I make myself quite clear. You will *not* be riding any of *my* horses.'

As the typewriter keys flew beneath Jancis' trained fingers, her brain was able to detach itself from the task before her, as she brooded on Keegan's final words.

He needn't think he had won that argument, intimidated her. He could forbid her all he liked, but horses and racing were in her blood, had always inspired her with a fierce joy and affection. She had grown up in a world where racing had formed the main topic of conversation, was the very stuff of which life was made. Somehow she was going to be on those early morning gallops. She'd show him she was as good ... and better ... than any of his lads.

For the first time, she was glad she had returned to The Kingdom. She had been exceedingly reluctant to do so, and her invidious position here would have as many drawbacks and irritations as she had expected, but it would give her a golden opportunity to wipe out a debt that had been long overdue, to make him eat his words ... those furious, sarcastic remarks ... about incompetent schoolgirls.

CHAPTER THREE

JANCIS was still typing when Keegan returned to the office. She studied with interest the man who accompanied him ... a square-cut, solidly built man of middle height, blue-eyed, fair-haired and immaculately groomed. He looked more like a successful businessman than a racehorse owner. It transpired that he was both.

'Miss King, this is Mr Mortimer, of Mortimer Plastics. I've recently taken two of his horses into training.'

The breezy blue eyes assessed Jancis, making it obvious that they approved of what they saw.

'And does the lovely Miss King have a christian name?' he enquired.

'Jancis,' she replied, smiling up at him.

'Mine's Nick,' he informed her, as a square, rather stubby hand enveloped hers.

'What sort of horses do you own, Nick?' Jancis ignored Keegan's restless movements. It was apparent from his scowling face that he did not approve of a mere secretary fraternising with his owners.

'Just a couple of flat racers at present,' Nick told her. 'A rather promising two-year-old colt, and a filly. Are you interested in racing yourself, Jancis, or is this just a job?'

'Very interested,' she said emphatically. 'Perhaps you didn't realise, Nick, but these stables used to belong to my father?'

'Oh . . . ah . . . yes.' He looked embarrassed. 'I did hear something. I'm sorry, I didn't make the connection . . . clumsy of me.'

'That's O.K. It's not your fault.' A quick, involuntary movement of eloquent brown eyes revealed where she believed the blame lay.

'Then perhaps you'd like to see my animals?' He laughed deprecatingly. 'You probably know more about them than I do!'

Nick Mortimer was perched on the edge of her desk now and Jancis took a perverse delight in disregarding Keegan's disapproving frown.

'I'd like that very much,' she said.

Nick rose, holding out an inviting hand, but Keegan forestalled him.

'I'm afraid it's not convenient for Miss King to leave the office just at present. As you can see, she's a little behind with her work. Perhaps some other time . . .?'

'Of course!' Nick apologised. 'I'm afraid I tend to get a bit carried away. Horses are a fairly new hobby of mine and it's always nice to meet a fellow enthusiast . . . especially such an attractive one.' He stood up, sketching Jancis a farewell salute. 'I shall look forward to seeing you again, Jancis.'

His warm manner betrayed that he was indeed looking forward, just as much to seeing Jancis herself, as to discussing his animals with her.

The friendliness, the obvious admiration of this very personable man was a pleasant contrast to Keegan's brusque reserve. Nick Mortimer was slightly older than Keegan, she judged, and obviously wealthy. Although his money did not lend any weight to her approval of him, she felt a warm glow of anticipation at the prospect of furthering her acquaintance with him.

Having speeded the departure of his new owner, Keegan returned to the office, holding out an impatient hand for the completed letters. As Jancis had expected, he had unfavourable comment to make, concerning her success with Nick Mortimer.

'I don't encourage familiarity between my employees and the owners,' he informed her, his eyes intently studying the papers before him, searching, Jancis was positive, for some error, some point on which he might legitimately criticise her work. But she was confident he would find nothing.

'So I gathered,' she remarked drily. 'A little unnecessary, surely. My father never . . .'

'As I've been forced to point out before, *I* am now the owner of these stables, and I make my own rules. There are certain confidential items of information, about the form of the horses in my care, which I should not wish to be discussed. Therefore . . .'

'Do you really imagine I should want to discuss such things as form, and time trials, with an attractive man like Nick Mortimer?' Jancis spoke ironically, beginning to clear her desk as she spoke. Despite Keegan's derogatory remark, about her being behindhand with her work, on the contrary, she had finished well ahead of the deadline he had given her.

'I feel sure Mr Mortimer, despite his interest in racing, is far too sophisticated to be so narrow-minded,' she continued.

'If you're implying that his interest in you is a more personal one, I'm forced to agree that you may be right,' Keegan said stiffly. 'However, my former remark still applies, and I must insist that you do not encourage his attentions.'

Jancis rose, her heart-shaped face flushed with anger, small hands clenched tightly at her side.

'Mr Leroy, what I do in my own time is none of your concern. Since you insist on being so stuffy, I won't talk to your owners in your time, but once I leave this office . . .'

'You're still on my premises,' he reminded her. The thrust was a shrewd one and she stared at him, frustrated rage rising in her throat, choking off all coherent speech.

'Why, you . . . you . . .'

He lifted that irritating, solitary eyebrow.

'Yes, Miss King, do go on?'

'. . . conceited, arrogant . . . insensitive . . .' The words jerked out, disconnected, barely audible to her listener.

Keegan leant back in his chair, studying her, she thought, as he would a piece of bloodstock he was about to acquire . . . appraisingly, critically, and overall, she sensed his quiet amusement at her impotent fury.

'You're not a man,' she accused him. 'You're a machine! All your mind can compute is racing odds . . . form. It doesn't seem to occur to you that . . .'

'That there's more to life than horses?'

He rose, coming round his desk to tower over her, causing an inexplicable tremor to shake her, uneasiness possessing her at his sudden proximity.

She was becoming irritated with herself over this continual embarrassing reaction on her part . . . so strong that she felt sure he too must be aware of it. She was *not* an immature teenager to tremble in a man's presence, nor was she afraid of him. So why on earth could she not treat him with the same cool aplomb that she had felt in dealing with Nick Mortimer?

'Oh, but you're wrong, Miss King . . . very wrong, which is why I suggest you stay away from Mr Mortimer. A woman's emotions are chancy things at the best of times, quite likely to override such unimportant things as loyalty, discretion . . .'

Oh, he was impossible! Why did men always have to assume that women were unstable, unreliable creatures, just because they *were* women? It was a typically arrogant male attitude.

'If you're implying that I'd reveal any of your precious "secrets" to Nick Mortimer, you're out of your mind!' Jancis had regained her composure, but her anger remained, now icily objective. 'You seem to forget, I used to work for my father, but it didn't interfere with my social life, nor did I ever discuss his business with my friends.'

'Naturally you were loyal to *your father*.' He emphasised the words. 'But I fear you have no such compulsion where I'm concerned.'

So that was what he expected . . . she might have guessed. It wasn't, as he had at first suggested, solely that she was a woman, whose emotional stability, according to him, was liable to be suspect. Oh no, he knew he deserved her hatred for his destruction of her father and was fully expecting her to exact her revenge. But did he really think that she would stoop to such methods, to strike at him through any opportunity she might have as an employee? Surely he ought to realise her detestation of him would make no difference to her integrity, so far as his business was concerned. But if that was what he *wanted* to think . . . Annoyance prodded Jancis into indiscretion.

'You're right, Mr Leroy. Where you're concerned, I feel nothing but contempt, and I shall choose my own friends without reference to you!'

Without a backward glance, she stalked out of the office, into the house, and made her way up to her room. She did not feel like going in search of her mother just then. Mary King's decided partiality for her employer would not incline her to lend a sympathetic ear to her daughter's indignation.

To Jancis' relief, Keegan did not appear at the dinner table that evening, and she gathered that he was dining out.

'A business matter,' Mary King said vaguely.

'With a prospective owner, no doubt,' Jancis said acidly, 'gathering more scalps to add to his belt.'

Alyson looked at her, light blue eyes curious.

'Don't you like my cousin, Jancis?'

'No,' Jancis said flatly.

A faint expression of satisfaction flitted across the younger girl's face, but she made no comment, and not for the first time Jancis wondered idly about the relationship between Keegan and his fair, frail cousin. Certainly he seemed very fond of the girl and she of him. Perhaps, one day, Alyson would be mistress of The Kingdom. Although Jancis had nothing personally against the girl, the thought was not a pleasant one. She supposed it was the idea of Alyson as mistress here, a place she still thought of as being rightfully her mother's. Goodness knows, the girl was welcome to him as a husband.

With Keegan out for the evening, it seemed a good opportunity for Jancis to visit the yard and weigh up the prospects of getting a ride. The lads would be opening up for evening stables and she was sure she could persuade the head lad to let her join the string next morning.

Fred Higgins had worked for her father since before she was born and she knew that the wizened little man had a soft spot for her. He had put her up on her first pony and from him she had absorbed the love of racing, her knowledge of horses. He would understand her need, her compulsion, to be involved with the animals themselves, and not just to be immured in the office, hidebound by paperwork and the more mundane aspects of the trainer's work.

Although it was evening, the sun was still warm on the cobbles and Jancis paused appreciatively to drink in the dry, sharp smell of hay and straw, mingled with the odours of leather, saddle soap and polish.

It was the first opportunity she had had, since returning home, to visit the yard, and she did so with the same apprehension with which she had entered the house. But here again, restoration had been made with a view to retaining its former character. The newly painted doors and windows, though pristine fresh, were exactly the same shade of blue; the central circle of turf, protected by white posts and chains, had been retained and was a smooth, lush green.

Jancis found Fred mucking out, busily flicking a pitchfork, throwing unsoiled straw to one side, while dirty straw, rank with ammonia and pungent droppings, was jerked on to a muck sack by the door.

'Miss Jancey!' Fred greeted her with delight and the familiarity of long acquaintance. He was the only person who had ever called her Jancey.

'Hallo, Fred. How's it going?'

Her enquiry referred not to the business of evening stables, but to the new ownership under which The Kingdom operated, and Fred interpreted her question correctly.

'To be truthful, Miss Jancey, it's going well . . . very well indeed. Don't get me wrong, you know I'd a million times sooner be working for your dad, but this fellow...' He paused.

'Yes, go on, Fred?'

Jancis was aware of a slightly breathless anticipation. Fred was a good judge of character, in both man and horse, and she valued the shrewd little man's opinion. Would he concur with her mistrust, her instinctive dislike for Keegan Leroy?

'Mr Leroy's a good gaffer, Miss Jancey. He don't suffer fools gladly, but he's fair. The lads know where they are with him ... and of course,' he added apologetically, 'he's got the money to put the old place back on its feet.'

He studied her again.

'You don't mind me speaking out, Miss Jancey?'

'No ... no, it's all right, Fred. I suppose you must speak as you find.' She laughed a little strainedly, surprised at what was for Fred enthusiastic praise. 'Even I have to admit that money seems to have its uses.'

'You getting on all right with him, miss, up there?' He jerked his head in the direction of the house.

'As well as can be expected,' she said wearily. 'I'll never get used to seeing him in Dad's place, Fred, and I shall never like him ... but I have to think of Mummy, and...'

'Ah, yes,' Fred nodded sagely. 'Your ma's been a different woman since Mr Leroy took over, and that's a fact. Seems to have given her a whole new purpose in life.'

Fred drew together the corners of the full sack, swinging it over his shoulder to carry it to the towering muck heap. He looked at her shrewdly.

'You'll be wanting a ride, no doubt?'

'Yes.'

Jancis studied Fred's gnomelike face anxiously. Had he received instructions from Keegan Leroy that she was not to ride the racehorses?

'Best go out with the first string in the morning, miss ... and pull the helmet well down over those bright curls of yours. Gaffer don't go out till the second gallop tomorrow.'

Fred strode away, the muck sack bouncing on his bowed shoulders, and Jancis stared after him, her eyes moistening sentimentally. Dear, loyal old Fred! He *did* know about Keegan's directive, but he also knew what riding meant to her. With a lighter heart, she turned to inspect the occupants of the many looseboxes.

'That's Mr Mortimer's colt,' Fred informed her on his return trip. 'Not a bad'un for a two-year-old, though a bit wild like. He's got a fair turn of speed. The gaffer gave him a trial against a couple of good three-year-olds, and he held his own. The gaffer won't take 'em into training unless they've got promise.'

'Careful about his reputation!' Jancis said a trifle acidly.

Fred eyed her askance, but made no comment.

'Which is Nick's filly?' she asked.

He led the way to the other end of the yard.

'You know Mr Mortimer, then?'

Jancis felt there was something more than just curiosity in Fred's enquiry. Having known her since infancy, Fred had never scrupled to advise her upon the suitability of her friendships, being as jealous of her welfare as her own parents.

'I met him for the first time this afternoon. I like him,' she said, a trace of defiance in her voice as she remembered Keegan's prohibition. 'What do you think of him, Fred?'

'Seems all right, on the surface,' Fred said grudgingly. 'Only time'll tell.'

Jancis relaxed. Dear old Fred! He was inclined to be cautious in his acceptance of new faces, which made his recent praise of Keegan all the more astonishing. How had the new owner of The Kingdom managed to pull the wool over the exceedingly astute eyes of his head lad?

Nick Mortimer's filly, The Linnet, was a three-year-old, a bright bay, with a shining summer coat.

Jancis approached confidently, but with caution. She found that firm, gentle handling and an air of confidence worked well with most horses. The filly snuffed her hand, nostrils quivering.

'How does she go, Fred?'

'Fair . . . fair.' Fred was as chary in his judgment of a new horse, as in assessing a new acquaintance. 'Long, smooth stride, a nice ride. Has a pretty good track record according to Nick Mortimer, but no wins to her credit as yet. What d'you think of her, Miss Jancey? Like to try her out tomorrow?'

'I'd love to, Fred.' Jancis eyed the filly critically. 'I'd like

to see how she goes. She's not got much character to look at
. . . significant markings, I mean. That head would look
more intelligent with a blaze, or a star.'

Fred shrugged. He judged a horse by its performance, not
by its appearance.

To Jancis' relief, Keegan was still out when she returned
to the house. She felt it would have been difficult to disguise
the suppressed elation she felt at the thought of an early
morning ride, of flouting his wishes. To her mother's
surprise, she declared that she felt in need of an early night,
since, though she could not tell Mary so, she intended to be
up early next day.

Mary was disappointed.

'I thought we'd have a nice cosy chat, dear. Alyson has to
go to bed so early . . .'

'I'm sorry, Mummy,' said Jancis. She felt despicable
deceiving her mother, but she couldn't be certain how strong
the alliance was between Mary King and her employer.
Mary might feel it her duty to tell Keegan that her daughter
intended to ride one of his horses, and Jancis was
determined that nothing was going to stop her trying out
Nick Mortimer's filly.

The next morning Jancis woke to the much-loved, familiar
sound of horses whinnying, the clank of buckets and voices
from the stableyard, the scrunch of hoofs on gravel.

She had intended to be up earlier, but some time during
the night her alarm clock must have stopped. There was
only time for a quick splash of cold water on her face before,
promising herself the luxury of a bath on her return, she
pulled on the clothing she had laid out the night before.

As Fred had advised, Jancis was clad exactly like one of
the lads, in breeches, boots and windcheater, the crash
helmet disguising her unmistakable coppery curls. Fred had
The Linnet ready for her and gave her a leg up into the
saddle, adjusting her stirrups.

She gave him a conspiratorial grin.

'Thanks, Fred.'

'Ah,' he nodded. 'But don't you get caught out, Miss
Jancey, or the gaffer'll have my cards waiting for me!'

The long string of horses made its way down the drive and

out on to the downs, large, windswept and beautiful in the early morning light. As they reached the sweet-smelling turf of the downland, the horses jigged in anticipation, their riders sitting more tensely.

At first, Jancis found her attention entirely concentrated on keeping her proper distance—the filly was eager and inclined to overhaul the animal in front. But soon she became used to her mount and was able to look around her, to recapture the thrill of early morning, the feel of a good horse beneath her, the sense of companionship ... of being with others who shared her enthusiasm.

When they reached the gallops, the riders drew their mounts up in a half circle around Fred, to receive their instructions. At last he came to Jancis. Deliberately, he did not use her name.

'You, ride at a canter for the first two furlongs, half speed gallop for the next two and then gradually slow up.'

Jancis nodded and turned her mount towards the inviting vista of turf. Soon there was nothing in the world but the muted pounding of hoofs on grass, the breeze flicking the corners of sheets, and she thrilled to the sensation of the rippling, living power of muscle and bone thundering along beneath her.

The Linnet's hoofs hardly seemed to touch the springy surface and Jancis laughed exultantly, head thrown back, the russet curls, which despite all her care insisted on escaping round the edge of her helmet, ruffled by the wind. Her hands, despite their smallness, were in perfect control of the filly.

All too soon the exhilarating gallop was over, the horses pulled up and turning for home at an easy pace, tails swishing leisurely. Half a mile from home, the riders dismounted to lead the animals in and Fred moved alongside, jerking his head towards the filly.

'Went well, didn't she?'

Jancis nodded, eyes shining.

'She's a beauty, Fred. Can I ride her again tomorrow?'

Fred refused to commit himself. Keegan, it seemed, liked to vary his routine, going out with the second string one day, the first on another. Jancis had to be content with Fred's promise that he would let her know when she could safely sneak in another ride.

She hated the thought that she was deceiving an employer, even though that employer was Keegan, and that she was allowing Fred to do the same. But it was all Keegan's fault, she thought indignantly. If it were not for his overbearing, intractable manner, neither of them would have been forced to compromise with their honour in this way.

In one sense, she would have preferred Keegan to know of her riding activities . . . at least then he would have to admit she could ride, that she rode well.

Back in the yard, Jancis was all set to do her share of the work, drying down the filly and feeding her. But Fred was adamant.

'Best not, missy,' he muttered. 'That *would* be asking for trouble. The gaffer's not daft, and if he caught you here, he'd be bound to guess you'd been out. Young David'll see to her.'

David was an apprentice jockey who had been taken on by Keegan in the last few weeks. Jancis had noticed him riding out with the others and liked the look of his young, fresh face.

It had been a relief, though somewhat of a surprise, to find that Sam Roscoe, her father's one-time jockey, who had defected to the Leroy stables, was no longer riding for Keegan. Fred, when questioned on the subject, had been unusually uncommunicative. Jancis could only suppose that the ambitious young man had moved on yet again.

Several times during the days that followed, Nick Mortimer dropped in at The Kingdom, ostensibly to enquire after his horses, but he made it obvious to Jancis that he also wished to further his acquaintance with her. True to her word, she did not actually encourage his visits to the office, but she refused to snub him, and despite Keegan's black looks, he did not make any actual complaint.

Nick had not asked her for a date as yet, but she felt it could not be long before this occurred, and she looked forward to the eventuality with pleasurable anticipation. In his presence she felt relaxed, assured, with none of the complicated contradictory emotions Keegan aroused in her.

She would dearly have loved to discuss The Linnet's

progress with Nick, but to do so would betray her intimate involvement with the filly's training.

There had been many occasions since that first morning when Jancis had contrived to go out on the early morning gallops and there was a growing sense of rapport between her and the bay filly. It had been impossible to keep her identity a secret for long and eventually all the lads were in on the deception. She was popular with them all, old employees and new, and in their youthful high spirits they all took great delight in the fact that she was putting one over on 'the gaffer'. She had struck up a lighthearted friendship with David, the young jockey, and on their return to the stables, he always undertook to attend to The Linnet. For her part, Jancis leant a willing ear to his eager confidences . . . about his ambitions as a rider, and about the girl he hoped to marry, once his income was assured.

'Poor kid,' he said. 'She's an orphan, lives with an elderly uncle. He treats her O.K., but he's a bit impractical and there's not much money. Ronny has to work hard. She has another uncle. I've not met him, but apparently he's filthy rich. She doesn't like him, though. I gather he's a bit of a rogue.'

Afterwards, Jancis supposed it had been almost inevitable that Keegan Leroy would eventually uncover her illicit activities.

One morning, at the completion of the gallops, she had just turned the filly's head for home, at a gentle canter, when she saw a lone horse coming towards her at a tremendous speed. She looked about her, but neither Fred nor any of the other lads was anywhere in sight. They must have turned back a furlong earlier and now be hidden from her by the swell of the downs.

It was immediately obvious that the approaching horse was riderless and that it would be useless to bar his way. She knew that there was only one thing to do . . . to turn and go with him, hoping that he would slow up gradually.

Not for one instant did it occur to Jancis to ignore the runaway. A racehorse was a valuable animal, and there was always the danger of injury, the beautiful creature having to be destroyed.

She turned the filly and increased her pace, taking the

same direction as the runaway. Looking back over her shoulder, she could see that he was gaining on her rapidly, and as he came alongside she increased her pace to match his, gently edging the filly closer and closer, so that the riderless horse was forced round in a gradual circle. They seemed to cover miles before the turn was completed and both horses were heading back in the direction of the stables.

By this time Jancis had recognised the truant. It was Nick Mortimer's colt, Fly-by-Night, which David had ridden out that morning. Still uttering soothing noises, Jancis rode on. Fly-by-Night seemed to be slowing from a gallop to a canter and then finally to a trot, as they came up with the rest of the string. He was dark with sweat and trembling all over, as Jancis leant across and secured the flapping reins in one shaking hand.

She sat quite still, totally unable to move, so great was the tension of the last few minutes. Then Fred was striding towards her, followed by a figure on a great, raking horse. The largest horse in the stables was needed to carry the man who bestrode it.

Jancis, curls inevitably escaped from her helmet during the tempestuous ride, knew she was discovered. Fred reached her, taking the reins of both the filly and the runaway into his gnarled hands. His weatherbeaten face was anxious.

'Are you all right, Miss Jancey?'

She forced a smile.

'I . . . I think so, Fred. What about David?'

'He's O.K. Took a nasty toss, but no bones broken.'

Jancis dismounted and was dismayed to find that her legs showed an ominous tendency to buckle under her. She was saved from ignominious collapse by a large, forceful hand, which gripped her elbow in a hold that was both supportive and painful.

She looked up into black, dangerous eyes, as, predictably, Keegan Leroy flared into angry speech.

'What the hell do you think you're doing, Miss King, playing at cowboys on one of my most valuable horses?'

Jancis' legs might be weak, but her courage was still indomitable. She snapped straight back at him.

'Playing, did you say, Mr Leroy? I wasn't aware that

rounding up a runaway was exactly play. As to the value of the filly, you'll find she's quite unharmed ... as, incidentally, is her stablemate. I believe Fly-by-Night is an equally valuable piece of horseflesh ... which might not have been the case if I hadn't. . .'

'Be quiet!' he quelled her attempt at self-justification. 'You had no business whatsoever to be riding the filly. I made myself quite clear on that point.' He turned to Fred, who had been an uneasy witness to this interchange. 'May I remind you, Higgins, that you're in *my* employ now. I think you have your loyalties a little misplaced.'

'Don't you dare to blame Fred!' Jancis attempted to shake off the iron hand that still held her, but she might as well have tried to escape the grip of a vice.

'*I* will decide where blame is to be apportioned. Higgins will see that the filly is returned safely to her stable. *You* will come with me.' Keegan marched towards his own horse, propelling Jancis before him.

Again she essayed a protest.

'I'm quite capable of riding The Linnet home myself.'

He did not even deign to answer her. Two steely hands gripped her waist, lifting her high in the air, and the next moment an indignant Jancis found herself riding before him, one muscular arm clamped imprisoningly around her slim waist, while the other controlled his powerful mount.

Inexplicable tremors shook her at the almost intimate contact. Damn the man! How could he contrive to be so hateful and yet so sensually disturbing? Why must her flesh and her brain always be in conflict over their reaction to him?

'*Will* you put me down?' she demanded, struggling in his grasp.

'No,' he said uncompromisingly, and urged his horse straight into a gallop, which rendered further attempts at escape almost certain suicide.

By the time they reached The Kingdom, Jancis felt as if every bone in her body had been shaken to pieces, the breathed jarred from her. She also felt intensely humiliated and a trifle apprehensive of what was to follow. The fear was not solely for herself, though that was present too, but for the head lad. Would Fred be penalised for his part in her escapade?

With a curt command, Keegan threw his reins to a hovering lad and marched her unceremoniously into the office, thrusting her down into a chair, where he towered over her, his whole attitude giving the impression of smouldering force barely held in check.

'How long has this been going on? And don't lie to me—I have ways of finding out.'

'Two weeks, off and on,' Jancis muttered reluctantly.

'The "off" being when I took the early gallops myself?'

She nodded.

He was silent for so long that she ventured a swift upward glance, to find his dark gaze fixed broodingly upon her. She flushed, furious with herself at her selfconscious reaction to his scrutiny. She wished he would have his say and be done with it.

The expected reprimand did not manifest itself. Instead he asked abruptly,

'Who taught you to ride?'

'Fred.'

A further silence, then:

'You realise you could have been killed? A frightened, runaway animal is an unpredictable creature. He might have turned on the filly. You could have been thrown, trampled underfoot . . .'

She nodded slowly.

'I realise that now, of course. At the time, I didn't . . .'

'Didn't think? Now do you realise why I don't employ girls in my stables? They're too impulsive, too easily swayed by their emotions.'

'Rubbish!' Jancis interrupted him, rising as she did so, to lessen the advantage which his great height gave him. 'Don't tell me any lad worth his salt wouldn't have done the same, because I won't believe you.'

He turned away from her, irritably ruffling a hand through his crisp, dark hair.

'No, I won't deny it. But my lads are insured against injury at work. You aren't. Suppose . . .' He turned towards her and she saw that his face was suddenly pale under the tan, the lines at the corners of his mouth more deeply etched. 'Suppose you'd been killed? How do you suppose I could have faced your mother with that news, after everything else she's been through?'

Jancis felt the blood drain from her own face. It was true. She had never considered the effect upon her mother, should she be involved in a riding accident. She had been accustomed to the saddle almost since she could toddle, had always been fiercely independent, though never reckless.

'I ... I ...'

'Didn't think!' Keegan repeated the condemnation.

Incensed by what she considered to be his insufferable air of superiority, Jancis abandoned her defensive attitude and returned to the attack.

'The same way *you* didn't think, when you destroyed my father? What sort of effect do you think *that* had on my mother? You're the last person with any right to remind me of what she's been through. So don't expect *me* to be touched by your so-called concern for my mother!'

'It didn't occur to you that I might also be concerned for your welfare, that I ...'

'Not for one moment,' she said emphatically. 'Why should my welfare be a cause of worry to you? I'm just the fly in your ointment of self-satisfaction, Mr Leroy. My mother is too easygoing, too trusting. *She* seems to have succumbed to your oily charm. Well, I haven't ... and while I'm here you'll never be able to forget that you were responsible for my father's failure ... because I don't intend to let you forget it ... and that you were probably responsible for hastening his death too. Oh no, Mr Leroy, with me out of the way, you'd be far better off, so don't try to pretend otherwise!'

'Have you quite finished?' he enquired stiffly.

'For the present, yes.' Her brown eyes held his defiantly.

'Then you may go. I hope ...'

Janice paused briefly in her step, struck by the hesitation, the alteration in his tone, the quality of which she could not quite fathom.

'I hope you won't have occasion to regret your accusations.'

His craggy features were strangely drawn in the harsh glare of the morning sunlight, which filled the little office with a brightness which merely seemed to emphasise the dark resentment in Jancis' heart.

'I shan't regret my words,' she told him, with a composure which now seemed to outweigh his own. 'But *you* may have cause for regret, Mr Leroy, before our association comes to an end.'

CHAPTER FOUR

LUNCH was an uncomfortable meal. Keegan was unusually reserved, even for him, while Mary King was quietly reproachful. It hadn't taken long for news of her illicit riding activities to reach the house, Jancis thought bitterly . . . for Keegan to regale the other two women with his version of that morning's escapade.

She was particularly irritated by Alyson's smug glances. The other girl was obviously delighted to see Jancis in disgrace with everyone.

'It was very naughty of you to disobey Keegan,' Alyson said, 'And I'm surprised at Fred Higgins, aiding and abetting you. He should have more loyalty.'

'He has,' Jancis snapped. 'Loyalty to me . . . and to Dad, which is more than can be said for some people around here!'

She was horrified to see the ready tears well up in Mary King's eyes.

'Jancis! Oh, how could you? Are you implying that I . . .' Her voice faltered into silence.

'Since you mention it, you don't seem to be missing Dad very much these days. I . . .'

'Jancis!' Mary stared disbelievingly at her daughter.

'I think you owe your mother an apology,' Keegan observed.

His tone was only mildly reproving, but Jancis turned on him. Her anger and resentment with Keegan Leroy, Alyson's smug comment, had been responsible for her unthinking words. Without their presence the words would never have been uttered, and had Keegan not chosen to intervene, she would have apologised immediately. Now his words goaded her into defiance.

'I don't need a lecture on behaviour from you!'

She lifted a small, stubborn chin at him. How dared he reprimand her as if she were a child!

He raised a cynical eyebrow.

'I'm afraid I can't agree with you there.'

Smouldering under his gaze, all too aware that she was behaving badly ... aware too of Alyson's intent, interested eyes, of her mother's unhappy face, Jancis pushed aside her plate and flinging down her napkin, rushed from the dining room.

As a child, in rare moments of unhappiness, she had always sought solace in the stables, and now her desperate need of solitude took her automatically in that direction.

The morning's work finished, the lads had departed to their various quarters, the afternoon hours their own; only one or two of them lived in, the rest lodging in the nearby village. They would not be back until it was time for evening stables, and the only evidence of life in the yard was the sound of the horses, the crack of a stamping foot, the snuffle of nostrils blowing into the mangers.

The Linnet was eating steadily, ears flicking as her jaws moved rhythmically. She seemed none the worse for her adventure.

Jancis slipped into the box and ran her hand down the filly's silky neck, proffering the square of chocolate the filly had grown to love and expect. Jancis had never before encountered a horse which was so fond of chocolate. She rested her head against the filly's nose, trying to draw comfort from the animal's demonstrative affection. Suddenly the Linnet moved restlessly, a hind foot snatched up in a kick-back gesture, and Jancis glanced round to see what had disturbed her.

Keegan stood in the open doorway, an unfathomable expression on his hawk-like features. Casually he moved into the box, running an expert hand over the filly's quarters and legs.

'Quite a love affair,' he commented, as The Linnet continued to nuzzle Jancis' neck and shoulder.

Jancis nodded, not trusting herself to speak. Tears were not far away, and she had determined long ago that she would not make a fool of herself in front of Keegan Leroy.

'You really are fond of horses,' he said. It was a statement, not a question, but Jancis nodded again.

Of course she loved horses. For as long as she could remember they had formed the main part of her life. As soon as she was old enough, she had gone with her father to race meetings, standing, her small hand clasped in his, by the parade ring, watching the jockeys mount and canter down to the post, the big, beautiful animals moving smoothly beneath them.

At the thought of those happy, carefree days with her father, the threatening tears spilled over and she turned away, hoping to hide them from the keen gaze of the man beside her.

It was a forlorn hope. A strong hand that could, it seemed, also be gentle, turned her towards him, the other lifting the small, pointed chin. Slowly his thumb traced lips that trembled ominously.

'You miss your father very much.' Again it was a statement.

Jancis could not answer, her eyelids pressed tight in a vain endeavour to stem those betraying tears that, against her will, trickled down her cheeks.

'But it must be much worse for your mother.' The voice was deliberately matter-of-fact, almost expressionless, but Jancis, already made uncomfortable by guilt, was sensitive to the implied reproach. Why did he have to be so reasonable . . . so right? It would be much easier to go on hating him, if he would only rant or shout at her.

'I know,' she whispered. 'And . . . and I wouldn't have spoken to her as I did, if it hadn't been for . . . for . . .'

'For my presence?' He sighed. 'Yes, I'm well aware of that.'

She stood immobile, unresisting in the grasp of the firm hands which still held her. There was a strange comfort in a man's touch and for a moment she had forgotten that this was the man, above all others, whom she most hated.

Eyes still closed, she did not see the movement of his dark head towards her, nor sense its nearness, until his lips brushed her tear-stained cheeks. It was a gentle, caressing touch, meant, she realised afterwards, only as a comforting gesture, as one might kiss a hurt child, but she could not disguise her instinctive response, as every nerve in her body leapt at that brief touch. In a moment of unbalanced emotionalism, she swayed against him, needing to feel the security of his arms about her, and was startled at his reaction to the intimate contact she had initiated.

The kiss that followed was no comforting caress, but a demanding invasion, which shook her to her innermost being, as Keegan's mouth lingered on hers with a marvellous intensity, its effect upon her already weakened defences amazingly erotic.

For a moment she clung, surrendering herself to this new, unbelievable sensation ... unbelievable because it was Keegan who aroused such feelings ... feelings which no other man had ever stirred in her. Then, too late, she remembered her dislike, her mistrust of the man whose arms held her, and with a quick, angry twist of her body she wrenched herself free, furious that Keegan of all people should be capable of arousing in her such ... such passion! The heat of shame warmed her cheeks and she backed away, putting the length of the loosebox between them.

Regarding him defiantly, she was aware of the unmistakable flicker of desire in those dark eyes and she realised, with a little surge of triumph that, for a second, she had breached *his* armour, that shell of cool indifference towards her ... discovered a momentary weakness in this hard, self-sufficient man. Here, surely, was the key to her revenge ... revenge for the humiliation her family had suffered, was still suffering at his hands.

If she could strike at him through his emotions, arouse his desire to a point where he must declare it ... plead with her for its fulfilment, and then spurn his advances ... It was a heady thought. Yet she was puzzled by the depression that it engendered. Why was she not more excited at her recognition of this instrument of vengeance Keegan had unwittingly given her? Moreover, why had she to force herself to feel a proper indignation at the incursion his lips had inflicted on hers?

Nevertheless, she was ready with words of icy condemnation, should he attempt to touch her again. But to her chagrin, he seemed to have regained his composure ...

regained it more readily than she had, still shaken by the compulsion of his physical attraction.

'Do you still want to ride?' Keegan asked abruptly.

Jancis stared at him in silence for a moment, finding it an effort to change the direction of her thoughts.

'Yes . . . yes, of course,' she replied at last. 'But I don't suppose . . .'

He raised a large hand in a silencing gesture.

'I thought you rode well today, in spite of your unnecessary recklessness.'

She opened her mouth to make an indignant protest . . . it had not been recklessness, but an instinctive knowledge of the right thing to do . . . but he forestalled her.

'Hear me out. Don't say anything to make me regret my decision. You may ride The Linnet whenever you wish, but no more heroics, hmm?'

Impulsively she moved towards him, forgetting for a moment her newly determined campaign against this man. Her brown eyes were alight, her piquant, heart-shaped face lovely in its radiance.

'You really mean it?'

For a moment he stared down at her, his dark eyes searching, and all her new-found instincts told her that with one sign of willingness from her she would be in his arms again.

Fiercely she renounced the tide of inexplicable sensation, the overwhelming weakness, which prompted her to give that sign. Despite his unexpected volte-face in the matter of her riding, Keegan was still the enemy, the buccaneering brute of a man who had ruthlessly possessed himself of all that had been her father's. He should not add her to his list of possessions!

She forced herself to turn aside, patting the filly's neck, giving herself time to choose her words.

'Thank you.' Coolly, she threw the words over her shoulder. 'It . . . it's very magnanimous of you.' Despite her attempt at casualness, a childlike bubble of excitement escaped her, as she moved towards him, neatly sidestepping his tall figure. 'I must go and tell Fred.'

'And apologise to your mother?'

Jancis paused on the threshold. This concern, this

gentleness he always displayed towards Mary King, still puzzled her. She had never expected such complexity of character in this man.

'You *will* apologise?' he persisted softly, moving towards her.

Something in his renewed proximity, in the dark eyes surveying her, made her feel a little breathless.

'Yes . . . yes.' She almost whispered the words. 'I'll . . . I'll apologise.'

She turned and hurried away. Keegan in this softened mood disturbed her and she was suddenly afraid, as she recalled her reaction to his kiss, his touch. She must not allow herself to be swayed . . . she must not yield an inch of ground in the state of hostility which existed between them. She was afraid of what might happen should all barriers be irrevocably removed.

Predictably, Fred was delighted by Keegan's removal of his ban and so was the young jockey, David.

'How are you feeling?' Jancis asked David, as they rode out next morning.

There was a new exuberance in her, able for the first time to enjoy a ride, unspoiled by the necessity for deception.

'A bit stiff,' David said ruefully. 'I took a heck of a toss yesterday. I don't mind the bruises so much, but . . .'

'But what?' she prompted.

'The boss was a bit scathing. Said I'd have to do better than that, if I want to work for him, and as my probationary period is nearly up . . .'

He looked very young and vulnerable as he bit his lower lip, and Jancis, remembering Ronny, his girl-friend, his hopes for the future, tried to reassure him.

David still looked doubtful.

'I've got my first big ride next week, on The Linnet,' he told her. 'The boss as good as hinted that my future depends on the outcome.'

'Then you must ride her as often as possible,' said Jancis, adding generously, 'I know . . . we'll swop for the next few mornings. I'll ride Fly-by-Night.'

David shook his head.

'I don't know. The boss might not like it.'

'I don't see how he can possibly object,' Jancis persisted. 'It's just as much to his advantage for you to do well. After all, that's a trainer's job . . . producing winners for his owners.'

David's scruples overcome, they changed mounts, Jancis riding Nick Mortimer's large, lively colt.

As they turned for home at the end of the gallops, Jancis saw that Keegan had ridden out to watch them and was now talking to Fred. As they drew nearer, she could see that he looked displeased, his dark face drawn into a now familiarly ominous scowl, one large hand waving aside Fred's deprecatory replies.

She was soon to learn the cause of his anger, as he wheeled his large, powerful mount towards her.

'I gave you permission to ride The Linnet, not any horse that took your fancy . . . and certainly not that one!'

Stumblingly, Jancis began to explain the reason for the exchange, but he cut short her excuses.

'Fly-by-Night is no horse for a girl. Have you no sense? You saw how he bolted yesterday, after throwing his rider.'

'No horse has ever thrown me yet,' Jancis retorted.

'Don't argue with me,' he ordered. 'In any case, your claim is scarcely likely to advance David's cause. He was all too easily thrown.'

Already sensitive about yesterday's events and anxious for Keegan's good opinion, David flushed bright scarlet. He dismounted hastily and led The Linnet towards her stablemate, intent on exchanging mounts once more.

But Jancis, infuriated by Keegan's manner of speaking to her before the lads and indignant on David's behalf, had no intention of submitting so tamely. So he thought the colt was no fit ride for a girl, did he? He was always so sure of himself. It was high time someone proved him wrong. She would show Keegan whether she could ride Fly-by-Night or not!

A touch of her heels and the colt jumped straight into a fast canter, startling the other riders by the suddenness of the action. His head turned towards home, Fly-by-Night was only too willing to oblige, and the ungainly colt's long stride ate up the ground.

Jancis forgot everything, even Keegan's certain fury, in

the exhilaration of the ride. She moved her hands forward on the colt's neck and he pricked up his ears, perceptibly lengthening his stride.

She was vaguely aware of the muted sounds of pursuit, but aware too that Fly-by-Night was still full of running, that nothing could catch him now ... not even Keegan's powerful hack.

Then the hedge loomed up ahead and with a gasp of dismay, she realised that she had no idea if the colt could jump. He was a flat racer, not a hurdler. But it was too late now to change her course.

Her heart beating a staccato counter-rhythm to the colt's stride, they approached the obstacle and Jancis tensed, using all her expertise, rising high in the stirrups, urging him on, willing him up and over. To her delighted relief, her mount made nothing of the hedge, flying through the air, soaring up and over, then sinking down to earth. It should have been a copybook jump, but disaster still lay in wait.

As Fly-by-Night landed, he pitched badly in a patch of mud and though he recovered himself almost instantly, the mistake was enough to unseat Jancis, sending her flying in a breathtaking arc, to land face downwards, yards from the hedge.

Feeling certain that every bone in her body must be shattered, she lay quite still, hearing the confused sounds of approaching riders, of shouting voices.

'Jancis! Jancis!'

It was Keegan's voice, breathless, anxious, as he knelt beside her, regardless of the soft mud adhering to the knees of his impeccable breeches. Dimly, she realised that this was the first time he had ever used her christian name.

'Jancis!' he repeated more urgently.

A gentle, probing exploration of her limbs ensued. Jancis knew she ought to move, explain that she was unhurt, but the touch of those strong hands was strangely pleasant, his concern disarming.

'No bones broken anyway,' Jancis heard Keegan say, and heard Fred's anxious voice reply:

'But she's unconscious.'

Jancis knew the time had come to face retribution. Slowly, very slowly, she eased herself on to one side and looked up at the two men kneeling beside her, concern showing on both faces.

Contrarily, seeing she was still alive, Keegan's expression changed to one of the utmost fury.

'Get up!' he hissed from between clenched teeth. 'You are without doubt the most pigheaded, reckless little fool it's ever been my misfortune to meet! Putting a flat racer at a jump! What do you use for a brain? It's fortunate for you that the colt wasn't injured!'

Painfully, Jancis got to her feet, incensed to see Keegan push aside Fred's proffered helping hand.

'Of course, it's immaterial to you that *I* might have been injured,' she muttered, unfairly ignoring the earlier anxiety in his voice as he had spoken her name. She attempted to brush the mud and grass from her clothes, but her legs were shaking and her head ached. She knew that for the second time in twenty-four hours she was in danger of breaking down before Keegan Leroy and ... even more lowering ... that she deserved every epithet he had flung at her.

He shrugged, answering her roughly.

'Since your own safety matters so little to you, why should it concern me? Fred,' he turned to the anxiously watching head lad, 'put this little fool up in front of you and get her home. I have a few home truths to tell young David!'

'It wasn't David's fault,' Jancis protested to Fred, as he gave her a leg up on to his own mount.

'I know that and you know that, Miss Jancey,' Fred said matter-of-factly, 'but somehow I don't think that will make the gaffer any easier on the lad.'

Despairingly, she looked after Keegan's receding figure, the purposeful set of his head and shoulders. Much as she disliked him, she could not even find relief in blaming him for her present condition. Once more she had allowed her emotions to sway her judgment and, unforgivable sin, she had at the time been in charge of a powerful and valuable animal. Even she could not justify her own rash behaviour, and despite his fondness for her, she knew Fred too could only disapprove of her action ... behaviour so contrary to the early training he had instilled in her. What was it about Keegan Leroy, she wondered, that drove her to such wild, uncharacteristic, foolhardy acts?

*

In all honesty, Jancis could not condemn Keegan for his coolness towards her in the days that followed ... a manner which contrasted all too obviously with his courtesy towards her mother and the indulgent affection he showed to Alyson.

Jancis was finding herself more and more irritated by Alyson's cloying personality, her dependence upon Keegan and the barely concealed delight the other girl showed at the animosity between her cousin and Jancis.

It was a relief when the weekend came round and with it the long-anticipated date with Nick Mortimer. True, it was only an invitation to accompany him to a race meeting, but as this was the event in which David was to ride The Linnet for the first time, Jancis was well content.

There had been an uninterrupted period of warm, sunny weather and she was conscious of looking her best, in a dress of cool mint-green, as she left the house and slid into the passenger seat of Nick's luxurious car. His bold blue gaze and appreciative intake of breath confirmed her confidence in her appearance.

'How is it that someone so incredibly lovely has managed to remain single?' he asked her, as the Silver Cloud slipped along the leafy tunnels of the country lanes.

Pleased, she flushed a little at his flattery.

'I suppose I've just never met the right person.'

'I hope you have now,' he said significantly.

For a moment she stared at him blankly, for a wild instant thinking he must be referring to Keegan. Then she realised he was talking about himself. Whatever could have put the other idea into her mind?

She was silent for so long that Nick darted a sidelong glance at her.

'Are you annoyed with me?'

'N-no, of course not.'

'That's good.'

For a brief second his hand rested on her knee, and though she suffered his touch without protest, she was bewildered by her lack of response. Nick was an attractive man. She had looked forward to a date with him and he had made no secret of his admiration for her. Yet she felt no eager rush of sensation, no desire for him to extend the caress, to initiate further intimacies, and she could not help comparing her present indifference with the primitive urges that had sprung to life, when she had been held fast in Keegan's arms ... could not help recalling the uneasy awareness that she felt just at the fact of his presence. Impatiently she tried to shake off the remembrance, this obsession that her body seemed to have developed, in direct opposition to all the promptings of common sense. But it was an effort to divert her thoughts, to pay attention to Nick's conversation.

The old fervour for racing had Jancis in its grip the moment they reached the course, one of a stream of crawling cars.

Here were the well-loved sights and sounds ... all the colour and noise of race day. Flags snapped in the stiff breeze, bookmakers cried their odds; milling around was the variety of characters that went to make up the racecourse scene ... officious car park attendants, voluble newspaper vendors, stewards, police, ambulance men, and above all, the horses ... gleaming, aristocratic thoroughbreds, being unloaded from their boxes, moving gingerly down the ramps, their ears pricking up, as they recognised their surroundings and caught the all-pervading excitement.

Nick had bought tickets for the main enclosure ... more expensive, of course, she thought with guilty pleasure, but the price included admission to the paddock.

It was inevitable that they should encounter Keegan. With two stables under his care, he had an entry in nearly every race and was very much in evidence in the paddock, giving last-minute instructions to the various jockeys riding for him and chatting to owners.

Jancis caught herself thinking how extremely attractive Keegan looked, when he was exerting himself to be affable. But of course, she mused cynically, it was in his interests to be pleasant, to butter up the wealthy men and women who brought their horses to him.

Nick consulted his race card.

'Do you fancy anything in the first race, Jancis?'

She shook her head.

'I don't bet. Dad always said it was a mug's game.'

He smiled tolerantly.

'Come on, just this once. I'll stake you, then the risk will be mine, hmm?'

It would have been churlish to refuse, and Jancis studied the proffered list of runners. A name caught her eye, and a thrill of certainty ran through her ... Bold Usurper. The coincidence was too good to pass up, for that was how she still thought of Keegan Leroy, she told herself ... as a usurper.

'That one.' She marked her choice.

'I'm surprised you didn't use a pin.' A sarcastic voice spoke in her ear. 'It would be just as effective.'

She turned, to find that Keegan, his pep-talk to the jockey completed, had moved to join them. He was insinuating, of course, that she knew nothing about form ... a pin indeed! ... though she was guiltily aware that her choice owed nothing to expertise, was just as much of a hunch as if she *had* used a pin.

'Oh,' she said lightly, 'I have a far more efficacious method. I choose a name that has a special significance for me.'

Her brown eyes met his challengingly and she saw his narrow, as he looked more closely at Nick's card and caught her implication.

He spoke with an air of would-be indifference, and only Jancis was triumphantly aware of the note of chagrin.

'You'd do better to keep a tight hold on your cash. That nag will never stay the distance.'

'But it isn't *my* money I'm risking,' she told him sweetly, 'and besides, I have a distinct premonition that I'm right. Usurpers aren't easily defeated, are they?'

She could tell that he was displeased by Nick's offer to stake her, but there was a little more to it than that. Smugly, she realised that she had succeeded in needling him, that he was distinctly annoyed by her pointed choice, her implication that she still thought of him as an outsider.

Nick left her side for a few moments, in order to place their bets with one of the many bookies, those noisy, colourful characters, standing on soapboxes beside their odds boards. Jancis expected Keegan to move away too, but, irritatingly, he stayed close beside her.

'Your acquaintance with the rich Mr Mortimer is

progressing satisfactorily, I see.'

'Yes,' Jancis agreed. She saw no reason to tell him that this was, in fact, her first proper date with Nick.

'He's not rich enough, though,' Keegan added enigmatically.

She looked up at him, a question in her eyes. What gave him the idea that she was the mercenary type . . . that she might be interested in Nick because of his money?

'Not rich enough to buy back the stables for you,' he explained.

Jancis stifled a gasp of outrage, forced back the angry reply. She would *not* let Keegan spoil the day for her.

'I never supposed he was,' she said coldly.

'No?' His voice was sardonic. 'I rather thought that would be your main purpose in life from now on . . . finding a way to oust me from your father's kingdom.'

His implication, that she would encourage the attentions of a rich man for such a purpose, added fuel to the flames of her already simmering anger; and, as always when roused, Jancis spoke with more feeling than wisdom, words that she was to have occasion to regret.

'It so happens I've no intention of marrying a rich man in order to solve that particular problem. When I marry, it will be for love, not cash. But if I *could* find some way to raise sufficient money to buy you out, I wouldn't hesitate for a moment.'

She was relieved when Nick returned at that moment, in time to prevent their exchange becoming still more acrimonious.

'The money's on,' Nick said with satisfaction, 'and I got good odds. If your hunch pays off, you stand to win a nice little sum.'

'If I win, I shall insist on returning your original stake,' she told him.

She would have done this anyway, but she spoke the words aloud for Keegan's benefit. She wasn't going to give him a chance to accuse her of scrounging from a rich client.

Nick's answering smile was complacent, as he tucked a proprietorial arm through hers.

'Never argue with a lovely lady, eh, old boy?' he asked Keegan.

Jancis felt a fit of the giggles threatening. Nick's remark struck her as being particularly fatuous. Moreover, his flattery, after Keegan's stringent treatment of her, seemed almost overdone. Anyway, Keegan was hardly likely to agree with the sentiment expressed. With her at least he did nothing *but* argue. She risked a sidelong glance at him and surprised a responsive glint of humour in his dark eyes, before he turned away to watch the runners go down to the post.

All eyes were now expectantly on the start, as the riders sorted their horses out into some sort of line, moving slowly towards the starter. The white flag went up, and over the loudspeaker system the commentator's disembodied voice announced: 'They're off!'

Bold Usurper had turned out to be a rather plain, gaunt-looking animal, and Jancis wondered if she had chosen wisely. Somehow it seemed important to the progress of her feud with Keegan that she should win. Anxiously she gnawed a fingernail as she tried to pick out the jockey's colours in the gaudy mêlée racing towards them.

As the field swept past, she could see that her horse was lying well up with the leaders, striding out easily, running well within himself. She felt Nick grip her elbow more tightly and she glanced up at him. He was as excited as she.

In the last furlong, Bold Usurper was gaining with every stride and at the line he was two lengths in front.

Eyes shining, Jancis turned to Nick.

'I've won!'

'You certainly have,' he agreed, 'and you've won a packet for me too. Let's go and collect our winnings.'

As she moved away with Nick, Jancis turned to look at Keegan, a gleam of triumph in her brown eyes.

His own expression was coldly remote.

'It seems I must congratulate you.'

'Yes, it does rather seem that way.' She spoke with an attempt at gaiety, but suddenly the petty victory seemed hollow, particularly as she remembered that her success meant The Kingdom's own runner had been defeated.

'Are you going to back The Linnet?' Nick asked her, two races later.

Jancis, her shoulder bag clutched closely to her side ...

she had never before carried so much money in it . . . nodded enthusiastically.

Nick's laugh was indulgent, triumphant.

'I believe you've been bitten by the gambling bug after all!'

'Take care it doesn't become a nasty virus,' Keegan warned.

Bother the man, Jancis thought. Why did he have to hang around, making sour remarks? Didn't she see enough of him at The Kingdom, without having him make an unwelcome third on her date with Nick?

Besides, with the two men together, she could not help making comparisons, and Nick did not come out of the exercise very well. His suave elegance seemed somehow overdone, almost . . . almost flashy, beside Keegan's well-cut but casual style, and she didn't want to award Keegan points for anything. Ostentatiously, she turned her shoulder on him.

In the paddock, David's face wore a look of strained anticipation. As Jancis already knew, much depended on the outcome of this, The Linnet's first race. She gave him an encouraging thumbs-up sign and watched sympathetically, as he leant down to receive Keegan's last-minute instructions.

Nick too was keyed up. Naturally, since The Linnet was his filly.

'If we win this one, it will be champagne all round,' he promised Jancis.

The tape swept up and the bunched horses surged forward. Jancis leant on the rail, her racing glasses unsteady in shaking hands. Every fibre of her being willed The Linnet to do well. The filly was two or three lengths behind the leaders, the two remaining runners having already dropped behind, to all intents and purposes out of the race. Three furlongs out, the filly moved up to the leader and at two furlongs, as instructed, David made his effort, giving The Linnet a light slap of the whip. Horse and rider went past the leader as if it were standing still and the filly continued to extend her lead, winning by a clear four lengths.

Bursting with excitement, Jancis turned to Nick, impulsively throwing her arms around his neck.

'She won! The Linnet won!' she told him unnecessarily.

Nick returned her embrace with interest, seeking out her lips in a long, lingering kiss, which oddly, for all his attraction, had no power to stir her and which, furthermore, was imbued with an intimacy she found she could not relish. He gave an exultant laugh as he released her.

'I think you must be lucky for me, Jancis,' he said. 'Stay around me, eh?'

As he released her to go and lead in his winner, Jancis met Keegan's brooding gaze and she realised that he had been a silent witness of their kiss, could not have failed to hear Nick's remark.

For her, the embrace had been only an expression of joyful well-being . . . not only for herself, but for David and for The Linnet. But Keegan, it seemed, had read more into her purely spontaneous act, and she remembered his insinuation that she was making up to Nick for his money.

As he turned away to speak to the jubilant David, whose grin spread from ear to ear, Keegan's expression, indeed his whole attitude, spoke of searing contempt.

CHAPTER FIVE

THE LINNET'S resounding victory, though in itself a cause for rejoicing, always marked for Jancis the beginning of the unpleasantness . . . the succession of incidents, which served to increase the hostility between herself and Keegan.

From being a simmering undercurrent to an already precarious relationship, their mutual antipathy was to flare into open warfare, with bitter recriminations and accusations being made on either side.

The day following the momentous race was a Sunday, and Jancis had readily agreed to Nick Mortimer's suggestion that they have a full day out together.

Casually, over breakfast, she mentioned her plans to her mother. But before Mary King had a chance to comment, Keegan intervened, his tone censorious.

'I don't recall being consulted about this.'

Jancis turned disbelieving eyes upon him.

'You may have succeeded my father in most things,' she said acidly, 'but that doesn't give you the right to monitor my private life.'

'I'm not speaking in loco parentis,' Keegan retorted, 'but as your employer.'

'Today *is* Sunday,' she reminded him.

'I'm well aware of that fact. It also happens to be one of my busiest days, when I catch up on my paperwork. And it's the day when a lot of owners visit the stables, for an on-the-spot report of their animals.'

Jancis' voice was ominously quiet and Mary King, recognising the familiar danger signals, watched her daughter apprehensively.

'Are you telling me that *I* have to work today?'

He flipped that irritating eyebrow.

'You catch on quickly, Miss King.'

'You've never asked me to work on a Sunday before,' Jancis pointed out, her tone still one of rigid but precarious control.

He shrugged.

'There's a first time for everything.'

She narrowed her eyes at him.

'I believe you're doing this deliberately. For some reason, you don't want me to go out with Nick Mortimer. You've always tried to discourage our friendship ... resented his interest in me.'

Keegan's reply was nicely calculated to fan the flames of her rising anger.

'*Resented?* His *interest*? Oh no, Miss King. That would imply far too personal an emotion, wouldn't it, such as ... jealousy? No, your love-affairs are a matter of complete indifference to me. It's your loyalty to the stables I demand.'

'I am not having an affair with Nick Mortimer!' Jancis snapped. Her self-control was at breaking point. It was just like him to make the implication, to impart an unpleasant flavour to what was an enjoyable, uncomplicated relationship.

'That sounds rather like pique,' he drawled. 'Mortimer not come up to scratch yet?'

Her cheeks flushed with fury, Jancis jumped up from the

table, her hand lifted to administer a stinging blow which would wipe the taunting expression from his face. But he parried the attempt effortlessly, catching her slight wrist in a crushing grip.

'Keegan! Jancis!' Mary King, a slightly bewildered spectator of their conflict, hastened to intervene. 'I'm surprised at the pair of you! Don't you think this argument is getting a little out of hand?'

Jancis, shaking uncontrollably, did not trust herself to reply, but Keegan, who had remained infuriatingly calm throughout the whole of their exchange, nodded gravely, as he released his furious captive.

'You're right, Mary—Jancis does tend to overreact. We'll remove ourselves and our disagreements to the office and leave you and Alyson to finish your breakfast in peace.'

Now he was blaming her . . . she was overreacting . . . the utter hypocrisy of him!

'*We* will *not* remove ourselves to the office,' Jancis snapped. 'You may do so, if you wish. *I* am going out with Nick.'

She did not wait for any further argument, but rushed from the room, slamming the door behind her.

Safe in the tranquil atmosphere of her bedroom, she brooded upon this latest unpleasantness, which had almost become an undignified brawl. Keegan certainly brought out the worse in her, she thought, humiliated at the knowledge that she had behaved like a fishwife . . . and in front of the smirking Alyson too. Well, it was his fault. He had no right to order her to work on a Sunday and she had no intention of being bullied or browbeaten into doing so.

She dressed for her date with deliberate care. A plain, wrap-around skirt in cream, topped by a tucked silk crêpe-de-chine blouse, in a warm shade of marigold, flattered her honey tan and emphasised the rich copper curls. Bronze court shoes and a matching bronze leather bag completed the outfit.

She descended the stairs, head held high in an attitude of defiance. She was rather deflated to find that Keegan had already left the house, having apparently accepted her rebellion . . . her assertion of her rights. Somehow she had not expected him to give in so tamely.

Nick's car was outside the front door, but there was no sign of Nick himself. Most probably he was in the yard, paying his horses a quick visit. Jancis debated whether to sit in the car and wait for him, but decided there would be more satisfaction gained from flaunting her defiant behaviour under Keegan's very nose. He wouldn't dare to censure her before Nick . . . wouldn't risk offending a valued client.

She strolled casually into the stableyard, quite aware that she was looking extremely good in the outfit she had chosen.

As she expected, she found Nick deep in conversation with Keegan, just outside The Linnet's stall. She moved to join them, but before she could utter the greeting she intended, Nick forestalled her, his square, good-looking face expressing rueful regret.

'Jancis—you look fantastic!' His blue eyes swept her from head to foot and she preened, only too aware of Keegan's silent but equally thorough appraisal.

Nick's next words banished the little smile from her lips.

'It makes me feel even more disappointed that you can't join me today, after all. Leroy tells me you've volunteered to work overtime. As a red-blooded male, I can't help feeling regret, but as an interested owner . . .' he shrugged resignedly, 'I can only applaud your dedication.'

Jancis flushed and opened her lips to speak the angry words of denial, but she was not allowed the chance. Smoothly, Keegan undermined her determination.

'Miss King *is* very dedicated to her work, of course . . . but then she has an important incentive. She has to consider her mother's welfare . . . the success of The Kingdom also safeguards Mary's home.'

Nick, taking Keegan's remarks at face value, smiled his appreciation of Jancis' thought for her mother, and only Jancis recognised that a subtle form of blackmail had been applied. Keegan was reminding her how easily he could dismiss both her and her mother. She had no doubt that any sort of scene in front of a wealthy owner would result in instant retribution.

Oh, Keegan was very subtle. He had achieved his ends in such a way that Nick could not possibly object. If there had been only herself to consider she would not have hesitated to expose his lies. She couldn't care less if he gave her the sack; with her qualifications she could get a job anywhere. But he had her cornered . . . knew she could not be so cruel as to destroy her mother's new-found contentment. She drew a deep breath in an attempt at composure, and realised Nick was speaking.

'I'll telephone you, Jancis, shall I? Make another date?'

She forced herself to give him a dazzling smile, to put enthusiasm into her voice.

'I'd love that, Nick. Make it soon, hmm?'

'You can be certain of that.'

Deliberately, she moved forward, offering her lips for a farewell kiss. Looking a little surprised, Nick was, nonetheless, willing to oblige, and Jancis shamelessly prolonged the moment, one hand curled caressingly around his neck.

As he drew away, Nick looked down at her, the expression in his blue eyes complacent. Obviously he attributed her behaviour to his own irresistible charm . . . blithely unaware of her true motive, that of showing Keegan her utter immunity to himself. It did not occur to her to wonder why this demonstration was so necessary.

'We—ell,' Nick breathed, 'our next date can't be *too* soon for me!'

'When you're quite ready, Miss King,' Keegan suggested stiffly. He turned on his heel and marched in the direction of the office.

Nick did not linger and with the restraint of his presence removed, Jancis fully intended to give vent to her feelings.

She had to run to catch up, but she was almost on Keegan's heels as he entered his office. She slammed the outer door and leant against it, facing him, brown eyes smouldering, her breasts heaving with mingled fury and exertion, further frustrated by the necessity of catching her breath before she could speak.

'How dare you!' she snapped. 'How dare you cancel my date like that? You knew very well that I intended to go out . . .'

'Then why didn't you contradict me?' Keegan asked coolly.

'You know damn well why not!' She advanced towards

him, fists clenched, small chin pugnacious. 'You lying, blackmailing, high-handed, obnoxious . . .' All her frustrations poured out in the insulting adjectives.

He acknowledged her description of him with a slight inclination of his dark head.

'And may I return the compliment by remarking that you're bad-tempered, pigheaded and rude . . . and now that we understand each other, shall we get on with some work?'

'Understand each other? Understand each other!' Seething at his retaliatory description of her, Jancis was in no mood to cease hostilities. 'Oh, I understand you very well, but you'll never understand me if you live to be a hundred. You don't think you've won that easily, do you, just because I held my tongue in front of Nick? You may have stopped me going out with him, because he's too much of a gentleman to disagree with you . . . and because you're a blackmailing swine, holding my mother's happiness over my head . . . but you can't *make* me sit at that desk . . .'

'Can't I?' he said grimly.

She tossed her curly head at him.

'Oh, you can probably force me to actually *sit* there . . . and knowing you, you wouldn't hesitate to use physical force . . . but you can't make me work.'

'My God!' His dark eyes were cynical. 'What frustration will do for a woman!'

'Frustration?'

She was puzzled for a moment, then could have kicked herself for the opening her naïvety had given him.

'It showed in every line of your body,' he told her contemptuously, 'when you kissed Mortimer. That's what's eating you, isn't it? You were looking forward to a whole day of . . .'

'I was looking forward to a day out,' she cut in before he could complete his unwarranted accusation. 'Looking forward to a few hours away from you. All right, so I enjoy kissing Nick Mortimer, but . . .'

'What's so special about *his* kisses?' Keegan jeered. 'Does he have some magic formula that other men lack?'

'They're infinitely preferable to yours, anyway,' she told him, with a reckless disregard for the probable consequences.

There was silence, and Jancis began to be afraid of the direction this conversation was taking. There was a gleam in Keegan's eyes that she mistrusted, and her last remark had almost amounted to a challenge ... a challenge she feared that Keegan would be unable to resist. He might dislike her, despise her even, but a man of his arrogance would not be likely to ignore such a deliberate slight on his physical attractions ... and there was only one way he could refute such a slur.

Her trepidation was not unfounded, and as he moved towards her, she realised that he had deliberately engineered this situation ... steered the conversation in this direction, deliberately provoked her intense retort. For some reason, he actually wanted an excuse to lay hands upon her, to kiss her.

She backed away, but the door she had so firmly closed now prevented her escape.

'Don't ... don't you dare!'

Her breath rasped in her throat and she felt the faint, excited prickling of her skin that his physical nearness always produced. The next moment she found herself imprisoned against the muscular wall of his chest, beneath which his heart thudded, a rhythm to which her own alarmed pulses swiftly and traitorously responded.

As a last resort, she braced herself, firming her lips against the expected onslaught. His kiss was likely to be a brutal assertive gesture, a retaliation for all her taunts.

Instead, his lips when they touched hers were warm, languorous, moving in a gentle yet demandingly persistent way, drawing a response that surprised her ... a response that was as basic and primitive as time past. Insidiously, brooking no denial, his lips parted hers, moving passionately, intimately, and against her will, she found her body curving against him, as his hands slid down her back; fondling her spine in a leisurely, hypnotically sensuous exploration.

She knew of course that it was only an instinctive, bodily response on her part to his undoubted sexual attraction which held her captive ... that such blatantly sexual desire, without the accompanying spiritual involvement, was not love. Yet some unfulfilled part of her being yearned for him to deepen his lovemaking, so that she felt an aching sense of disappointment and anti-climax when he pushed her firmly away from him.

'Feel like making comparisons now ... giving me an assessment?' Keegan asked mockingly.

She gasped. It had been a deliberate campaign, aimed at breaching her bristling defences ... an entirely successful campaign, and the memory of her unresisting response sent a wave of shameful heat across her cheeks.

'You cold-blooded, calculating bastard!' she whispered.

'Calculating, maybe ... scarcely cold-blooded,' he taunted. 'Or perhaps you'd like a further demonstration, before you tell me how I rate?'

At the thought, her heart leapt in a frightening, willing assent and she felt her senses quiver, as if he had indeed touched her once more.

She breathed deeply, in an attempt to regain her composure. Somehow she must show him how little his kiss had affected her.

'All right,' she conceded, 'so you've proved that you have experience, a certain knack of arousing a physical response in a woman ... so what?'

'So you enjoyed it,' he accused. 'Don't try to deny it. Your mouth, your whole body responded to me, begged for more.'

Jancis' quick wits came to her rescue and she laughed mockingly, knowing that in his intensity, nothing could be more infuriating.

'I must be an even better actress than I thought.'

'What do you mean?' he asked suspiciously.

She shrugged.

'I thought that as my compliance was a fundamental requirement, to ensure my mother's future, I would appear to comply.'

'Are you seriously asking me to believe that you feigned all that pulsating emotion?' His tone was sceptical.

She tried to meet his look, to brazen it out, but her eyes faltered before the knowing mockery in his. She made a gesture of helpless dismissal. He was reaching out for her again and she knew she had no defence against him, that once in his arms, she could not help but betray herself still further.

The imperious knock on the door behind her was her salvation. The first of a long string of owners had arrived, descending on the stable for the usual tour of inspection. For the moment she was reprieved.

In the days that followed, Jancis was torn between pique and relief that Keegan made no move to follow up his unlicensed familiarity, his calculated violation of her peace of mind. Having proved his point, Keegan, it seemed was content to let the matter rest. But Jancis found it impossible to regain her unruffled tranquillity. Yet it was just as impossible to rekindle the fires of her hatred. She felt as if something very precious had been stolen from her ... she could not say what. Was it the resentment, the implacable desire for revenge which she had nursed for so long, or something more intangible, the loss of which was infinitely more disturbing?

Despite Jancis' own private turmoil, the day-to-day work of the stables progressed as usual. The Kingdom's reputation was growing ... increasing with the almost phenomenal number of wins achieved by the horses under Keegan's care; and this almost universal success made The Linnet's sudden fall from grace all the more disappointing and puzzling.

To her surprise, Keegan had made no further attempts to baulk Jancis' outings with Nick Mortimer, and thus she was with the owner to witness the filly's downfall. The day had not started well for Jancis. She was already tired, owing to an unusual disturbance in the middle of the night.

She was uncertain what had first awakened her, but she woke with the sure knowledge that something was wrong in the stable yard. There was a distant, fugitive sound of clattering hoofs, followed by shrill neighing. The same sounds which had disturbed her appeared to have alarmed the occupants of the numerous looseboxes, and as Jancis hurriedly put on her dressing gown and ran downstairs, she met Keegan, torch in hand, also on his way to investigate.

There was no time for embarrassment at this nocturnal encounter. The prime consideration of both was for the animals in their care.

As they entered the yard, a rhythmic banging noise

assailed their ears. Already sure of what they would find, Jancis followed Keegan, as he traced the sound to the box occupied by Fly-by-Night.

'He's cast!' Keegan announced briefly.

Jancis knew that large, ungainly horses, if restive or alarmed, were prone to such accidental falls and that once down in their boxes were totally incapable of rising unaided, often resulting in severe self-inflicted injuries.

The big, rangy colt was lying on his side, kicking the wall of his box, threshing wildly and sweating with fright.

Jancis made to open the door.

'Hold it!' Keegan commanded. 'I'll go and wake Fred.'

'That might take ages,' Jancis argued. 'Fly-by-Night could have injured himself badly by then. Surely between us, we can . . .'

'You're not going in there! This is no job . . .'

'For a girl!' she finished for him. 'For heaven's sake, we've been through all that before! This isn't the first time I've encountered this situation. I know exactly what to do.'

Brushing aside his restraining hand, she entered the box.

'Of course, if you're afraid . . .' she taunted.

Swearing under his breath, Keegan followed her.

'Do exactly as I tell you,' he ordered. 'And if I say get out, you move . . . fast!'

Working closely together, avoiding the thrashing hoofs, they grabbed the colt's tail, high up, tugging steadily, in unison, until, inch by inch, they turned the powerful creature round . . . away from the wall. Finding his legs free, Fly-by-Night scrambled to his feet, snorting and shaking his head.

Jancis held the colt's head and directed the torchlight as Keegan unbuckled the rug and roller and examined him for damage.

'Seems all right, as far as I can tell in this light,' he announced at last. 'But I'll look him over again, first thing in the morning.'

The colt settled, Keegan made a brief inspection of the other stalls. With the cessation of the insistent drumming of the frightened colt's heels, the other horses seemed to have calmed down. Satisfied that nothing else required his attention, he indicated to Jancis that they should return to the house.

One hand securely under her elbow, he guided her across the uneven surface of the yard, and in spite of herself, she could not suppress the shiver that ran through her at his touch.

'You're cold,' he said, and she nodded, glad that he had attributed the involuntary movement to the night air and not to its true cause.

'Hot chocolate?' he asked, as they entered the house, 'or something stronger?'

'N—nothing for me, thanks.'

She was anxious to escape from this uncomfortable intimacy. Somehow Keegan seemed more alarming, more of a threat to her self-control, alone together in the middle of the night ... and she was all too aware of the decided informality of their clothing.

'Sure?' he asked.

'Quite sure.' She edged towards the stairs and safety.

'Jancis!'

She stopped, one foot on the bottom step, and looked back at him, her attention arrested by the fact that, only for the second time in their acquaintance, he had used her first name.

'Thanks for your help.' He hesitated. 'You're ... you're quite a girl.'

'Don't you mean, "not bad for a girl"?' she riposted, unwilling to accept his remark as a compliment.

Keegan in a mellow, affable mood was too disconcerting, too much of an encroachment upon her defences, the armour she had hitherto believed to be impregnable to the charm he could exert when it suited him. It would be against all her principles to find something likeable in him, with all the complications such weakness might lead to.

Nevertheless, their nocturnal encounter had disturbed her sufficiently to keep her awake, and it was with dark shadows under her eyes that she rose to meet the day which was to herald The Linnet's crushing defeat.

Jancis had been looking forward to this The Linnet's fourth appearance on the race track. Since the filly's win followed by a further two successes she had ridden another horse out to the gallops, feeling that it was only fair to let David establish his own rapport with The Linnet, since he would be riding her in all her forthcoming races.

Today, The Linnet was entered in a mile and two furlongs for fillies and mares. Keegan had issued a casual invitation to her to accompany him to this second August meeting at Newcastle. But she had already promised to go with Nick Mortimer.

Unaccountably, she felt a little dejected at having to refuse what amounted to Keegan's proffering of the olive branch. But then, she reminded herself, it was just as well. Whatever the physical sensations he aroused in her, she was not going to be weak enough to yield ... to allow mere sexual attraction to alter her long-conceived opinion of him.

Standing at the ringside, they took stock of The Linnet's chief opponents. There were some very showy, good-looking animals among the competition, but Jancis was unperturbed.

'It's performance, not looks, that counts,' Jancis reassured Nick, when he expressed doubt over their chances.

He shook his head.

'I don't know, Jancis. I just have this feeling ... and between you and me, I could have wished for a more experienced jockey.'

Jancis sprang immediately to David's defence, but she could not help noticing that he too looked a little worried, as they went over to wish him luck.

'Cheer up,' she told him, as she gave The Linnet's neck an affectionate slap.

Normally, the beautifully-mannered filly would have responded with a huffle of pleasure, nosing Jancis in the hope of a titbit ... sugar, or her favourite chocolate. Instead, she went tense, the veins on her neck standing out, and she began agitating with her feet, turning her head aside and snorting anxiously.

David shook his head dubiously, as he tried to control the restless animal.

'She doesn't feel right today, Jancis. She keeps acting up like this. Something's wrong.'

'Horses have their off-days, like people,' Jancis comforted him. 'She does seem a bit nervy, but perhaps she's just sensitive to atmosphere. I'm sure horses know when they're going to race.'

Though she had tried to reassure David, secretly Jancis was a little concerned. Despite their apparent toughness, thoroughbred racehorses were delicate creatures, unlikely to go through their entire career without at least one period on the 'unsound list'. It was possible that The Linnet was sickening for something.

'Are you going to back her?' she asked Nick.

'Yes, I suppose so.' But he looked doubtful. 'She doesn't look on top form. Do you think we'd better cover ourselves by backing something else in this race?' He pointed to a chestnut mare with a white star on her forehead. 'How about that one?'

Jancis studied the mare and then the jockey. With an unpleasant start of surprise she saw that the rider was Sam Roscoe, her father's one-time jockey, who had also recently left Keegan's employ. If she had been at all tempted to follow Nick's lead, this discovery made up her mind for her. She shook her head.

'You can, if you like. I'll stick to The Linnet.'

There was the usual tense, excited chatter, the last-minute laying-on of money, as the horses left the paddock. Jancis looked contentedly around her . . . as always, enjoying the atmosphere of race day, fascinated by the motley assortment of folk that made up the crowd. There was the usual rash of brilliantly coloured hats . . . the eternal headscarf; tweedy men in ancient, well-cut suits. She shook off the slight unease which The Linnet's temperamental behaviour had caused. Once the race began, she would settle down.

Nick had returned from placing their bets. The Linnet, he told her, was starting at nine to two, second favourite in a field of twenty.

'But I backed the chestnut too,' he confessed, 'though it seems she's a complete outsider.'

The Linnet seemed a little stiff going down to the start and Jancis hoped that she *would* loosen up, when she sensed that she had some strong opposition. But, from the first, it was obvious to them all that something was badly wrong.

After the first furlong, The Linnet was lying tenth and Jancis hoped to see her work her way up through the field, but soon she was being challenged by the back markers and instead of responding, the filly went on at the same plodding pace, with none of the light but powerful grace she had shown last time out.

'Show her the whip, you young idiot,' Keegan muttered at Jancis' side. 'What's he playing at? He's not giving her a chance. Better to come to the front too soon than too late.'

'It's not David's fault,' Jancis protested. 'Look, he's riding her for all he's worth. She's just not responding.'

The showy chestnut ridden by Sam Roscoe was leading the field, a good two lengths clear, ears pricked, looking as if she were merely cantering, while the others galloped.

'Oh, come on, Linnet!' Jancis groaned.

But two furlongs from home, The Linnet put her head up, a sure indication that she could do no more, and Jancis chewed anxiously at her lower lip. What on earth was wrong with the filly?

'What's he doing?' Nick demanded angrily, more inclined to attribute his horse's failure to her jockey. 'He's letting her drop herself out. Look, they're leaving her for dead!'

Keegan shook his head in impatient disbelief.

'I just don't understand it,' he admitted.

All three of them hurried down to the unsaddling enclosure, to question the dejected David.

'She just blew up on me, Boss.'

'Nonsense,' Nick snapped, before Keegan could reply. 'I don't believe you were trying, young man.'

'I tried everything I knew, Mr Mortimer,' David insisted.

To Jancis' indignation, Keegan seemed to support Nick.

'Are you sure, David? I know she was carrying a penalty after her success in her last three races, but that shouldn't have made so much difference to her performance.'

David dismounted, shoulders drooping, too dispirited to argue, or defend himself further.

Jancis helped Fred to box the filly. They sponged her down, dried and cleaned her and put on the travelling rug.

'What do you think went wrong, Fred?' Jancis asked the elderly head lad, as she held a bucket so that The Linnet could drink.

Fred shrugged, as he hung the hay net.

'Search me. After last time out, I'd have thought she was a dead cert.'

So at least *Fred* didn't blame David, she thought thankfully. She'd trust his instincts any time.

On the journey home, Nick seemed to have recovered from his annoyance, adopting instead a philosophical attitude.

'Good thing I did back the chestnut, eh? She romped home. *You* should have followed *my* hunch this time, Jancis.'

She shook her head positively.

'Even if I'd fancied the mare, I wouldn't back any horse Sam Roscoe was riding,' she told him.

He shot her a questioning look.

'Oh, how's that?'

Jancis recounted Sam's defection from The Kingdom, adding that he had not remained long in Keegan's employ either.

Nick shrugged.

'I can understand you feeling bitter, but I don't know much about the fellow, except that he rides occasionally for a chap called Louie Dutch. All I *do* know is that he's a damn good rider. That chestnut won me a packet this afternoon.'

When Jancis, still concerned about the filly's health, went down to the stable that evening, to see if The Linnet had eaten up, she found the young jockey perilously close to tears. Keegan, it seemed, had held a searching post-mortem.

'I *was* trying, Jancis,' David assured her.

'I know that,' she assured him.

'The boss didn't believe me,' he said despairingly, 'and neither did Mr Mortimer.'

'Oh, I'm sure you're wrong,' she said. 'I know Nick was disappointed, but . . .'

'He as good as accused me of pulling the filly,' David said flatly. 'He said there was no other earthly reason why she should run such a lousy race.'

'That's ridiculous. Why would you deliberately lose?'

'For money!' said David. 'He asked me if I had a bet on any of the other runners.'

'He asked you that? But he knows jockeys aren't supposed to bet.'

'They're not supposed to,' David said grimly. 'But unofficially they do.'

'And *did* you have a bet?'

'No, thank goodness . . . not today. But I have in the past, and the boss knows it, so he's not likely to believe me.'

A new line of thought occurred to Jancis.

'What do *you* think went wrong, David?'

He hesitated, then:

'If I didn't know better, I'd say The Linnet had been got at.'

'You mean . . .?'

'Tampered with in some way . . . doped . . . or even given a bucket of water just before the race. Even that would have been enough to slow her up.'

'But who would do such a thing?' Jancis was horrified. She had heard such things spoken of—unavoidably, having been brought up in a trainer's household, but no breath of trouble of that nature had ever touched The Kingdom.

David shrugged.

'Someone who didn't want her to win, obviously.'

'Or someone who wanted *another* horse to win?' she asked.

'Yes.'

'Sam Roscoe!' Jancis said triumphantly. As David stared at her blankly, she explained. 'He was riding the chestnut that won, and on her previous form, The Linnet was the only runner there likely to touch it.'

'Anything's possible, I suppose,' David said slowly. Then he shook his head. 'No, he wouldn't have had the opportunity. Either Fred or the boss was with the filly, right from the time we unboxed her until the race.'

Jancis bit her lip thoughtfully. There *had* to be some explanation, something which would exonerate David . . . account for the filly's poor performance.

'It could have happened before The Linnet even got to the racecourse,' she said slowly. She grew excited, as a theory began to form. 'What about last night? Yes . . . suppose all that commotion in the yard last night wasn't just because of Fly-by-Night getting himself cast? Suppose something else happened, something which upset him . . . caused his fall. There could have been a disturbance, someone . . . a stranger nosing around the yard, looking for The Linnet's box. The horses would be bound to act up, and . . .'

'Yes,' David was ready to snatch at any possibility, 'you could have a point there. But I don't see how it helps me,' he added dejectedly. 'It's all surmise, after all. We can't prove anything.'

'Not this time, perhaps, but next time . . .'

He stared, aghast.

'What makes you think there'll *be* a next time?'

'Call it a hunch,' said Jancis. Her vivid little face alight with enthusiasm, she continued, 'Say I'm right, suppose it *was* Sam Roscoe . . . no wait,' she added, as David seemed about to protest. 'He used to work for Keegan, and Fred was pretty cagey when I asked him why Sam left the Leroy stable. Suppose Sam has some sort of grudge against Keegan Leroy.'

David brightened.

'I think I catch your drift. But why The Linnet, specifically? If Roscoe has a grudge against the boss, any horse would have done.'

'Except that Sam was riding the horse that won today,' Jancis pointed out. 'But in case you're right . . . in case any horse would have done . . . we'll keep watch before our next race . . . overnight, in the yard. Well?' she demanded impatiently.

'I'm game,' David said slowly, 'but shouldn't we tell Fred what we suspect . . . or the boss?'

'No!' Jancis said positively. 'Keegan would only forbid it. For one thing, he has a bee in his bonnet about you being to blame, and another thing, he thinks girls are useless. He'd say it was no job for a girl.'

'He could be right,' David agreed. 'Oh, I don't mean that bit about girls being useless,' he added quickly, seeing Jancis' indignant expression, 'or about me being to blame. What I mean is, it could be dangerous . . . not safe for a girl.'

'We'll only be there to keep watch,' Jancis explained patiently. 'Look, I promise I won't tackle Sam . . . if it is Sam . . . or anyone else. All we want to do is to find out if someone *is* interfering with our runners. *Then* we can tell the others, when we have proof.'

David was not formed in Keegan's mould and Jancis readily overcame his objections. All that remained was to wait for the eve of The Kingdom's next big race.

CHAPTER SIX

SILENCE, tangible as thick velvet, blanketed the stableyard, a silence broken only by the occasional restless stamp, or a scrape from a horse's hoof. Somewhere near at hand came the hoot of a hunting owl and, down in the distant village, the bark of a dog.

Jancis had suggested to David that they keep their observation from the loosebox immediately next to The Linnet's . . . its rightful occupant being absent overnight . . . on the way to a racecourse in Scotland. They were prepared for a long wait, with a blanket apiece, sandwiches and thermos flasks.

It had seemed a good idea in the bright light of day, but now, in the small hours of the morning, with every faculty at its lowest ebb, Jancis felt a little nervous. Just what were they getting themselves into? she wondered. David had been right; this could be dangerous. The kind of intruder resolute enough to sabotage a horse was unlikely to deal gently with anyone discovered observing his actions. She was uncomfortably aware also that Keegan would most certainly disapprove of their presence here, would list tonight's activities under the heading of rash escapades . . . a practice to which she seemed to be increasingly prone since Keegan's arrival at The Kingdom.

Every time a horse snorted, she gave an involuntary start. There was no moon and the dark corners of the yard were full of menacing shadows, any one of which might conceal a prowler.

'Are you scared?' David's whisper was a faint thread of sound in her ear.

'No—no, of course not.'

If she admitted to fear, David might insist that they abandon their vigil.

The scrape of a boot on the cobbled surface of the yard sent Jancis' heart fluttering into her mouth, and she grabbed

David's arm. She could tell by the tensing of his muscles that he too had heard the sound.

'Someone's coming . . . coming this way,' he muttered.

The wavering light of a torch could be seen, moving slowly along the boxes, getting nearer and nearer to their place of concealment. Was the nocturnal visitor looking for The Linnet? It seemed so.

'Quick, get down!' Jancis hissed.

They threw themselves flat, straw prickling their hands and faces, the dust getting into nose and mouth. Suddenly, before she could stifle the involuntary reaction, Jancis sneezed.

The next moment she and David were illumined in the beam of a powerful flashlight.

'Right. Outside, the pair of you!'

Jancis was almost relieved to hear Keegan's angry voice . . . but not for long.

Sheepishly, they emerged from the loosebox to find both Keegan and Fred confronting them, and Jancis made futile attempts to detach the clinging straw from her clothes and hair. Dazzled by the lamplight, she could not see the expression on Keegan's face, but his words, and the savage tone in which they were uttered, left little to the imagination. She could picture the harsh condemnation in those dark, hawk-like features.

'Even the most charitable interpretation of your presence here I find a distasteful one. But I assume this was *not* a romantic interlude?'

Jancis heard David gasp. That such a construction could be put upon their presence in the yard had obviously not occurred to him. Nor had it occurred to Jancis, David being considerably younger than herself.

'You have a mind like your own muck-heap!' she retorted.

A long arm shot out and she felt her shoulder taken in a painful grip.

'Believe me, by the time I've finished with the pair of you, you'll wish you *had* been indulging in a little promiscuous dalliance, instead of sabotaging my horses!'

Jancis wrenched furiously at the hand which held her, incensed by this unmerited accusation. Oh, it was unfair . . . being accused of the very thing that they were trying to prevent!

'If that's what you believe, then you've not only a filthy mind, but a sick one. David and I were here to *protect* the horses, not to . . .'

'It's true, Mr Leroy . . . Mr Higgins.' David's voice sounded very young, very nervous, and, distracted for the moment, Keegan turned the full lash of his icy fury upon the young jockey.

'You, get back to your quarters, now . . . and be in my office at eight o'clock prompt. Fred, take over here.'

Without waiting to hear David's reply, or to see if he had obeyed the peremptory command, Keegan swung round, propelling Jancis before him. He was always marching her around in this captive fashion, she thought angrily. She seriously contemplated kicking his shins and making an attempt to break away, but she knew she would not be allowed to escape so easily and retribution would be all the fiercer.

To her surprise, they did not enter the house, but turned instead towards the side door of the office. A faint frisson of fear slid down her spine.

'Why have you brought me here?' she asked, her tone belligerent, in an attempt to conceal her apprehension. She rubbed at her arm, as he released her and turned to close the door and draw the curtains, before switching on the main light.

'Because in here we're less likely to disturb the rest of the household . . . and because I want some answers, before you and that young fool David have had a chance to get your heads together and concoct a story.'

He pushed her down into a chair and pulled up another, facing her, so close that their knees were almost touching, his proximity a menace to her already quivering nerves.

'Right,' he said grimly. 'Start talking.'

Jancis regarded him helplessly. To her annoyance she felt her lips beginning to tremble. Why did he always have to misunderstand her? When she tried to annoy him, he remained exasperatingly calm, yet when she tried to do him a good turn . . .

'There's nothing to tell. What I told you was the truth.'

'I'm beginning to wonder if you know the meaning of that word,' he said acidly.

'That's rich, coming from you!' Jancis made a spirited attempt at a retort. 'After the way you lied to Nick Mortimer about my time off.'

'Mortimer's not a suitable companion for you ... too experienced, too old for you.'

How dared he make such arbitrary decisions on her behalf!

'He's not much older than you,' she retorted.

'But then we're not discussing my suitability, are we?' Keegan asked mockingly.

No, she thought miserably. She wished they were ... but obviously such an idea was the farthest from Keegan's mind.

Keegan's full lips were compressed into a grim line.

'Let's stop wasting time, shall we? Don't think you're going to distract me by trading insults. The Linnet is racing again tomorrow ... today, I should say. If she does badly again I shall know what to think, shan't I?'

'You can think what you like!' Jancis shouted the words at him. 'We didn't *touch* The Linnet. I told you why we were there ... to keep watch, in case anyone *did* try to tamper with her, or any of the other horses.'

'And who were you expecting this mythical "someone" to be?'

Secure in his own arrogant assessment of the situation, he asked his question in a sarcastic, disbelieving drawl.

Jancis bit her lip. She had no proof, only a hunch ... a suspicion that Sam Roscoe might be involved, might have some grudge against Keegan Leroy. But her innate sense of fair play made it impossible for her to accuse anyone without proof ... unlike Keegan, she thought bitterly, who accused and sought proof afterwards ... so she said nothing.

'I suggest that you intended to stop The Linnet again, with some crazy idea of revenge for my alleged sharp practice against your father.'

'No!' Jancis protested. 'I ...'

'And I further suggest,' he continued inexorably, 'that you've suborned that rather gullible young man to your cause.'

'I haven't! I wouldn't ...'

'You've told me often enough, in no uncertain terms, that

you'd seize any opportunity to get back at me. Haven't you?'
He rapped out the question.

'Yes, but . . .'

'And only recently you informed me that if you could find
a way to raise enough money . . .'

'You're mad,' Jancis gasped, 'if you think I . . .'

'What did you do?' Keegan continued his indictment. 'Get
your boy-friend Mortimer to back that chestnut on your
behalf? A bit ironic, after you'd nobbled *his* entry.'

'No . . . no . . .'

'And what do you fancy for tomorrow, Jancis? Or was I in
time to put paid to your little game?'

'Stop it! Stop it!' Jancis drew a sobbing breath. Somehow she
had to stem this stream of vile accusations. 'I didn't have
anything to do with The Linnet losing last time . . . and if she
does lose tomorrow, it won't be anything to do with me, or
David.'

Keegan looked at her narrowly.

'So, you admit there'a chance she might lose?'

'Of course there's a chance!' Jancis raged at him. 'No horse is
a certainty until it's passed the post. *You* should know that.'

Keegan relaxed in his chair, arms folded, thoughtfully
assessing her flushed cheeks and tear-bright eyes. She
watched him, still on the defensive. She realised now the
folly of her open defiance of him, when she had declared
aloud her intention of avenging her father. She should have
conducted her campaign more discreetly, more subtly.

Campaign! What campaign? she asked herself drearily. So
far she seemed to have achieved precisely nothing. Any
aggravation which she had caused Keegan Leroy had been
purely accidental . . . a result of heedlessness, emotional
response, rather than deliberate action on her part . . . and
now this night's work, which, ironically, she had under-
taken with the best of intentions, had backfired on her.
Through no fault of her own, Keegan thought the worst
of her, and Jancis now knew that this was not at all what
she wanted.

Unexpectedly, Keegan leant forward and as he raised his
hand, instinctively she flinched. But his intention was only
to remove some stray pieces of straw which had become
entangled in her bright curls. The intimacy of the thoughtful

little gesture was curiously disarming, making her throat ache with sudden unshed tears.

But he had noticed her recoil and frowned slightly.

'You thought I was going to strike you,' he said accusingly. 'Just what *do* you take me for, Jancis?'

He had used her name again, unwittingly, she was certain, and the sound of it, pronounced in his deep, resonant voice, was infinitely disturbing. Bemused, she stared at him with troubled fascination, her eyes searching his strongly etched features as if she had never seen him before. Perhaps she hadn't, she thought wonderingly ... perhaps she had never really seen Keegan Leroy properly, but only through the eyes of prejudice. She tried to summon up the old antagonism, the bitter hatred of her father's usurper, but she couldn't. Dismayed, she tried to analyse her feelings. What *was* this wave of sensation which flooded through her in Keegan's presence, making coherent thought impossible? What had become of her fierce resolution? She had the lowering sense of having been cheated, betrayed, by her own emotions. It was impossible, yet it had happened. Imperceptibly, without her being aware of the fact, she had undergone a change of heart. Somewhere along the way, she had fallen in love with Keegan Leroy ... and she had not realised it, until this moment, when everything was lost ... now, when he believed her capable of a despicable, underhand act of vengeance.

She had not realised that the startled wonder in her eyes could be mistaken for terror until, with a gesture of impatience, Keegan rose to his feet.

'You've no earthly reason to fear me. I'm not in the habit of striking women. Whatever you may think of me, I haven't descended to those depths ... yet.'

His voice was curiously bitter. Almost, she thought, as if he were hurt. Only you couldn't hurt Keegan Leroy. He was too hard, too self-satisfied, too self-sufficient. If he knew how she felt about him at this moment, he would only laugh. He hadn't cared when she had hated him ... he would care even less if he found that she loved him.

'You'd better get to bed,' Keegan said wearily. 'This discussion is getting us nowhere.'

He might not have made any progress in his cross-examination of her, Jancis thought drearily, as he ushered her through the communicating door to the house, but the last few minutes had resulted in considerable enlightenment, as far as she was concerned. He was still in the dark, but she had emerged into a blinding, dazzling light of revelation . . . of self-knowledge.

The next day being a working day, neither Jancis nor Nick Mortimer was free to watch the filly race and Jancis wondered how on earth she would endure the long hours, waiting for Keegan, Fred and David to return. There would be plenty of office work to occupy her, but how was she going to concentrate? Not only was there the possible outcome of the race to trouble her, but now she had another cause for mental turmoil . . . her discovery of her changed feelings for Keegan.

She was bewildered by the depths of these newly recognised emotions . . . the longing, both mental and physical, tinged by despair, and there was no way these deep-felt cravings of hers could ever be assuaged. From the very first, she had deliberately set out to annoy Keegan, and it seemed her efforts had been all too successful

But what else *could* she have done, she asked herself, believing, as she still did, that he had ruined her father? She must fight against this new love . . . she must remain loyal to her father's memory. She smiled bitterly, as she recalled how she had intended to arouse Keegan's desires, then reject him. How ironic that the situation should have been reversed . . . now she would give anything to win his love and two . . . no, three barriers stood between her and the attainment of her desires. Keegan's growing dislike and distrust of her, loyalty to her father, and Alyson . . . even if the other two could be surmounted, there would always be Alyson.

The day loomed endlessly before her and yet, when Keegan unexpectedly ordered her to down tools and accompany them, Jancis was not sure which was the greater of two evils. To remain behind would be intolerable, but to accept would mean a journey of considerable length, alone with him, in his car. David and Fred would be travelling with the filly. But she knew she had no choice. Keegan's manner made it quite obvious that he would brook no refusal and, prudently, Jancis decided not to protest.

With a sudden return of her normal optimism she reflected that perhaps, though The Linnet might not win, she might run well ... well enough to dispel any suspicion that she had been sabotaged. She would make the most of this time in Keegan's company. Perhaps, she thought wistfully, an opportunity would occur for her to present herself in a better light than hitherto, to demonstrate that she could be pleasant company, to effect an improvement in their relationship.

She could not help feeling the irony of her situation, as she recalled the many occasions on which Keegan had shown great forbearance with her rebellious behaviour, his magnanimity, when, after her flagrant disobedience of his orders, he had admitted her skill as a rider and allowed her to go on exercising The Linnet.

Why had she been so blind? she wondered. Her mother had very soon discovered the gentler, more considerate side of Keegan's nature. Yet was this a mask, which he could assume at will? He could still be utterly ruthless. The doubt remained to niggle, like an aching tooth. He was still the man whose successful rivalry had ruined her father.

Still enmeshed in this web of inner conflict, she went out to the car. She felt Keegan's eyes assessing her appearance ... the wand-slim figure, to which the lightweight jersey dress she had chosen to wear clung revealingly, the vivid blue making her coppery curls more chestnut by comparison.

It was impossible to gauge his reaction to the care she had taken, and as he made no comment, she slipped into the passenger seat, feeling rather deflated. She had not really expected a compliment, she told herself, but it would have been nice. Nick would have said something, but his flattery came all too easily. A hard-won compliment from Keegan would have been just that much more valuable.

'I suppose you're wondering what David told me?' he said, as he swung the powerful car out on to the main road.

Jancis shook her head. He wasn't going to catch her like that.

'I *know* what he told you ... what I want to know is whether or not you believe him?'

Keegan shot her a glance in which were mingled exasperation and an emotion she could not quite fathom.

'I wish I knew. Heaven knows I'd like to believe him, *and* you, but . . .'

'But?' She tensed herself for his reply.

Keegan ran one large hand through the crisp dark waves at the nape of his neck, a gesture which held her eyes as if mesmerised. In imagination, her own fingers felt the texture of his hair against their soft skin.

'But . . . Oh, hell, Jancis, I just don't know. Let's wait till after the race, shall we?'

'And suppose The Linnet does badly again?' she persisted, dreading his answer, yet needing to know.

With a suddenness, which, despite the safety harness, jolted her in her seat, he braked and pulled the powerful car into a layby. He switched off the engine and sat silently, drumming his lean fingers on the steering wheel. After what seemed endless moments, he turned in his seat to look at her.

'You tell me,' he suggested.

Jancis shrugged.

'I suppose the accusations will begin all over again,' she said bitterly. 'It's so easy, isn't it, to believe that I'm involved in some way . . . just because I . . .'

'No, Jancis!' He contradicted her. 'It isn't easy to believe . . . it's very hard. Do you think I *want* to believe it's you?'

His gaze was compelling, and afterwards she could never be sure who had moved first, but suddenly he was holding her against his lean, firm body, the soft material of her dress no barrier to sensation, as her breasts were crushed against the hardness of his chest. Slowly, experimentally, he parted her mouth with his own, so that a frantic response throbbed in her veins and dormant longings she had tried for so long to suppress sprang to life beneath the insidious movement of his hands.

He pulled her still closer, deepening his kiss, until she clung helplessly to him, her lips fighting a sweet duel with his, her hands exploring, caressing, while, with one part of her mind, she wondered at her own temerity, her own utter lack of shame. After what seemed like an eternity of these intoxicating sensations, his breath rasped painfully in his throat and a deep shudder seemed to vibrate through his whole body, as, gently, he pushed her away from him.

'*Now* do you think I want it to be you?' he asked.

Still drugged, half senseless with the ardour he had aroused in her, she put up a trembling hand to trace the outlines of his mouth, still moist with the kisses they had shared.

'It *isn't* me,' she assured him softly. 'Even if I still hated you, I couldn't do that to The Linnet. I'm very fond of her.'

He was still, and Jancis held her breath. How much had he gathered from her impulsive, unthinking speech.

'Even if you still hated me?' he queried. 'What does that mean?' As she did not reply, he continued, 'Jancis, is there something you want to tell me?'

His eyes had an odd expression and now uncertain of his motives, she avoided his gaze. Had she allowed herself to be fooled once more by the undoubted physical attraction he held for her ... was he just using his sexual powers as a weapon, deliberately trying to undermine her defences, catch her off guard? He had elicited nothing by his earlier questioning of her. Was he now resorting to other methods? Suppose he still mistrusted her ... suppose he had simulated passion, in an endeavour to weaken her resistance, hoping that she would break down and confess her complicity. Even in the security of her innocence, it was still an unpleasant thought, and indignation welled in her at the idea that he could be so devious.

'It merely means,' she said, her voice sounding stiff with the effort of controlling her unruly emotions, 'that I've decided you're not *quite* as bad as I thought. You're ... you're very fair in your dealings with the lads ... most of them,' she qualified, remembering his suspicions of David. 'Fred likes you, and Fred doesn't give his friendship easily, and ... and you've been very good to my mother.'

'Is that all?' He was still strangely quiescent.

'Yes, of course!' She forced a laugh, trying to make a jest of it. 'What more do you want ... a medal?'

'No.' Keegan answered her curtly and with an abrupt gesture he started the motor, putting the engine into gear with less than his usual smoothness, so that it grated slightly. 'No, I suppose I must be thankful for small mercies.'

*

It was growing dark when the grimly silent racegoers returned to The Kingdom. One look at Jancis' face, as she entered the drawing room, told Mary King and Alyson all they needed to know.

'The Linnet lost again?' Mary said.

Jancis nodded wearily, slumping down on to the settee and kicking off her shoes. She was bone-weary and depressed.

'How . . . how's Keegan taking it?' Mary asked.

'Very badly,' said Jancis, thinking, as she did so, that she was considerably understating the case. Keegan had been absolutely furious. To do him justice, he had contained his fury until he, his head lad and his jockey were out of earshot of any bystanders. But his language had been blistering and it was obvious from his manner towards David that he gave no credence to the young jockey's repeated claims that the horse was just not responding to his efforts.

Even Fred seemed to be regarding David grimly, and though Keegan had not said anything to her on the return journey . . . indeed, not a word, condemnatory or otherwise, had passed his lips . . . Jancis was uncomfortably aware that all his suspicions must have been rekindled.

So much for his statement that he did not want to believe the worst of her! If he really meant that, he would trust her anyway, would know she could not be so despicable. Yet why *should* he trust her? she argued with herself . . . even the greatest of friends sometimes found they had been deceived in each other, and she and Keegan were not even friends, despite the various uneasy truces through which their relationship had passed.

Just what was wrong with the filly? As Jancis well knew, there were tranquillisers and dope which could slow horses up and which could work quickly, or with delayed action, to suit the perpetrator's plans. But for the life of her she could not see how The Linnet could have been tampered with this time. Though the fact would carry no weight with Keegan, she knew that she and David had been on watch most of the night, and after their discovery by Keegan, Fred Higgins had remained in the yard until dawn. There had certainly been no opportunity at the racetrack for anyone to go near the filly, let alone to administer anything harmful.

'Does Keegan still think David had something to do with the horse's performance?' Alyson asked.

She had been silent until now, her shrewd, prominent, pale eyes taking in every expression on Jancis' woebegone face. She alone seemed undismayed by The Linnet's failure.

Jancis frowned. She had not told her mother of Keegan's suspicions ... that he also believed her to be involved, but now Alyson's revelation and the natural bitterness that she felt, caused her to break into angry speech.

'Not only that. He believes *I* had a hand in nobbling The Linnet.'

Mary stared aghast at her daughter, and for the first time since her return home, Jancis heard her mother criticise Keegan Leroy.

'He must be mad to think you'd do such a thing!'

'Why?' Alyson spoke with a slightly smug expression on her peaky face. Mother and daughter stared at her as she continued. 'He knows Jancis has always hated him and that she resents his ownership of the stable. Why *shouldn't* he suspect her?'

Usually gentle and considerate with the frail girl, Mary leapt to her daughter's defence, speaking sharply.

'Nonsense, Alyson! You ought to know better! Anyone with any charity or common sense would realise Jancis couldn't do a thing like this. It's not in her nature.'

Alyson's rather prominent pale blue eyes filled with facile tears which she allowed to spill over, breaking, as they did so, into noisy sobs, just as Keegan entered the room.

With a look of concern, he was immediately by her side.

'What's upsetting *you*, chicken?'

'Oh, Keegan!' she sobbed. 'I'm so sorry about The Linnet, and I didn't *mean* to annoy Mary, but ... but I *had* to stand up for *you*, didn't I?'

The beastly little hypocrite, Jancis thought. The other girl hadn't given two hoots whether their horse had lost or won. In fact, she was probably delighted that it had lost, so that Keegan would have further reason to doubt his jockey and ... in particular ... his secretary.

Keegan sat down beside Alyson, drawing her closely into the circle of his arm, wiping away her tears with his own handkerchief.

Somehow the sight of this small intimacy inflamed Jancis' already smouldering anger.

'Oh, stop those crocodile tears, Alyson! I question whether you *were* defending Keegan. It sounded more as if you were attacking me!'

'Jancis!' Keegan spoke sharply. 'Alyson isn't robust enough for these acrimonious scenes. Vent your feelings on me, if you must, but be good enough to leave her out of it.'

'She's robust enough to *start* trouble,' Jancis muttered rebelliously.

Keegan darted her a contemptuous look, then spoke affectionately to his cousin.

'Come on, Aly love. You're best away upstairs, out of this. It's long past your bedtime. I'll take you up.'

'I couldn't go to bed until you came home, Keegan,' Alyson sobbed breathily. 'Not until I'd heard how The Linnet got on.'

As Keegan left the room, carrying his cousin, Jancis turned to her mother.

'What does he see in that whey-faced, puling little shrimp?' she demanded, bitter, searing jealousy lending an uncharacteristically spiteful edge to her tongue.

But it was obvious that Mary was already experiencing guilt over her own reproof to Alyson.

'She *is* family, Jancis, not very strong . . . and Keegan is devoted to her, as you well know. You really shouldn't upset her.'

'Do you think he intends to marry her?' Jancis asked bluntly. Somehow her mother's opinion seemed vitally important and she waited painfully for Mary's reply.

Mary King considered her question gravely.

'I don't really know . . . I have wondered. It would certainly be a great thing for Alyson . . . a secure home, strong, capable husband . . .'

'And what would Keegan get out of it?' Jancis asked scornfully. 'What possible use would she be to him as a wife . . . an invalid who has to be carried everywhere? What sort of marriage would that be, for a healthy, vital man like Keegan . . . and besides, she doesn't like horses.'

Jancis had never made any secret of her opinion of people

who did not feel as strongly as she about her favourite animals.

Mary looked at her thoughtfully.

'You sound almost as if ... Jancis, you're not ... not falling in love with him yourself, are you, because ...'

Mendaciously, Jancis denied the suggestion.

'Me?' She laughed harshly. 'You know very well I've always detested him ... and the feeling appears to be mutual.'

Mary sighed wistfully.

'Of course it would have been nice, if you and Keegan had fallen in love ... so right somehow. It would have solved all our problems and this would really be your home again. Still, as it is, I suppose it's just as well. Because the more I think about it, the more I believe a marriage between them *is* a likelihood. Alyson's health may well improve ... I'm sure she's better than she was ... and she needs a strong protector. And of course she *does* have something to offer in return ... her money.'

'Her money?' Jancis echoed. This was the first indication she had received that Alyson was rich.

Mary nodded. 'Alyson's parents were very wealthy, and she was their only child. Running a stable, as we know to our cost, is an expensive, sometimes risky business. I should imagine more capital would always be welcome.'

Jancis was silent, digesting the unpalatable facts her mother had laid before her. The more she considered them, the more dejected she felt. The combination of The Linnet's second disastrous race and this unwelcome intelligence of Alyson's wealth, following so immediately upon her newly discovered feelings for her employer, brought home to Jancis just how little she herself had to offer a man like Keegan Leroy. Apart from his distrust of her, she had done nothing to engender feelings of friendship, let alone love, and despite her share of the sale, she could not compete with Alyson in terms of wealth.

But I am healthy, she argued with herself, and I'm good with horses. We could have a good partnership, I know we could, if only he were in love with me.

Keegan's return to the drawing room did away with all opportunity for daydreaming, or for any further discussion and both women watched him apprehensively, as he crossed the room to lean against the mantelshelf.

Pointedly, it seemed to her, he ignored Jancis, directing his words to Mary.

'I should be obliged if you'd ensure that nothing of a similar nature occurs in future. Alyson is an affectionate, sensitive girl. She feels things very strongly.'

Jancis turned to stare unseeingly out of the uncurtained window, into the night sky. Didn't he realise that other people beside Alyson felt things just as strongly, could be just as affectionate, wanted to be . . .

Mary spoke quietly, reasonably.

'I'm sorry if Alyson was upset, Keegan, though I do think she takes things to heart more than is necessary. I'm just as much to blame as Jancis, but you could scarcely expect me not to defend my own daughter. Jancis tells me you have some dreadful suspicions of her, and Alyson seemed to share them. It isn't like you to be so unfair, so easily prejudiced. Surely you have no proof?'

'No proof,' he agreed grimly, 'but a lot of circumstantial evidence, plus the very real fact that your daughter dislikes and resents me . . . always has done. She has made no secret of the fact that she would do anything . . .'

'Anything but injure a horse!' Jancis swung round to interrupt him. 'I happen to like *horses* . . . and no horse ever injured my father.'

'Mary,' Keegan said courteously, 'would you excuse us? I think it's time I had a long talk with your daughter. There are certain things which need to be straightened out.'

Mary King paled, her hands fluttering in agitated protest.

'Keegan, you're not going to tell her . . . not just yet! Wait a little longer, please . . . you . . . you promised me you'd wait until . . .'

'Until the right moment,' he agreed. 'But in view of all that has happened recently, I judge that moment to have arrived.'

Jancis looked from one to the other in bewilderment. What on earth were they talking about? What was this secret Keegan and her mother apparently shared . . . had kept from her? Something disturbing, evidently, to judge by her mother's behaviour.

Keegan walked to the door, holding it open.

'Mary!' It was quietly spoken, but nonetheless it was a command.

Reluctantly, Mary King moved towards him, her eyes pleading, as she gazed up into his inflexible face.

'You . . . you'll be kind . . . gentle with her? Remember, she had no idea. You won't . . .?'

As she reached his side, he patted her arm in a gesture which was obviously meant to be reassuring. Perhaps it did reassure Mary, for she smiled up at him tremulously.

'I expect you know best, Keegan, but . . .'

Firmly he thrust her through the door, closing it behind her, and turned to face Jancis.

'Now, Miss King!'

He had reverted to the old formality, she noticed with a sinking heart . . . a habit of his when greatly annoyed. She was afraid now . . . afraid of whatever revelations he might be about to make.

'I . . . I don't want to hear anything that *you've* got to say.'

She walked towards him, wishing that there were more than one exit to the room.

'Please let me pass.'

Deliberately, he folded his arms and leant against the door.

'You're not leaving this room until you've heard what I have to say. It's time someone told you a few home truths . . . the real facts of the case, Miss Jancis King.'

CHAPTER SEVEN

JANCIS watched Keegan warily, as he blocked her escape; long, lean and dangerous, his ruggedly hewn features were set in lines of ruthless determination. Everything about him hinted of strength . . . a strength she knew she would be unwise to challenge, and fear of him stabbed through her . . . not the fear of physical violence; even in anger Keegan was not deliberately ungentle, but of the devastating effect his mere presence had upon her. Loving him as she did, she did not know if she could bear this much longer . . . this

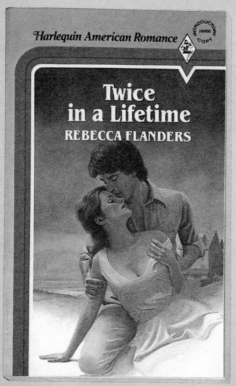

TWICE IN A LIFETIME

Rebecca Flanders

CHAPTER ONE

BARBARA sat in the crowded airport lounge, waiting for her flight to be called, and fingered the letter of invitation from her sister somewhat uncertainly. Barbara was twenty-six years old, self-sufficient, and mature, and she had been managing her own life since the first day she had left home for the independence of the state university. But, sitting alone amid the bustle and confusion of excited travelers, she felt somewhat like a lost and frightened child. She had felt that way a lot since Daniel had died.

She had been widowed a little over a year, and she knew her sister, via long-distance conferences with their mother, was worried about her. Perhaps with good cause, Barbara had to admit uneasily, for although most of the time Barbara managed to convince herself she was getting along just fine, there were still feelings of bitterness and periods of black depression she did not seem to be able to control. Of course it was a tragedy to be widowed so young, and everyone commiserated, everyone claimed to understand what she was going through. The real tragedy was that no one understood. No one could understand what it was to lose the one and only love of her life, not just a husband, but a lover and a friend... Most people would go their entire lives without ever finding what she and Daniel had shared, and to have their life together severed so abruptly and so cruelly was more than unfair, it was incomprehensible...

But Barbara wasn't meant to be alone for long. Follow her as she rediscovers the beauty of love. Read the rest of "Twice in a Lifetime" FREE.

Experience *Harlequin American Romance*...

with this special introductory FREE book offer.

continual battle of wills, this denial of her heart's promptings.

'This interview is likely to be a protracted one,' Keegan observed. 'I suggest that you sit down.'

'Thank you, but I prefer to stand.' She lifted her chin defiantly. 'Besides, I don't intend to stay long. I can't think of anything you might say which would be of interest to me.'

Except that you love me, her heart groaned within her . . . the one thing she would never hear him say . . . and she was forced to set her mouth to hide the trembling caused by the hopeless wish.

'No?' The glint in his eyes was unreadable and she licked her dry lips nervously, the movement of her tongue an unknowing provocation to the tall man watching her.

'No!' she said, with more firmness than she felt.

Being alone with him once more brought to mind all too vividly those few moments that afternoon in his car, and her own shaken response to his kisses. She found herself trying to imagine those lips on hers now . . . Would she have the will to resist, if he repeated his onslaught?

He moved towards her, so close now that her breath caught in alarm, but it was only to force her down on to a chair.

'You *will* sit down and you *will* listen to me,' he told her. 'I don't want to restrain you forcibly, but I will if I have to.'

The mere touch of his hand had sent shock waves through her body and she was beset by contradictory emotions. But uppermost was panic . . . the need to escape this unsettling proximity. She could not bear the thought of his triumph, perhaps even his scornful pity, should he realise just how much he affected her. There was resentment too, that he should dare to treat her this way . . . force her to listen to him. But, she had to admit to herself, she had another weakness, other than the weakness of the senses . . . curiosity, albeit unwilling, as she wondered what he could possibly have to say . . . something moreover which had roused her mother sufficiently to venture a nervous protest.

Jancis knew that to argue would only prolong the moment, increase the tension that stretched between them. Deliberately she made herself relax in the chair, forcing a tone of insolent unconcern into her voice.

'You've no right to treat me this way, of course, but since you're stronger than I am . . .' She shrugged. 'Let's just get it over with, shall we?'

'No *right*?' Keegan's tone was one of barely restrained violence. 'No right to defend myself against your persistent accusations of malpractice, your continual implication that I deliberately set out to ruin your father?'

It was impossible to remain relaxed. Jancis sat bolt upright in the chair, glaring at him.

'All right, it may not have been a deliberate campaign, I'm prepared to grant you that much . . . but it happened, nevertheless, and you can't tell me you weren't to blame.'

His dark eyes blazed at her.

'Maybe not blameless, in so far as I was your father's nearest competitor . . . but it didn't *have* to be me. Anyone with a reasonable degree of competence could have put your father out of business.'

'How dare you call my father incompetent! He was a sick man . . .'

'So you've told me before, and I haven't denied it, have I, nor was I accusing him of incompetence. You're too quick to take offence, where none is . . .'

'Then just what are you trying to say?' she demanded.

'Simply this . . . that I am not guilty of sharp practice, that in no way was I your father's enemy. That in fact I tried to be his friend, to help him . . . but it was too late. Things had gone too far. Both his health and his financial problems had deteriorated too much.'

'*You* . . . tried to be his *friend*?' Jancis put all the scorn she could muster into her voice. 'If that's your idea of friendship, I'd hate to see what you do to your enemies!'

With an abrupt movement he jerked her from the chair, his fingers digging mercilessly into her shoulders.

'Take care that I don't give you a demonstration!' He ground out the words from between clenched teeth. I think *you* are the only enemy I have. I hadn't planned to tell you this for a long time, maybe never. I was hoping that . . . But I'm no martyr and I'm sick of your snide remarks, sick of sparing your delicate feelings. You don't deserve any such consideration!'

His nearness and its effect upon her terrified Jancis, and

she swayed limply beneath his hands. She didn't want to fight him any more, didn't want to hate him. She was devastated by his words ... that he considered her his enemy. If only he knew! But, certain that he intended to make Alyson his wife, she did not want to entertain these feelings for him, which caused the blood to beat frantically in her veins. That could be even more dangerous to her peace of mind than her former animosity. If you could stop hating someone, surely to goodness you could stop loving them as well, she thought despairingly. If only she could put about a hundred miles between herself and Keegan!

'Let me go,' she implored him.

'Not until you've heard what I have to say.'

'I don't want to know ... please ...'

But he continued, inexorably.

'Your father came to see me, six months before he died. He was at his wits' end ...'

Vainly, Jancis struggled in his grasp, not wanting to hear the words which would destroy all her illusions, demolish her reasons for hating this man ... the only defence she had left against him.

'He begged me to help him, and ... well, to cut a long story short, he mortgaged The Kingdom to me. So in fact, the stables were mine the moment he died.'

Jancis stood very still, brown eyes wide with horror.

'No, no, I don't believe you,' she whispered, 'Daddy wouldn't beg ... he wouldn't ... not to you!'

'But he did. Oh, don't worry,' Keegan reassured her, the hard edge to his voice softening a little. 'You don't have to take your father off his pedestal. What he did was for your sake ... and your mother's. He insisted that a clause be inserted into our agreement, that if anything happened to him ... and I think he knew that he was dying ... I should take you both into my care.'

'Into your *care*!' Roused from her momentary torpor, Jancis stormed at him. 'You call working for you, as menials in our former home, taking care of us?'

'Would you have accepted my help in any other way?' Keegan asked bluntly. 'Would *you* have accepted my charity?'

She was silent. She could not argue with the truth. If she

had known of her father's agreement with Keegan Leroy, she would have gone to the farthest ends of the earth, rather than be beholden to him for anything ... even now, when her hatred for him had evaporated in the warmth of other emotions, his revelation had come as a tremendous and unpalatable shock.

'Does ... does my mother know about this?'

Keegan nodded.

'And, I might add, stood up to the knowledge better than you're doing. She, at least, appreciated your father's foresight for the two of you.'

At the thought of her father, knowing he was dying, humbling his pride to go cap-in-hand to Keegan Leroy, Jancis felt a sob rising in her throat. She struggled to crush her feelings, to hold back her grief until she was alone, but already the tears were streaming down her cheeks and her head fell forward in an attitude of defeat.

She heard Keegan's breath catch suddenly in his throat. The grip of his hands slackened, became gentle, as he gathered her against him, holding her closely, one hand stroking the sensitive nape of her neck. Completely undone by his unexpected gentleness, she allowed her emotions full rein, her face pressed hard against the strength and warmth of his chest, the harsh sobs racking her slight form.

For a while he allowed her to luxuriate in her grief, his hands still gentle, stroking her hair, cupping her head as it rested against him.

But as she clung even more closely, pressing herself against him for the reassurance of his nearness, she became aware of a restlessness in him, an unaccountable trembling, before he bent over her, scooping her up with one hand under her knees and carrying her towards the settee, where he held her across his thighs, gently forcing her face away from its place of concealment, lowering his head, his lips moving over her eyelids and damp cheeks, then taking her mouth in a gentle but persistent kiss.

Her distress had left her feeling absurdly vulnerable and his kisses promised consolation ... and something more besides. She nestled trustingly against him, her mouth responsive, tasting the salt of her own tears upon their moving lips. Her lips parted, allowing him, inviting him, to explore her mouth, tentatively at first, then with increasing passion.

A hand that could be hard in anger was now all gentle strength as it closed over her breast, the intimacy of the gesture suffusing the whole of her body with a sensuous warmth.

With fingers that trembled slightly, she felt for the lower ribbing of his sweater and slid her hand up beneath the soft wool, until it encountered the hair-roughened, muscular hardness of his chest. She tangled her fingers in the luxuriant growth, feeling his ribcage lift and fall shudderingly beneath her touch.

His mouth was devouring her, his hands becoming increasingly daring in their caresses . . . caresses which brought her throbbingly alive, and yet his hunger seemed unappeased by her now feverish response, by the fervour with which she returned his kisses.

Jancis knew that in a few more moments his love-making would become more insistent, more demanding, more impossible to deny . . . that they were both approaching the point of no return. Common sense, until now drugged by the consuming fire of their desires, re-awoke within her. What was she doing . . . what was she letting *him* do? Somehow she must fight this fever of the senses.

Keegan didn't love her. His embrace had begun as a comforting gesture, but he was a man, with all the natural appetites that implied, and these had been aroused by her helplessness, her clinging dependence upon him.

Clinging dependence! The words reminded her of Alyson, and just the thought of the other girl gave her the strength to fight the waves of passion that threatened to overwhelm her, to swirl her away on an irresistible tide, which would not ebb until she had given herself entirely to him.

But, almost certainly, Keegan planned to marry Alyson . . . even her mother thought so. There was no doubt that he loved Alyson, and even if he didn't, he would be foolish to miss the chance of adding his cousin's fortune to his own . . . and Keegan was anything but foolish. He was a hard-headed businessman. This was why she could be so certain that his urgent lovemaking did not arise from anything so irrational as emotion.

She struggled in his arms and sat up, straightening her skirt, endeavouring to smooth her tumbled hair. His eyes, glazed with smouldering desire, met hers and he made as if to pull her back into his arms.

'No,' she said breathlessly, 'Keegan, please, you mustn't . . . we mustn't . . .'

'Why not?' His voice was thick with unfulfilled passion. 'What is it? Do you *still* hate me, Jancis? Even now . . . now that I've explained?'

Desperately she fought against the longing to fling herself back into his arms, to submit to whatever demands he might make of her. But pride, self-respect forbade it. True, she no longer hated him . . . far from it . . . but she could not tell him so. She must look beyond superficial sensualities . . . and the emotions she stirred in him were undisguisedly physical, as indeed were her own reactions to him. There was no doubt that her body was responsive to his undoubted masculinity . . . that much she admitted to herself, it was pointless to deny it . . . but her heart, her mind . . . She scarcely dared to think of it, much less reveal it to him, that these two more logical organs also cried out for his domination, that mentally, spiritually, as well as physically, she loved him.

But it would be wrong to allow such intimacy to develop between them, with no other foundation than this mutual ravishment of their senses. There must be more . . . much more . . . something which Keegan could not offer and without which she must not submit.

He repeated his question, his deep voice tortured.

'No,' she told him, her own unsteady, 'I . . . I don't hate you.' He was entitled to this much of the truth. 'I think I'd stopped hating you a long time ago.'

'Well, then?'

He relaxed and ran a provocative hand over the contours of her hip, almost melting her into surrender; but Jancis forced herself to continue.

'But there was still this lingering resentment, for my parents' sake, but now you've explained . . .'

'And now that I've explained?'

His fingers were running along her spine, so that she had

to resist her body's urge to arch towards him. She fought for self-control.

'Now that you've explained, I know that I've been unfair, and I apologise. I'll do everything I can to make amends.'

'Everything?' His voice was husky and his dark glance with its passionate message made her shudder.

She dragged her gaze from his.

'I meant I'll tell everyone that I was mistaken ... that you ...'

'Everyone else knows.'

Jancis stared at him incredulously.

'Everyone?'

He nodded.

'Then why didn't anyone tell me?' Jancis asked angrily. 'Why did they let me go on thinking that you ... let me make a fool of myself?'

He sighed.

'Because I forbade anyone to tell you. I ... I was idiot enough to hope that you'd work it out for yourself. That you'd realise I wasn't capable of the behaviour you attributed to me.'

His voice had regained a little of its old bitterness and she slipped from his now unresisting arms, taking two or three irresolute steps away from him, pride and indignation warring with her conscience. Then, resolutely, she turned to face him.

'Keegan, I'm sorry ... truly I am. But I wish you'd told me ... that someone had told me, instead of letting me go on treating you the way I did ...'

She retraced her steps, brown eyes steady, facing him frankly.

'Can you forgive me?'

'Easily,' he said, his eyes intent upon her solemn little face.

Jancis held out a tremulous hand.

'Will you shake hands with me?'

He laughed then, but not in mockery. It was a sound of delighted, genuine amusement, and his laughter altered the whole expression of his face, his lips curving upwards, the laughter lines around his eyes deepening.

'Isn't that a little formal, Jancis, after ... after all this?'

His shrug was expressive and his raised brow, the discomfiting gleam in his eyes made her blush hotly.

He stood up and closed the gap between them, his hands capturing her face, his index fingers sensuously probing the sensitive skin behind her ears, thumbs at the corners of her mouth. There was still that unmistakable flicker of desire in his eyes, as he backed towards the settee, drawing her down beside him, kissing her gently, coaxingly.

'Jancis,' he pleaded, 'please, I need you . . .'

She wanted to give in to the passionate longing for him that shuddered through her, but with an effort, she evaded his lips . . . for her own sake she had to be cruel.

'Keegan, stop it! You're . . . you're taking too much for granted. Just because I'm willing to bury the hatchet, to be friends, it doesn't mean I . . .'

'Oh, come on, Jancis,' his smile was incredulous, 'don't tell me you're completely indifferent to me. Just now, you wanted me as much as I want you. *I know.*'

If he had continued to coax, she might have weakened, but his self-confident assurance gave her the spur she had needed to resist, to hold to her principles. She would *not* share his favours with Alyson.

She jumped up, lips curved in a sarcastic smile, which it cost her dearly to assume.

'Oh, I can enjoy a little flirtation as well as anyone,' she told him lightly. 'But you were getting a little too intense for my liking. Besides . . .' surreptitiously, she crossed her fingers behind her back, 'somehow I don't think Nick would approve of . . .'

'Mortimer?' In his turn, Keegan rose, black eyes snapping angrily. 'What has he to do with this?'

'I *am* dating Nick,' she reminded him.

'I'm aware of that, and you know my opinion . . . but I wasn't aware that you'd given him permanent rights over you? Jancis, don't . . . don't lie to me.'

This conversation was becoming dangerous. Soon, Jancis felt, she would be forced into making a false claim . . . a claim she might find it impossible, embarrassing even, to substantiate. She would look very foolish if Keegan chose to confront Nick.

She edged towards the door.

'No, no permanent rights, but basically I'm a one-man-at-a-time girl . . . and at the moment that man happens to be Nick,' she lied.

'You could have fooled me.'

Keegan regarded her morosely, but made no further attempt to detain her, and with a little gasp of relief Jancis gained the comparative safety of the hall. She could not have held out against him for much longer, denied the compulsion of her own senses, her racing pulses.

The sound of the door re-opening behind her lent strength to her shaking legs and she fled upstairs, hearing, as she did so, the drawing room door close again with unnecessary force.

It was not until she was on the point of sleep that Jancis recalled something which puzzled her. Keegan had said . . . and her brain had not really registered his words until now . . . that the stables were mortgaged to him, had become his upon her father's death. But at their first encounter, *after* Jack King's death, Keegan had spoken of 'buying' the stables.

'You and Keegan seem to be getting on better these days.' Mary King made use of one of their rare moments of privacy to quiz her daughter.

'Let's say we've decided to call a truce,' Jancis said casually. 'But I still think you might have told me the whole truth,' she reproached her mother, 'instead of letting me find out from *him*.'

Mary sighed.

'Yes, I didn't like deceiving you, dear, but it was one of Keegan's stipulations . . . that it should be left to him to tell you, when he saw fit. It didn't seem much to promise, after all he'd done for us.'

'Yes, and that's another thing,' Jancis said. 'Why did he talk about buying The Kingdom, when it was already his?'

Mary King looked quizzically at her daughter.

'Can you imagine your reaction, if you'd realised the stables already belonged to him? You'd have refused to live here, and Keegan wanted you to stay. He said he had his reasons.'

'What reasons?'

'I don't know, dear. I'm not that much in his confidence.'

Jancis shook her head in puzzled disbelief. Why on earth had Keegan been so determined that she should stay at The Kingdom . . . determined enough to conceal the fact that he already owned the stables, to bluff her into staying for her mother's sake?

'I'll never understand that man,' she muttered, 'never, as long as I live!'

'Well,' said Mary King, 'thank goodness you know everything at last. Perhaps now we can all live together harmoniously.'

If only her mother knew, Jancis thought, with a painful twist of her heart. There was no way she dared to go on living in the same house as Keegan Leroy. She knew him well enough now to be sure that he would not throw her mother out on to the streets. Thus, she need not hesitate to leave herself, as soon as possible . . . as soon, in fact, as she could get another job. She just could not risk a repetition of last night's encounter. There was no future in these alternating moments of hope and despair, of temptation and rejection of all that he offered. Nor could she stay here and see him married to Alyson. She shuddered at the thought; and, if she needed another incentive, despite justifying himself to her, he had not mentioned The Linnet's deteriorating form . . . had not retracted his accusations. She, apparently, was not entitled to the trust he had demanded from her.

During the following week, Jancis scanned the situations vacant column of the *Times Educational Supplement*. She had decided that she would prefer, if possible, to return to teaching Business Studies. Apart from the racing world, it was the way of life she knew best.

Meanwhile an uneasy peace reigned between her and Keegan. He had made no attempt at further persuasion, but sometimes she surprised an expression in his dark eyes, that seemed to express a torture as deep as her own, which disturbed her, setting her vulnerable heart leaping frantically in her throat.

Though Keegan had not dismissed David, it was very evident that he still mistrusted the young jockey, and he had given instructions that David was not to be allowed to ride in any major races. Since her second inglorious defeat, The Linnet had not been entered in any events, but was being rested for a week or two, with only gentle training, in the hope that this would help her to regain her lost form.

However, a resounding win with a hurdler, a horse recently purchased and owned by Keegan himself, had put him into a better frame of mind, and lads and jockeys alike breathed a little easier, when 'the gaffer', as they called him, made his regular daily tour of the yard.

It was only in the house that a state of tension still seemed to continue.

This was the state of affairs which existed until the morning when David failed to report for duty. The young jockey had been visibly unhappy of late, and though Jancis had tried to cheer him up, her efforts had been signally unsuccessful. The day before his non-appearance, he had confided in her that, following The Linnet's last race, Keegan had demanded that the racecourse vet carry out a dope test. It would be several days yet before the results were known and, despite his protestations of innocence, David was terrified that the tests would be positive, for he knew this would be the death knell of his career.

'My conscience is clear,' he told Jancis, 'but even Fred seems to doubt me. He asked me an awful lot of questions after that race . . . was I mixed up in any trouble of any sort, whether I was in debt . . .'

Jancis felt helpless before David's depression.

'I'm sure Fred was only trying to help,' she told him. 'He likes you.'

'He used to,' David said gloomily. 'Now he's almost certain I'm a wrong'un, and all my rides are off, indefinitely.'

'It's ridiculous!' Jancis protested. 'He must be crazy to think you'd do anything to jeopardise your career. Anyway, I'm sure the tests will be negative, and then . . .'

'It won't make much difference.' David seemed determined to be pessimistic. 'You know what they say about giving a dog a bad name. It's the same in racing. Even if the suspicion is unfounded, some of the mud sticks. Owners go round saying there must have been something in it. I tell you, Jancis, I feel like leaving the district, getting out of racing altogether. Trouble is, it's all I know . . . and then there's Ronny to consider. I can't leave her. We were thinking of getting engaged soon.'

There was no great alarm, when David didn't turn up for the early gallop. Everyone assumed that he had overslept, or was ill, in which case he would get a message to Fred somehow.

But as the day passed without any message, verbal or written, Fred sent one of the other lads down to David's digs, with a curt enquiry.

The lad returned, agog with the information he had obtained. David's bed had not been slept in and his landlady had not seen the young jockey since the previous morning.

'Sure sign of a guilty conscience,' Fred rumbled angrily, as he stood just inside the office door to make his report. 'The lad's done a bunk. I thought better of him than that!' He seemed as much annoyed by his bad judgment of character as by David's defection.

'Surely there must be some other explanation?' Jancis pleaded. 'I'm sure David's trustworthy. He desperately wants to ride winners, to make a name for himself.'

Keegan was more cynical.

'And to make money! These lads are all the same . . . meet a girl and they're in a hurry to get rich. If he's fallen in with some of the undesirables of the racing world . . .'

'I'm sure he hasn't,' Jancis persisted.

But both Fred and Keegan ignored her repeated opinion that David had gone away only because he was hurt, bewildered, unhappy . . . and Keegan lifted the telephone, with the avowed intention of informing the police.

Without stopping to weigh the consequences of her action, Jancis flung herself round her desk and depressed the receiver rest.

'Please, Keegan,' she begged, 'wait a bit longer . . . give him a chance. I *know* he's innocent. I have the strongest feeling . . .'

'I haven't much faith in your convictions,' he retorted, 'I seem to remember you once had rather strong feelings about me.'

She flushed scarlet.

'That . . . that's not fair! You . . . you said you'd forgiven me.'

Jancis scarcely noticed when an embarrassed Fred sidled towards the door, closing it carefully behind him.

Keegan leant back in his chair, thrusting his hands into his trouser pockets, an action which stretched the material tautly across his thighs, making Jancis acutely aware of their firm muscularity. Hastily she looked away.

'So, I agreed to forgive and forget. But it didn't get me anywhere, did it?' His dark eyes were challenging.

'Do you always have to have an eye for an eye, a tooth for a tooth?' Jancis enquired furiously, all the more angry because of her conscious reaction to the suggestion in his words.

But at least, while he was arguing with her, he was not telephoning the police, she thought, searching feverishly for further distraction.

'Did you expect a reward?' she taunted him.

'I thought it might lead to an improvement in our relationship,' he admitted.

'It did . . . it has.'

'And yet you're more concerned about a defecting jockey than about any detrimental effect his disappearance might have upon my stables.'

'Oh, do try to think about something besides business . . . and money. Don't you ever think about people?'

'There are certain people I'm only too willing to think about,' he agreed readily, 'and one person in particular.'

He rose so swiftly from his chair that she had no time to retreat.

'I think about you, Jancis, very often,' he said softly, one hand lifting to touch the bright curls which rioted softly about her heart-shaped face. 'I'd give anything to know that you thought about me sometimes.'

She fought determinedly against the insidious weakness his words induced . . . but perhaps they could be put to advantage. She was on dangerous ground, but she had to use every means at her disposal to help David. So instead of moving away, which instinct told her might be safer, she looked up at Keegan, brown eyes softly luminous.

'Then, just for me, won't you give David a little longer . . . please?'

A smile of unwilling admiration twisted his well-shaped mouth.

'You little siren!' he murmured, his hand moving down to touch the pulse in her neck, that leapt like a startled thing at his nearness. 'Just how far would you go, I wonder,' he mused aloud, 'for the sake of your friend?'

Jancis swallowed. This conversation was getting out of hand. She had only intended to ask a favour, on the strength of their suspended hostilities ... their precarious new friendship. But Keegan had read more into her words than she had intended. He had asked how far she would be prepared to go.

Warily she eyed him ... just how much did he intend to demand as the price of David's reprieve?

CHAPTER EIGHT

FOR MINUTES, Keegan kept Jancis in suspense, holding her wide gaze with his own darkly probing eyes. Then he gave a short laugh and moved away from her, his tone mocking.

'Don't worry, I shan't demand the ultimate sacrifice.'

The very fact that she *had* feared such an ultimatum, had feared her own inability, in the last resort, to resist his lovemaking, made Jancis' voice sharp, as she retorted.

'Nothing was farther from my mind!'

The lift of that sardonically independent brow indicated his doubt of her assertion, but he did not contradict her. Instead he asked:

'So what's to be done about young David, then?'

Relieved at this return to a safer theme, she gave the question her full consideration.

'There may be a perfectly good reason why he hasn't turned up. He may have been called away ... somebody ill at home ... or he could have been involved in an accident. Won't you at least give him a day or two to get in touch?'

Keegan moved restlessly about the office, his craggy features further contorted in thought. Unobserved, Jancis watched him avidly; just for these few moments letting her imagination roam, unbridled, studying every dear, familiar facet of his appearance, from over-long dark, wavy hair to the muscular length of his breeched legs.

Finally he turned towards her, his expression rueful.

'I probably need my head testing, but . . . all right, I'll give him three days . . . no more. After that . . .' His gesture towards the telephone spoke for itself.

'Oh, thank you.' Jancis had scarcely expected such an easy victory and impulsively, she moved towards him. 'I promise you, you won't regret it.'

'I won't?' His dark eyes were quizzical, his well-shaped mouth twisted wryly.

Confused, Jancis felt a tide of colour once more suffusing her face and neck.

'I didn't . . . that is . . . why do you keep . . .? You know very well, what I meant . . . I . . . oh!'

Her courage failing her, she turned and fled, leaving Keegan to shake his head over his own uncharacteristically easy capitulation.

Mary King was the only person who seemed unsurprised by Keegan's decision.

'It's just like you, giving the lad the benefit of the doubt,' she said warmly, as they sat at dinner that evening. 'I do hope the poor boy hasn't come to any harm, though.'

'Of course he hasn't,' said Alyson, in her light, breathy voice. 'I think Keegan should have reported his disappearance to the police immediately.' She turned to Keegan, her voice carefully neutral, the spite in her eyes for Jancis' benefit only. 'I suppose Jancis talked you out of it. Of course, she and David are rather close friends . . . just how close I'm not sure.'

Heatedly, Jancis repudiated the other girl's insinuation.

'Have some sense, Alyson! There's nothing like that between me and David . . . he's too young, and besides, he has a girl-friend, whom he hopes to marry some day. But I like David, and . . .'

'Oh, sorry! Of course, I forgot,' Alyson interrupted, her voice honey-sweet, gently self-deprecatory. 'It's Nick Mortimer you're interested in.' She laughed lightly. 'I can't keep trace of all your men-friends.' She managed to make

Jancis sound wildly promiscuous. 'Nick's a better catch than a struggling jockey, I can quite see that. All the same, I still think your defence of David is rather strange. I don't know much about horse-racing, but . . .'

'Then why don't you keep your silly mouth shut, and leave this to people who *do* know something?'

Immediately Jancis was annoyed with herself for allowing Keegan's cousin to get under her skin, and she was uncomfortably aware of the censure in his gaze.

'There's absolutely no reason to be offensive,' he remarked, as Alyson's baby blue eyes began to fill with easy tears. 'Alyson is just as entitled to her opinion as anyone else.'

'Yes, dear,' Mary King said gently, 'perhaps you should apologise. I'm quite sure Alyson didn't mean to imply . . . well, she's just concerned on Keegan's behalf, as indeed we all are.'

Jancis bit back an angry retort. Alyson *had* meant to insult her, but to continue the argument would only be to play into the other girl's hands by antagonising Keegan.

'Very well, I'll apologise,' Jancis said stiffly. She rose from the table, addressing no one in particular. 'If you'll excuse me, I'm going down to the yard. With David away, they'll be short-handed at evening stables.'

She hurried from the room. Not for the first time in her life, she cursed her quick temper and ready tongue. She knew very well that Alyson welcomed any opportunity to show her up in a bad light in front of Keegan. So why couldn't *he* see it? she wondered. Was he so besotted with his fair, frail cousin that he didn't recognise the petty spitefulness of her nature? Granted, the girl was not strong, but Jancis was sure Alyson over-accentuated her fragility, playing on the sympathy of those around her and using it, moreover, as a cover for malicious sniping at Jancis.

Only that morning Alyson had proudly displayed a letter from her cousins in Australia. Jancis thought it a pity that it had not been they, instead of Keegan, who had offered the younger girl a home.

As she worked alongside the lads that evening, Jancis moved through her tasks like an automaton. Her thoughts were on

David, as she tried to think of some way in which his name could be cleared and his whereabouts ascertained, before Keegan's three-day reprieve expired.

But it was not until the next morning that the discovery of a clerical error gave her an idea.

When The Linnet had first joined Keegan's string of horses in training, her programme of races had been made out for several weeks in advance. Recently, Keegan had given orders that the filly's name be withdrawn, but one entry had been overlooked. It was unusual for Jancis to make such an error and there was still time to cancel the declaration. Jancis was torn between her obvious duty as Keegan's secretary and her inclination as David's friend. The idea that this discovery had given her ... it was crazy ... it certainly came under Keegan's definition of rash escapades, but why not let the filly run? she reasoned. Keegan need not know . . . not until afterwards.

He was going away for two days, to see his own horse run at Ludlow. Between them, she and Fred could take The Linnet to Newmarket ... for she would need the head lad's collusion . . . and she would ride The Linnet herself. The more Jancis thought about it, the more the idea appealed to her. She had ridden The Linnet regularly from her very first introduction to The Kingdom stables and she knew that the filly loved and trusted her.

If she put her plan into operation, one way or another this present impasse would be resolved. Either the filly would run well, in which case someone had tampered with her on the two previous occasions, or she would give another bad performance. In the latter case, and with David's mysterious absence, at least the failure could not be laid at his door.

At first, when Jancis put her idea to Fred Higgins, the head lad was obdurate in his refusal.

'Me? Put one over on the boss? Not on your life, Miss Jancey! It's more than my job's worth, or yours ... or your ma's come to that.'

But Jancis shook her head stubbornly.

'Keegan wouldn't throw Mum out ... and he'd know you weren't to blame, Fred. One thing I've learned about him, he is fair. But if you won't help me, I'll manage somehow. I have to do this, Fred . . . for David. Keegan can throw me out if he likes.'

She did not add that it would be almost a relief to be summarily dismissed, saving her the heart-searching she must surely go through, before she took the irrevocable step of handing in her notice.

As she had been almost sure he would, Fred weakened.

'You know I can't let you go it alone, Miss Jancey,' he sighed, 'but I can't help thinking . . . a new job will be hard to get at my time of life.'

Impatiently Jancis shrugged aside the elderly man's fears. Nothing could possibly go wrong with her plan. They would be leaving The Kingdom after Keegan's own departure and would be back well before he returned. If The Linnet lost her race, they need not say anything . . . but if she won, then there would be nothing to lose by confessing their deception; the ends would have justified the means.

Jancis did not reveal her plan to her mother . . . she dared not take anyone but Fred into her confidence. Most of all, she must beware of Alyson's keen, prying eyes.

The race at Newmarket was to be over a mile and two furlongs, and to begin with things went according to plan. Jancis, with Fred driving the horsebox, left at first light, before even the most punctual of the lads could arrive for the morning gallops. They were well enough trained in their duties to carry on without the head lad for one day.

The journey itself was uneventful and as they drew nearer to their destination, Jancis felt an upsurge of optimism, not unmingled with apprehension at the thought of the race before her . . . an optimism shortly to prove unfounded.

In the paddock, The Linnet again showed uncharacteristic signs of temperament. Fred stood at her head, one hand behind each of the snaffle reins, while Jancis tightened the girths. The filly laid back her ears and gnashed her teeth, causing Fred to shake his head anxiously.

'I don't like it a bit, Miss Jancey and that's a fact. She's acting awful strange lately. She never used to fuss in the paddock. It's almost as if someone has been ill-treating her.'

'Just let me find out that somebody has!' Jancis said fiercely.

'Perhaps we should withdraw her after all?' Fred muttered, as the filly sidled and plunged in an attempt to rear up.

But then came the call, 'Jockeys out, please,' and before Fred could demur further, Jancis was in the saddle, and adjusting her goggles.

The horses circled the parade ring for the benefit of the punters, the sun sparkling on the multi-coloured throng of jockeys. Rugs and name sheets were removed, leading reins slipped and the horses' heads turned towards the start. An expectant hush fell over the onlookers, as the riders came under the starter's orders, and then they were off, thundering over the springy turf.

At first, Jancis was aware only of the wild beating of her own heart, but then, as she became calmer, she thrilled to the familiar sensation of rippling muscles beneath her and began to mutter words of endearment, of encouragement to the filly, even though she knew the pricked-back ears would be deaf to all but the thud of her opponents' feet.

At first The Linnet seemed to be holding her own, but before the race was much advanced, Jancis found herself dropping further and further back, having a hard time of it to keep her mount going. A good animal, she knew from experience, would put its head down and battle on, whatever the opposition, but The Linnet was already beginning to throw up her head, giving unmistakable indication that she did not relish further effort.

Jancis tried everything she knew, encouraging her with hands, heels and the swing of her whip, but she had to admit that the filly just wasn't trying . . . in fact hadn't got it in her to stay the course.

Suddenly, without any warning, The Linnet stumbled and, to her utter dismay, Jancis found herself unshipped and falling. She kept her head, however, maintaining a firm hold of the reins, intending, as she had been taught, to pull The Linnet round in a tight circle, until a steward could come to her assistance. But The Linnet, thoroughly alarmed, reared up and as Jancis hung on, the filly fell, trapping Jancis' leg beneath her.

With The Linnet injured and her own badly bruised leg tightly strapped, there was no way now that her escapade could be concealed from Keegan, and it was with trepidation that Jancis awaited his return from Ludlow on the following day.

She knew that, as always after an absence, he would visit the stables first and that Fred would have no choice but to report The Linnet as being injured . . . and the cause. It took all her courage, but Jancis decided that she too would face Keegan in the yard. She could not leave Fred to bear the full brunt of his rage. Besides, she could not bear the thought of meeting Keegan under her mother's anxious, reproachful gaze, with a gloating Alyson looking on.

Alyson had already taken great delight in predicting Keegan's reaction to the accident and what she termed Jancis' dishonest behaviour.

The trouble was that Jancis' own innate honesty made her admit . . . though not to Alyson . . . that she had indeed been underhand.

As the Range Rover, towing a horsebox, went slowly past the window, Jancis left the office, bracing herself for what was bound to be an unpleasantly acrimonious encounter.

It would carry no weight with Keegan that her actions had been prompted by a desire to help. All he would recognise would be wilful deception on her part and its consequences. He would have every right to berate her. She only wished she felt better able to face his anger. Her own disappointment at the utter failure of her plan . . . and her injured leg . . . had combined to depress her usually resilient spirits.

Wincing a little at the pain from her bruised leg, she made her way slowly across the cobbled yard. Fred was already waiting for Keegan, as he stepped from the Range Rover, stretching a little after his long drive. Despite her apprehension, Jancis felt the familiar thrill run through her, at the sight of his tall, athletic figure, the springy dark hair, which he now rumpled with a heart-tuggingly habitual gesture.

Then she saw his shoulders straighten, his head jerk up in angry disbelief, as Fred spoke, before he outstripped the elderly head lad, striding rapidly towards The Linnet's stall.

Keegan had completed his examination of the filly by the time Jancis had limped the length of the yard, and, as he re-emerged, his eyes, black as agates in their anger, went straight to her pale, anxious face, the chin already tilted in anticipation of his attack. But she faced him unflinchingly, ready to take the furious censure she knew she deserved.

To her surprise, he did not rush immediately into angry speech. Instead, his gaze swept her from head to foot, his eyes flickering only for a moment, as he noted her bandaged leg. Then he turned his back upon her, completely ignoring her, as he spoke to Fred.

'Has the owner been advised?'

Fred shook his head. The gnarled little man seemed even more bent and bowed, his wizened features lacking their usual cheerful aspect. He too seemed to find Keegan's silkily controlled reception of Jancis more alarming than a violent outburst. His faded eyes watched his employer's face, their expression like that of a dog that expects a blow. Jancis knew he must be wondering if Keegan would dismiss him.

Suddenly she could bear the precarious calm no longer.

'It wasn't Fred's fault.' Despite herself, her voice wobbled ominously. 'I *made* him help me. I . . . I'll ring Nick, tell him it was all my fault.'

Keegan rounded on her then, still cool and tight-lipped in his anger, but nonetheless menacing.

'You will do no such thing! I don't relish my owners thinking that I allow an employee . . . and a girl at that . . . to have a say in the running of my stables.'

'I see that, but . . .' she began.

He ignored the interruption.

'Regardless of where the fault lies, this accident will be considered by everyone as a breach of my duty . . . the duty cast upon every trainer . . . to ensure the safety of all horses under his care.'

'But it isn't fair that you should take the blame for something I did behind your back,' she protested.

'It's a little late in the day to realise that,' he told her grimly.

With a curt, dismissive nod to the unhappy Fred, Keegan turned and strode towards the office, while Jancis followed, stumbling over the uneven cobbles in her attempt to keep up with him.

'You *mustn't* blame Fred,' she insisted. 'He didn't want to run The Linnet, but I persuaded him.'

'And you can be very persuasive, as I know to my cost. Well, you needn't think I shall be so complaisant in future. As far as I'm concerned, this latest scrape of yours releases me from my promise. As soon as I've spoken to Mortimer, I shall contact the police, report David's disappearance, and tell them of my suspicions. I was a fool to let you persuade me otherwise.'

'Oh, no!' Jancis was horrified. How could he be so unfair? How could he break his promise? 'It's not David's fault that I . . .'

'Isn't it?' Keegan paused in his stride for a moment, to survey her. 'Hasn't this whole situation arisen from his gross mishandling of that filly, followed by his very suspicious disappearance? No, Jancis, my mind is made up. That lad must be found and brought to book, and this time neither argument nor blandishments will persuade me otherwise.'

Miserably she followed him into the office, watched him as he dialled Nick Mortimer's number. She could only hear one side of the conversation that followed, but the expressions which crossed Keegan's rugged features told their own story, and she moved restlessly from one foot to the other.

It was distressing to have to listen to Keegan, that normally arrogant, self-assured man, explaining, apologising . . . to Nick; and it increased Jancis' feelings of stricken guilt that Keegan made no mention of her part in The Linnet's accident.

She looked at him imploringly, as his dark eyes met hers for an instant.

'Let me speak to Nick,' she mouthed.

But he shook his head, momentarily placing one hand over the mouthpiece.

'Sit down . . . and be quiet!' he hissed the words at her. 'I'll deal with you later!'

He looked and sounded as if he hated her. Jancis turned away, shoulders drooping.

It was impossible to sit down, when the only chair was immediately facing him. She limped painfully towards the window, staring unseeingly across the yards, where the lads, blissfully unaware of tensions at management level, were finishing their morning stint.

Drearily she reflected that she had added yet another nail to the coffin of her truce with Keegan . . . now, when she least desired to be at odds with him.

In all the weeks since he had taken over The Kingdom, Keegan had treated her deliberate antagonism with patient tolerance, slowly but surely winning first her reluctant respect and admiration, and finally her love.

The pain in her heart, combined with the dull throbbing from her bruised leg, undermined her indomitable spirit, the pluck with which she usually faced life, and an involuntary sob escaped her.

She had not even noticed that Keegan had concluded his uncomfortable telephone conversation, and his hand on her shoulder, swinging her round to face him, startled her, making her shake uncontrollably with mingled fear and another, more deeply felt emotion. Her eyes, misty with the threatening tears, met his apprehensively.

'What . . . what are you going to do?' she whispered, her soft, trembling lips scarcely able to form the words.

'With you?' he asked, a wry grimace twisting his well-shaped mouth. 'God alone knows . . . I wish I did.'

He continued to stare down at her, hands resting lightly on her shoulders, and her colour began to rise, until at last she was forced to look down, no longer able to sustain the steady assessment of those dark eyes.

Keegan made a sound midway between a groan and a choked laugh, then, almost roughly, pulled her against him.

'What *am* I to do with you?' he repeated softly against her curly head.

Love me, just love me, every part of her yearned to speak the words aloud, but she knew she never would. It was sweet torture to be held thus, to feel the strong thud of his heart beneath her . . . to know that it did not beat for her. She knew she should move away, that to rest like this in his arms was only prolonging her own agony, increasing her fevered longing to be wholly possessed by him. Yet a delicious torpor held her spellbound, as if she must extract every ounce of sensation from this suspended moment in time . . . the most she would ever receive of him, could ever expect to receive.

Her nostrils flared slightly, as she breathed in the almost

heady male scent of him . . . a mixture of tweed, of horse-leather, the tang of after-shave. If she lived for a thousand years, she thought, her senses would never forget this heightened awareness. She choked back a sob at the thought of the empty years ahead, with only her memories for company . . . how could flesh and blood endure this unfulfilled, painful longing which stabbed through the most intimate recesses of her being?

Keegan felt the sudden spasm, as she tried to suppress the despairing grief that threatened to overwhelm her, and led her towards the hitherto despised chair, firmly sitting her down. He crouched before her, his face disturbingly close to hers, and almost absently smoothed back the rumpled curls from her strained, tear-wet face.

'There's no need to make quite such a tragedy of it.' He sighed. 'Oh, Jancis, when will you ever learn not to be so independent . . . so impetuous? Just what did you hope to gain by running The Linnet, eh?'

Jancis shook her head in a dazed fashion. Somehow his proximity always banished all coherent thought, now making it difficult to remember just how she had rationalized her plan of action.

'It . . . it just seemed like a good idea. I thought it might solve the problem of The Linnet one way or the other . . . why her form had deteriorated so badly. I thought, if *I* rode her . . .'

'So you *do* have your doubts about young David?' he said gravely.

'No . . . yes . . .' She passed a hand through her hair, further disordering the russet curls. 'Oh, I don't know any more . . . Yes, I do, though.' For an instant her brain cleared and a spark of her old defiance showed momentarily. 'She ran badly for me too, so it couldn't be David, could it?'

Keegan stood up and paced restlessly about the office, his face tired and drawn, and Jancis experienced a pang of guilt that he should have to face all this vexation after his early start and long drive. She longed to smooth the furrows from his brow, the deeply etched lines that framed his mouth.

He swung round and came back to her, remaining upright this time, but one long, lean finger tilting up her chin, so that she was forced to meet his eyes squarely.

'Tell me something, Jancis ... I know he's younger than you, but *are* you in love with David? You denied it to Alyson, but ...'

'Good heavens, no!' Her eyes expressed such astonished incredulity that it was impossible for the man watching to doubt her sincerity, and his own expression lightened. But he persisted, nevertheless.

'So you've no personal reason for believing so strongly in his innocence?'

'Yes, of course I have.' Her tone was indignant and his eyes narrowed. 'David is a friend. You don't have to be in love with someone to believe in them ... somehow, you just know when somebody is genuine, and straight, and ...' Her voice faltered away.

'Woman's intuition?' His voice was bitter, a bitterness expressed in his next words. 'So what happened to your instincts where I was concerned?'

She bit her lip, looking at him with genuine contrition in her brown eyes.

'Oh, Keegan, I'm sorry about that ... truly I am, and I *have* already apologised for the way I treated you. I suppose if I'm honest with myself, I began to realise, long before I would admit it, that you were a good man ... kind, trustworthy. But Daddy's death ... losing The Kingdom hurt so much ...'

Her lips quivered, for her memories still had the power to wound.

'Then why do you still fight me ... hold me at arm's length?'

His eyes blazed with a sudden intensity and he pulled her from the chair more roughly than he intended, his face instantly concerned, when she winced, as her leg came in contact with the solidity of his.

'Does your leg pain you very much?' he asked gently.

'A bit,' she admitted.

'Let me see,' he demanded.

'Oh ... oh no, it ... it's all right, really. The ... the doctor said it was only bruised.'

Ignoring her protests, he swung her lightly on to the desk top, deft fingers removing the pins which held the bandaging in place.

Jancis flushed scarlet, remembering the full extent of the bruising, which ran from ankle to hipbone. Surely he would not attempt to remove the full length of binding?

'Keegan, please . . .' she begged, as his hands moved higher, the feel of their firm, warm flesh exquisite agony against her own.

Mercifully, after a swift glance at her rosy face, he stopped at the knee and with a gentle finger traced the extent of the ugly bruising already exposed. His touch sent tongues of fire leaping along her nerve ends and she closed her eyes against the unbearable ecstasy.

'Sorry,' he apologised. 'Did I hurt you?'

She wanted to tell him that it was not pain, but torture . . . torture of the most insidious kind, one which she would be prepared to endure eternally.

Efficient as any doctor, Keegan rebound her leg, hands and eyes intent upon his task, so that she was able to study his downbent head with hungry absorption. There would be so few moments like this left to her.

She was still determined to leave The Kingdom, as soon as a suitable opportunity arose. How could she stay here, feeling as she did, to see him make Alyson his wife? She determined then and there to redouble her efforts to find alternative employment, whatever the cost to her in terms of unhappiness.

The rebandaging completed, he set her once more upon her feet, his voice rough, as he bade her to take more care of herself in future. If only his polite concern were prompted by some deeper, more personal feeling! Jancis sighed involuntarily, as he moved away, round his desk, his hand on the telephone receiver.

His next words shocked her out of her bemused state.

'I have to contact the police.' His voice was almost apologetic. 'You *do* see that, don't you, Jancis? For the lad's own sake, the reputation of the stables . . . for everyone's protection, this matter has to be cleared up once and for all.'

She stared at him in disbelief. With his manner so much softened towards her, she had not really believed he would carry out his threat.

'Keegan . . .' she began.

His upraised hand silenced her.

'No, Jancis,' he said firmly, 'you won't dissuade me again. This is something I have to do ... it's a question of duty, integrity.'

'And money,' she snapped at him. 'You're frightened that the same thing will happen to you that happened to Dad ... that owners will take their horses away ...'

'Of course!' He sounded surprised. 'I've made no secret of the fact that business and sentiment don't go together.'

'And yet you agreed to keep Mummy and me here at The Kingdom, when you didn't need to. If you'd waited a bit longer, till Daddy died, you could have bought us out anyway. Would you call that entirely businesslike?'

For the first time since she had known him, Keegan appeared discomfited, a dull brick red creeping up under his tan.

'That was different,' he muttered. 'I had my reasons.'

'Which of course you're not prepared to divulge?'

'Certainly not to you,' he agreed. 'The only person in whom I confided was your father. Even your mother only knew part of the story.'

'Yes, and that's another thing,' Jancis told him. 'You sneer at what you call my persuasiveness. It seems you too can be convincing, when it suits you. You certainly talked my mother into deceiving me about a lot of things. Well, I'll tell you something, Mr Keegan Leroy, if you do this to David, I'll never forgive you, never speak to you again ... not that that will worry you, I suppose!'

With her limp, it was impossible to make a dignified exit and she was uncomfortably aware of Keegan's gaze upon her retreating back, as she attempted to stalk from the office. But what she could not be aware of was the pain in the depths of those dark eyes, or the deepening of the etched lines from mouth to jaw, as, slowly, he dialled the number he required.

CHAPTER NINE

JANCIS' only desire was to gain the privacy of her own room, to give herself a chance to resolve the inner fever of conflict, the ferment of emotionalism that had ebbed and flowed within her, during the last half hour.

Dread of Keegan's anger had turned to a fear far more potent, that of herself ... of her compulsive reactions to his vibrant sexuality, the challenge he posed to all her resolutions. She knew a numbing certainty that she must put as much distance between herself and Keegan as possible ... a certainty that was at variance with her doubt that she would have the necessary strength of character to do so, to liberate herself from his physical dominion over her.

But she was not destined to have the time she needed for sober reflection, before a new crisis was upon her.

Mary King intercepted her daughter, as she limped her way painfully towards the stairs.

'Oh, there you are, dear,' Mary said in tones of profound relief. 'There's someone to see you ... a young girl ... and she seems very upset.'

Dismayed, Jancis shook her head. She was in no fit state to cope with her own emotions; the thought of confronting similar turmoil in another filled her with consternation.

'I can't see anyone now, Mum, please. Tell her, whoever it is ...'

From the open drawing room door, a small figure erupted; long golden hair bounced around a small but determined tear-stained face.

'Miss King? Jancis King? I *must* speak to you ... now, please! It—it's terribly important. I'm Veronica—Ronny!' Then, as Jancis still stared blankly, the girl moved closer, adding in a murmur that reached Jancis' ears only, 'David's girl-friend.'

The small girl's face puckered and it seemed that at any moment she might burst into tears again.

With a nervous glance over her shoulder, almost as if she

expected Keegan to materialise at this intelligence, Jancis hustled Veronica back into the drawing room, closed the door behind them and coaxed the girl to sit down.

'Is it about David . . . do you know where he is, Veronica? or do I call you Ronny?'

The small girl nodded.

'Ronny, please.'

'*Do* you know where David is?' Jancis asked again.

Once more, Ronny bobbed her head, large grey eyes swimming in tears. She would be a very pretty girl, Jancis decided, without the blotches that recent tears had made on her clear, ivory skin.

'D-David said you were the only one here who believed in him.' A hiccupping sob escaped with the words. 'Y-you do still believe he's innocent, that he didn't do all the horrible things they've accused him of . . . you haven't changed your mind?'

'Horrible things? What things? Who's accused him?'

'Mr Leroy . . . Fred Higgins. They've been rotten to David.'

'Now, hold on!' Jancis felt impelled to spring to Keegan's defence . . . and Fred's, of course, she told herself. 'Nobody's actually accused him, but Keegan is suspicious, naturally . . . after all, his reputation is at stake.'

Why was it so easy, she wondered, to recognise that fact, when defending him to someone else, but impossible to admit the justice, when Keegan himself made the same claim?

Veronica's small hands rent and twisted a pitifully inadequate handkerchief. Jancis sat down beside her.

'Now listen,' she said firmly. 'Personally, I *do* believe that David is innocent, that he had nothing to do with The Linnet losing those two races. Does that make you feel any better?'

Veronica's face relaxed into a mistily grateful smile.

'So,' Jancis continued, 'suppose you tell me where David is?'

Veronica's small, slender body was tense once more.

'Promise me first that you wont tell Mr Leroy?' she demanded.

'Oh, but . . .' Jancis was dismayed. She was in enough

trouble with Keegan, had deceived him too many times already.

Veronica half rose, her tear-stained face set mulishly.

'If you don't promise, I won't tell you anything. David is afraid Mr Leroy will hand him over to the police.'

'But if David is innocent,' Jancis argued, 'he has nothing to fear. Once we know where he is everything can be cleared up.'

Veronica was on her feet now and moving towards the door.

'If you don't promise not to tell Mr Leroy, *I* won't tell *you* anything,' she repeated.

'Oh, very well,' Jancis sighed, 'I promise.'

It seemed, she thought ruefully, that she was destined always to be deceiving Keegan. But this time she had no choice, she comforted herself; the deception was not of her own making.

Reassured, Veronica sat down again, though on the extreme edge of the settee, still poised as if for instant flight.

'He—he's locked up.'

'Locked up?' Jancis echoed the words disbelievingly. Who on earth would want to lock up the young jockey, and why?

The other girl saw the incredulity in Jancis' eyes.

'Oh, you must believe me, you must!' Her voice broke on the words.

'Go on,' Jancis said quietly. 'Why is he locked up, and where?'

'He . . . he's in a disused loft, over an empty stable at Dutch's Dyke.'

Jancis recognised the name of the stable . . . an establishment considerably smaller than The Kingdom, run by a trainer named Louie Dutch and situated about twenty miles away.

'How do *you* know this?' she asked curiously.

'I . . . I just do know,' Veronica muttered, for the first time avoiding Jancis' eyes.

'Ronny,' Jancis said firmly, 'if you want me to help David, to trust you, you *must* tell me *everything*.'

'I . . . I know the . . . the people who own it.' The words came reluctantly. 'I . . . I've been there. I've spoken to David.'

'Then why on earth didn't *you* let him out?' Jancis demanded in exasperation.

'I couldn't,' said Veronica, her grey eyes desperate. 'There . . . there were reasons. You . . . you don't understand.'

'How can I understand, if you don't tell me everything you know? You're keeping something back, Ronny. Why?'

Ronny's lips set obstinately.

By the uneasy shifting of Veronica's eyes and the heightened colour in the other girl's face, Jancis knew that she had certainly not heard the whole truth. However, the news of David's whereabouts would have to suffice . . . it was a start at least.

'Well, do you know *why* the people at Dutch's Dyke have got him locked up?' Jancis persisted.

'He said it was because he'd found something out . . . about . . . about The Linnet.'

'Found out what?' Jancis had to restrain herself from screaming the words; her patience was wearing thin. She was having to drag every detail from this exasperating girl.

'I don't know,' Ronny said miserably. 'He didn't have time to tell me any more. He . . . I mean someone . . . was coming. I . . . I had to get away. David told me to come and tell you. He . . . he said you'd agree to help us . . . you'd know what to do.'

Jancis wished she felt as certain of her own capabilities. Normally independent . . . recently to the point of recklessness . . . she suddenly felt a ridiculous urge for a strong man to lean on, to take the decisions.

'Look,' she said, 'I know you don't want me to tell Keegan anything, but I think you ought to know that he was phoning the police when I left the office.'

Veronica jumped up, her face whitening.

'He . . . he's here? Mr Leroy's here? I thought he was away!'

'He got back about an hour ago.'

'But the police mustn't know,' Ronny insisted. 'It would only be David's word against . . . against the owner of Dutch's Dyke. Look, I have to go. He mustn't see me here . . . Mr Leroy, I mean.'

Again Jancis noticed the slight hesitation in the girl's speech and once more felt positive that Ronny knew a great deal more than she had revealed.

But since her mention of Keegan, Veronica seemed increasingly anxious to be gone.

Parked in the front drive was a small but expensive sports car . . . not the sort of car Jancis would have expected David's girl-friend to own, not when she recalled David's description of Ronny's straitened circumstances. *Had* the young jockey lied to her after all?

Veronica started the powerful engine and looked up anxiously at Jancis.

'You will help us?'

'Yes, of course,' Jancis nodded. She couldn't refuse, despite her increasing misgivings. She must give David the benefit of the doubt . . . not to do so would make her as bad as Keegan. 'But we must have a proper plan. I mean, I can't just walk in and . . .'

'Ring me this evening.' Veronica mentioned a telephone number. 'But if anyone else answers, put the phone down quickly, promise?'

Suddenly her eyes widened, as she gazed somewhere over Jancis' right shoulder and with a sudden increase of revs and a grinding of gears, the small car shot away and Jancis jumped back hastily, as it left a spray of gravel in the wake of its tortured tyres.

She could guess only too well what had caused Veronica's sudden alarm, and she turned to see Keegan at the top of the front steps, one hand shading his eyes, as he stared after the speeding car.

'Who was that?' he asked, moving down to stand close beside her.

Jancis felt her nerves tauten and quiver, almost as if he had touched her. How flimsy were her defences against this man!

She improvised rapidly.

'An . . . an old girl-friend, someone I hadn't seen for a long time.'

'Funny,' he muttered, 'I could have sworn it was . . . oh well, never mind.' He turned away and re-entered the house.

Jancis was about to call after him, to ask if he had indeed telephoned the police, and if so what their reaction had been. But then she checked herself. She didn't really want to know. If he *had* contacted the police sheer pride would force her to keep her threat. She would have to refuse to speak to Keegan, and somehow she did not feel equal to the increased tension such a state of affairs would be bound to bring in its wake. Already too many dark threads of hostility were woven into their relationship.

With her new knowledge of David's whereabouts to burden her, plus the fact that she was about to deceive Keegan once more, the afternoon seemed intolerably slow.

Dinner that evening was a silent meal. Keegan seemed disinclined for conversation, though several times Jancis disturbed an oddly pensive expression in his eyes, as they met hers; Mary King was not one to chatter unrestrainedly, without encouragement of some kind, and Jancis felt almost too nervous to eat, anticipating the moment when she must telephone Veronica and commit herself to a plan of action which could well turn out to be a risky one.

If the owner of Dutch's Dyke was desperate enough to imprison David, to what further lengths might he not go, if he thought she had uncovered his crime? It seemed pretty obvious to her that Louie Dutch must have been the one responsible for The Linnet's loss of form . . . and now that she had leisure to reflect, she recalled Nick saying that Sam Roscoe often rode for Louie Dutch. Things were beginning to add up.

After dinner, Keegan disappeared in the direction of the office and, exasperatingly, the telephone seemed to be in constant use for most of the evening. It was almost nine before Jancis found an opportunity to make her call, using the house extension. Even then it was made with frequent, anxious glances over her shoulder, in case anyone should overhear.

She dialled the number Veronica had given her. The ringing tone went on and on interminably. Jancis was about to put down the receiver when at last someone replied. It was a gruff, masculine voice that answered:

'Dutch's Dyke stables.'

Jancis could not have spoken had she wished to do so. The shock was too great. It seemed so incredible that Veronica should have given her the telephone number of the actual place where David was held prisoner.

Impatiently, the voice repeated itself, and remembering Ronny's warning, Jancis was just about to replace the receiver, when she heard, in the background, a girl's voice say:

'Oh, I think that must be for me.' Then, unmistakably, Veronica's voice.

'Hallo!'

'Ronny? Thank goodness!' Jancis exclaimed. 'I'm sorry I couldn't ring before, but . . .'

'Oh, that's quite all right, my dear. Yes, you can still have your riding lesson at three o'clock tomorrow.'

Belatedly, Jancis realised that Veronica was talking for the benefit of the owner of the gruff voice, and the other girl continued to prattle on in this fashion for some time. At last she said:

'I'm sorry about that, Jancis.' Her voice had dropped to a husky whisper. 'I hope you realised that he . . . someone else was still here. Listen . . . I haven't much time. He'll be back,' Ronny continued. 'Come here tomorrow afternoon, in riding kit, and say you've come for a riding lesson. Then I can take you round the stables without anyone thinking it suspicious.'

'Tomorrow afternoon? That might be difficult,' Jancis demurred. 'I have to work all day . . .'

A movement, glimpsed from the corner of her eye, proved to be Keegan, on his way through from the office, and immediately she felt the pull of the senses his presence always induced.

'What's your problem?' he enquired. 'Need some time off?'

He sounded genuinely concerned, which made Jancis feel even worse about deceiving him.

She covered the mouthpiece, ignoring Veronica's anxious questioning.

'Yes, my . . . my friend has to go away again, the day after tomorrow . . .'

'And you'd like to visit her tomorrow?'

Jancis nodded, hating the lies she was being forced to tell.

Instead of the curt refusal she expected, Keegan waved an airy hand.

'No problem! Take the afternoon off. Take the whole day off if you like.'

He passed on his way, leaving a startled Jancis staring after his tall, heart-stopping figure, her features contorted with the helpless agony of wanting. If only . . .

Suddenly she realised that Veronica was still making agitated noises from the other end of the phone.

'Sorry about that, Ronny,' she said, 'but I was just arranging to have the afternoon off.'

'Was Keegan Leroy there?' Veronica asked suspiciously.

'Yes,' said Jancis, 'but he was only passing by. He doesn't suspect a thing, honestly. Look, I'll see you tomorrow, about three . . . O.K?'

As she replaced the receiver on its rest and turned away towards the stairs, Jancis was surprised to see Alyson loitering in the drawing room doorway. It was the first time she had ever seen the girl move around the house unaided. Jancis' eyes narrowed. She had always suspected that Alyson overplayed her alleged fragility.

'*Another* boy-friend?' Alyson asked in her high, rather plaintive voice. 'Is this one rich too?'

Jancis was only thankful that the abbreviation of Veronica's name could pass for either male or female. Alyson could make what she liked of the results of her snooping. Abruptly, she brushed past the other girl. When alone, neither girl made a secret of their mutual dislike.

'Wouldn't you like to know?' Jancis taunted.

It did not occur to her that Alyson might make malicious use of her eavesdropping.

Once or twice the following morning, Jancis felt Keegan's dark enigmatic eyes on her as they worked their way through the usual mound of paperwork. Every time she met his gaze, her heart seemed to become lodged in her throat. She was becoming increasingly vulnerable to him . . . even to be in the same room was delightful torture. She felt sure that he was waiting for her to say something about her plans for the afternoon, but she decided that the less she said, the fewer lies she would be forced to tell.

The only reference she made to the subject was to ask if she could finish half an hour earlier for her lunch, in order to give her time to catch the little country bus which made a tortuous detour around several villages before passing her destination.

'I'll run you to wherever you're going if you like,' Keegan volunteered.

Alarmed at this idea, which might destroy all her plans, Jancis rejected his offer more vigorously than was necessary and was rewarded by seeing him lapse into an angry, offended silence.

'I ... I'm sorry,' she ventured. 'I didn't mean to sound rude or ungrateful, and it's very kind of you to offer, but I'll enjoy the bus ride. I don't get much opportunity to go out on my own, and ...'

'Away from me, you mean,' he suggested, his dark eyes narrowed, and she realised that far from placating him, she was only making matters worse.

'If that's the way you want to take it,' she conceded wearily, too worn down by this constant battle between them to argue further.

'And you're off to see a girl-friend?' he said, 'the one who called here yesterday?'

'Yes.'

'I see.'

There was patent disbelief in his voice and Jancis realised, with a sense of shock, that he thought she was meeting a man. Obviously Alyson had been busy, she reflected cynically.

After its customary meanderings, the bus set Jancis down on a long, lonely stretch of road, with only the Dutch's Dyke Stables and a badly delapidated pair of cottages in sight. Everything in the area, in fact, seemed to be in poor condition, from the drunken, peeling sign which said 'Racehorses—Dead slow' to the stables themselves, with their cracked walls, warped door and window frames, the drunken roof, with its patchwork of missing tiles.

Dutch's Dyke was certainly not in the same class as The Kingdom. There was no sweeping, gracious approach to the house, with the stableyard set behind. Instead, the stables flanked the road, divided from it by only a crumbling brick wall. There seemed to be an overall air of depression about the place, and Jancis shuddered at the thought that, but for

Keegan, The Kingdom might have been reduced to this parlous condition.

Only a few of the boxes seemed to be in use, and to Jancis' prejudiced eye, the heads protruding from them looked vastly inferior in appearance to those of the thoroughbreds being trained by Keegan. Except ... except for that of a rather showy chestnut, with a white blaze. Jancis drew a swift breath ... the chestnut, surely, which had beaten The Linnet at Newcastle ... the chestnut which Sam Roscoe had ridden.

As Jancis closed the sagging gate into the yard, Veronica ran from one of the looseboxes.

'Thank goodness you've come!' she breathed. 'I was so afraid you wouldn't, that you'd change your mind. You haven't told anyone else?'

Jancis shook her head.

'Come on, the riding horses are in the other yard, around the back of the house. Put your riding hat on and keep your head down as we pass the house. You don't want to be recognised.'

'But surely no one here knows me ...' Jancis began.

'Just do it!' Veronica hissed.

She hustled Jancis past the run-down house, at a speed which made Jancis grimace, for her leg, though slowly improving, was still tender.

A hack, already saddled and bridled, stood at a hitching post and Veronica led her towards it.

'Now, you must pretend you've never ridden before,' she explained. 'Then I can give you your first lesson here, in the yard, so you can see ...' She paused in mid-sentence.

'See what?' asked the mystified Jancis.

But in a deliberately loud voice, Veronica began enumerating the various pieces of harness and instructing Jancis in the correct manner of mounting, as if she were the veriest beginner.

The reason for this caution became evident, as an elderly man shambled across the yard and into one of the looseboxes, darting a penetrating glance at them from beneath shaggy brows.

'Did you notice what he was carrying?' Veronica hissed. 'Food ... for David. He feeds him ... when he remembers,' she added in a choked voice.

'So that's where . . .?'

'Yes, but don't stare. They don't trust me, because they know David is my boy-friend, and if they knew who you were. . .'

Her voice rose again, admonishing for some imaginary mistake in her technique as the elderly man made his return journey.

'Isn't there any way we can talk to David?' Jancis asked, as Veronica led the horse slowly round the yard, while Jancis tried to look like an uncertain beginner.

Veronica shook her head.

'No, not now . . . not in broad daylight.'

'Then how . . .?'

'I've worked out a plan. When your lesson is over, you must pretend to go away, then come back and hide until it's dark. They only check up on David in the daytime.'

'Then why haven't you . . .?' Jancis began.

Veronica shook her head.

'They lock me in my room at night. Not that there's any need. They know I daren't do anything, because of . . .'

'You *live* here?' Jancis was astounded, 'but I thought . . . I thought you just worked here.'

'Louie Dutch is my uncle,' Veronica explained sadly. 'He and my other uncle are the only two relatives I have in the world.'

Jancis remembered the expensive sports car Veronica had driven the previous day. A car like that just didn't tie in with the pervading air of poverty at Dutch's Dyke.

'Uncle Louie is a darling,' Veronica explained, 'but he's a terrible businessman. The stables haven't paid for years, but he adores horses . . . it would break his heart to have to sell up.'

'I know how he feels,' Jancis said wryly.

So Veronica thought her Uncle Louie was a darling. That didn't make him sound like the sort of man to be mixed up in this shady business . . . or to keep a young lad locked up.

'But my other uncle is terribly rich,' Veronica continued. 'He . . . he allows Uncle Louie enough money to keep him going here, but not enough to make him independent, so Uncle Louie has to do what he says. It was Uncle Nicholas who made Louie keep David here.'

'Then I suppose it was your rich uncle who bought you the sports car?' Jancis said.

'Yes. Damn him!' Veronica spat the words out viciously. 'He thinks he can make me forget about poor David by buying me expensive toys like that. But I'd sooner be poor and married to David, get him safely away from here, than have all of Uncle's money.'

As they spoke, they had circled the small yard over and over again until Jancis was quite dizzy.

'Don't you think I've had long enough for a beginner?' she asked hopefully.

Startled, Veronica looked at her watch.

'Goodness, yes! It must look like a normal, everyday lesson, or they'll get suspicious.'

'They?'

Veronica scowled.

'Yes, Uncle Nicholas is here now ... blackmailing and bullying poor old Louie, as usual.'

Jancis was a little worried about the idea of being away from The Kingdom for so long. Her mother, in particular, would begin to worry once it grew dark.

'I said I was going out just for the afternoon,' she said, as, for the sake of appearances, she handed Veronica some money. 'If I'm missing all evening, someone may ...'

'You've *got* to come back,' Veronica whispered urgently. 'You must ... you promised to help. You can't let David down now, he's depending on you. Now go quickly, please ... catch the bus, but get off at the next stop. Walk back over the fields ... there's an old barn in the field next to our paddock, where you can hide until it gets dark.'

Despite her misgivings, Jancis knew Veronica was right. She couldn't let her ... or David ... down. So, promising to do as the other girl suggested, she strolled away down the road towards the bus stop.

There was some time to wait before the bus was due and she sat on the grass verge to review what Veronica had told her. She had no doubt now that Louie Dutch and Sam Roscoe were both involved in a vendetta of some kind against Keegan. Perhaps some of Louie's owners had transferred their business to The Kingdom ... a similar pattern which had caused the deterioration of her father's business; Louie, if Veronica was to be believed, was only a tool in the hands of his rich relation, but it wasn't too difficult to guess at Sam Roscoe's motives. Quite probably Keegan had dismissed the jockey for some misdemeanour ... she couldn't see Keegan Leroy putting up with Sam's behaviour, the way her more tolerant father had done.

She thought too about Veronica. In one way, she could understand the other girl's timidity, her failure to help David herself. After all, if Veronica was fond of her Uncle Louie, she would not want to see him ruined, made homeless, which apparently could happen, if the rich uncle was crossed. On the other hand, Jancis knew that if their positions were reversed, if it were Keegan who was incarcerated in that dismal place, she would have released him first and worried about the consequences afterwards.

But then, she realised, the circumstances would be rather different. Keegan was himself a wealthy man, with a certain local prestige, whose accusation against the real villain would be believed. Poor David, already in his boss's black books and with nobody of any substance to support his story, would be in no position to save Louie Dutch from the wrath of his rich relation.

The sound of an engine starting up roused Jancis from her reverie and she looked up to see an expensive-looking limousine nosing its way out of the entrance to Dutch's Dyke. The car was forced to wait until a slowly moving tractor had passed by, and the startled Jancis had time to realise that she knew this car. As it turned towards her and swept past, she ducked her head down, as though absorbed by something in the vegetation amongst which she sat.

It took her some time to recover from the shock of her discovery that Veronica's rich Uncle Nicholas was none other than Nick ... Nick Mortimer ... and the owner of The Linnet.

CHAPTER TEN

THE SHOCK of her discovery was so great that Jancis sat completely motionless for some time after the familiar Silver Cloud had passed. It was utterly incredible ... that Nick Mortimer, the pleasant, good-looking man, who had seemed so genuine and open in his business dealings with Keegan, and had made no secret of his admiration for herself, should also be Veronica's rich Uncle Nicholas.

Yet, if Veronica were to be believed ... and Jancis had no reason to doubt that the other girl was speaking the truth ... he was also the man responsible for David being kept prisoner, and ... and this was the most puzzling of all ... responsible for The Linnet's loss of form.

Why, for heaven's sake, should the man want to ruin his own horse? It just didn't make sense. But one thing was certain ... if she had been doubtful before about returning to Dutch's Dyke after dark, she was now equally positive that she *must* do so. Loyalty to her friends was now reinforced by the irresistible lure of curiosity; and, she had to admit, she was also motivated by indignation. How dared Nick Mortimer bamboozle then all in this way? Had he just been using her, using their friendship to ingratiate himself at The Kingdom? She smiled wryly. If so, then he had made a serious mistake. Far from making him more popular with the owner of The Kingdom, he had only succeeded in antagonising Keegan, who actively disapproved of her familiarity with Nick. Thank goodness, she thought, she had not been in love with Nick Mortimer ... at least she was spared that humiliation.

The empty barn Veronica had mentioned was not a pleasant retreat. It was obvious that it had not been used for some considerable time, and the mouldy remnants of straw and animal feed smelled most unpleasant. Small rustlings and scufflings convinced Jancis that there were mice about, possibly even rats, and it took all her courage and determination to remain inside the building, until the rapidly fading light told her it was safe to emerge.

As Veronica had said, the field in which the barn stood immediately adjoined Louie Dutch's paddock, which in turn backed on to the stableyard where Jancis knew David to be imprisoned.

The sky was heavy with scudding clouds, through which the moonlight slid in surreptitious trickles, casting more shadows than it relieved, but Jancis had just enough light to make her way around the dark edges of the yard, until she reached the empty loosebox. She could just distinguish the rear of the house, where a solitary light burnt in an upper window, and she wondered if that was Veronica's room.

She could just imagine how the other girl must be feeling now . . . wondering if Jancis had kept her promise, wondering if David were free yet.

Jancis was not lacking in courage, but she wished that Veronica were with her now. The inside of the loosebox was in total darkness and she had no torch. She wished it had occurred to Veronica to provide one. Thickly festooned cobwebs drifted across her face, making her choke back a scream.

Now she began to wonder how she was supposed to communicate with David, much less rescue him. Would he hear if she called? Would anyone else hear?

A rustling noise from above her made her start, an irresistible thought of bats, or of owls roosting in the rafters, crossing her mind. Instead, as she looked up, she saw a faint glimmer of light showing through a crack in the roof about six feet above her head. Then, faintly, she heard a voice, muffled, but unmistakably David's.

'Is . . . is there anyone down there?'

Yes,' she hissed back. 'It's me . . . Jancis!'

'Thank goodness! I'm nearly going out of my mind up here. For heaven's sake hurry up and let me out!'

'How?' she asked.

'There's a trapdoor, just above the old hayrack. Years ago it would have been used for dropping hay down from this loft into the rack. It's bolted on your side, but if you can get it open, I'll drop down.'

'Is that the only way into the loft?' Jancis asked.

'No, there is another entrance, but it's locked and he keeps the key in his pocket. Now listen ... they've left me this old candle stub. If I hold it down by the floor, near the trapdoor, so that the light shows through a crack in the boards. ...'

Thankful for her thick riding breeches, which gave some protection to her bruised leg, Jancis managed to swing herself up on to the old manger, hearing it creak ominously beneath her weight. From there, she was just able to reach the trap.

As David had hoped, the light from his candle was just sufficient to show her the location of the bolt.

'I think it's rusted in,' she told him, after a while. 'I can't shift it.'

'Damn!' He was silent for a while. 'What we really need is oil.'

'Or a strong man,' she said feelingly.

If only she had been able to take Keegan into her confidence. He would have made short work of the rescue operation.

'Maybe a bit of candlegrease would do the trick,' David suggested, 'Suppose I blow the candle out and poke it down to you, through the floorboards ... there's a gap here just wide enough.'

The faint gleam of light vanished, as David extinguished his candle.

'Right!' he said. 'Now, for Pete's sake, don't drop it ... it's all we have.'

With the candle stump safely in her hand, Jancis began smearing was over the bolt. She couldn't see what she was doing and could only hope she was spreading it in the correct place. Finally, when the small piece of wax was exhausted, she tried the bolt again. At first she thought her efforts had been a waste of time, but then slowly, agonisingly slowly, the big bolt began to move.

With a shower of dust and straw, the trapdoor swung down, narrowly missing Jancis' head, and the next moment David had slithered through.

Protesting at this extra weight, the old hayrack gave up its tenuous hold and crashed to the floor, carrying them with it. To their terrified ears the noise sounded tremendous, and they lay scarcely daring to breathe. Surely someone would come to investigate? But only a horse whickered softly in the next stall.

They sorted out their tangled limbs and rose rather shakily.

'Are you all right?'

'Are you hurt?'

They spoke together, then hastily muffled the hysterical giggles of relief.

'Now what?' Jancis asked, as she brushed herself down. 'I suppose we'd better get away from here as quickly as possible?'

'Not yet,' said David, surprising her. She had expected him to be only too eager to get away from the scene of his imprisonment. 'We have to wait until the last light in the house goes out,' he explained. 'That will be Ronny's signal that her Uncle Louie is in bed.'

'N-Nick's not there, then?' Jancis asked nervously.

Strange to think that she should now be mortally afraid of a man whom she had once considered her friend.

In the darkness, she sensed David's glance towards her.

'So you know about Mortimer? I'm sorry,' he said awkwardly. 'I know that you and he . . .'

'It doesn't matter, honestly,' she assured him. 'How long have you known?'

'Only a couple of days.'

'What do we do when Ronny's light goes out?' Jancis asked. 'Surely we could slip away before that?'

'No,' said David. 'You see, I intend to ride out of here. For one thing, it's a long walk home, and for another . . .'

'Ride?' Jancis queried.

'Mmm. Ronny left a halter on the mare in the next box . . . the same one you rode this afternoon. She shouldn't give you any trouble.' He paused, then drew a long breath. 'And we're going to take a racehorse with us.'

'*What?*' Jancis felt she must be a trifle lightheaded. 'You can't steal . . . or even borrow . . . a racehorse, just like that!'

'It won't be stealing exactly. You see, it's The Linnet.'

'But The Linnet was safely in her loosebox when I left home. She couldn't possibly be here . . . she's resting, not fit.'

Quickly Jancis explained how the filly had come by her injuries.

David stifled a laugh.

'You're a tremendous girl, Jancis . . . a real sport. I wouldn't have liked to be in your shoes, though, when the gaffer found out.'

Feelingly, Jancis agreed that it had not been a pleasant experience.

'Even so,' David persisted, 'I *know* that the filly they have here is The Linnet. I've been going out with Ronny for several months now,' he explained, 'and any free time I had, I'd come over here to help her muck out. Her uncle's getting on a bit and he only has one part-time lad nowadays. A few days ago I was here, helping out as usual, and I started to go into one of the stalls. Louie came rushing out of the house just like someone demented, and told me to get away from there. Naturally I was curious, and when he went off to the pub, I took a look. There was a bay filly in the box, and she was a dead ringer for The Linnet.

'Well, to cut a long story short, I got caught. The old fellow popped back . . . forgotten his pipe, he said . . . and nabbed me. Before I knew where I was, I was locked up in that loft.

'Hours later, it seemed, old Louie came back, and who should walk in with him but our friend Mortimer!'

'And you really had no idea that Nick was related to Ronny?' Jancis asked.

'Not till that moment,' said David.

'But what were they going to do with you? They surely didn't think they could keep you locked up for ever?' A sudden dread assailed her, making her feel quite faint. 'David, they weren't going to . . . to . . .?'

'Kill me?' He laughed, a breathy sound. 'Nothing so melodramatic, fortunately. No, Nick Mortimer may be a blackmailer and a bully, but he's also a coward . . . most bullies are. He wouldn't have the guts for murder . . . and to do him justice, I don't think poor old Louie would have stood for him going that far.'

'Well, what then?' Jancis asked.

'As I'd discovered their little fiddle, they planned to swop the fillies over again, at the first opportunity. You were right about one thing, by the way. They took The Linnet the night Fly-by-Night was cast ... and substituted the other filly.'

'But what would have happened to you, David?'

'It wouldn't have mattered then, if they'd set me free. It'd only be my word against theirs. As far as Fred and the gaffer were concerned, The Linnet would miraculously recover her form. They would have been even more convinced that I'd deliberately thrown those two races.'

'Ronny's light's gone out,' Jancis was able to report a few minutes later.

Cautiously, they sidled out into the yard, Jancis going into the next box to bring out the little mare.

'Ronny said to set the mare free when we're well away,' said David. 'She'll find her own way home.'

The bay filly which David claimed was The Linnet was led from her stall without incident and moving on the unkempt grass verges of the yard, they led both horses until they reached the road.

'I know a short cut across country,' said David, as they mounted. 'No need to follow the road.'

The clouds had been swept away by a stiff breeze, allowing the moonlight full play over the countryside and it was a relief to reach the downs, the horses walking with long strides and outstretched necks. As soon as they reached the boundaries of The Kingdom, Jancis dismounted and turned the mare to face the opposite way. With a sharp slap on its flank, it needed no further encouragement to set off for its own stable. She felt rather sorry for the pleasant little animal, having to return to its squalid surroundings.

The house was in complete darkness as they entered the yard, David leading the filly. At the unusual sounds of night-time activity, sleepy heads appeared over loosebox doors. Most of the boxes were full and in the half-light just before the dawn, the intelligent face in the end box was certainly indistinguishable from that of the filly they had abstracted from Dutch's Dyke.

'You're quite sure you heard right?' queried Jancis in sudden doubt. 'They look identical to me ... but which is which?'

'We'll wait for daylight,' said David, but he too sounded

less sure of himself, as they put the filly in a vacant box.

It was no use going to bed; Jancis knew she would never sleep. Instead she and David sat in the kitchen, drinking endless cups of coffee and talking in muted whispers.

Mary King, coming down to prepare breakfast, found them still there, heads resting on their arms at the kitchen table.

'What on earth ... Jancis ... David!' Then, suddenly realising, 'David! You're back! Where on earth have you been? We've been so worried. Does Keegan know?'

'Mummy!' Jancis interrupted her mother, half laughingly, half impatient. 'It's a long story and I promise we'll tell you all about it ... but there's something we have to do first, in the yard.'

With Mrs King's protests still ringing in their ears, they went out. The sun had not warmed the grey early light yet and they shivered a little, as they led out the two bay fillies.

Ten minutes later they were looking at each other with puzzled eyes.

'I can't see a ha'porth of difference,' David admitted.

'David! Jancis! Where has he come from? What's going on here? What are you doing with those two horses ... what the blazes ...'

Keegan broke off in mid-sentence, as he confronted the identical animals. Mary King, full of the news of David's reappearance, had lost no time in summoning the master of The Kingdom.

Rapidly, Jancis related David's discovery that an identical filly had been substituted for The Linnet, his imprisonment and her subsequent rescue of the young jockey.

She had expected disbelief from Keegan, angry condemnation of their actions, but instead he circled the two animals slowly, assessing their points, stopping to run a hand over their necks, examining their mouths and teeth. Tensely, they watched him. At last he turned towards them, his face a study in bafflement.

'There's not a hair to choose between them so far as I can see.' He looked at them grimly. 'Well, you've either uncovered an audacious fraud, or you've stolen somebody's horse ... I wouldn't care to decide which. Box them up again and come into the office. I want the full story from you again, young David. As for you . . .' he looked at Jancis, 'you'd better get some rest. You look dead on your feet.' He shook his head in grim amusement. 'You really do take the biscuit, for getting into scrapes.'

'Biscuit!' Jancis shrieked. 'Of course . . . chocolate biscuit!' The two males looked at her, then at each other.

'It's all right,' she exclaimed, 'I haven't gone mad. Wait right there, both of you.'

She hurried into the house, returning a few moments later with a biscuit in each hand. Going over to the animal which for the last few weeks they had all supposed to be The Linnet, she patted the filly's neck and at the same time offered her a biscuit. The filly sniffed disdainfully at the dainty morsel, then turned her head aside uninterestedly.

Jancis moved over to the filly abducted from Dutch's Dyke and repeated the process. This time the biscuit was eagerly removed from her hand, the filly munching with evident enjoyment.

Jancis and David stared at each other, triumph showing in both faces.

'Of course,' said David, 'I should have remembered . . . the old girl's potty about chocolate in any form.' He turned to Keegan. 'Sir . . . this one is definitely The Linnet!'

Hours later, after a lengthy interview with the police, following which Keegan accompanied them on an official visit to Dutch's Dyke, the whole matter had been cleared up.

Louie Dutch had owned twin bay fillies . . . The Linnet and her sister The Skylark. When The Skylark had broken down after only one race, Nick Mortimer, Louie's brother-in-law, had placed the superior Linnet with Keegan, in order to establish a good name for her. Then, one night . . . the night the colt had been cast in its box . . . Nick and his accomplice Sam Roscoe had substituted The Skylark. Nick knew that racegoers who believed the filly to be The Linnet would put their money on her. He meanwhile, would back another horse, getting a very good price . . . as indeed he had on the day of the second August Meeting at Newcastle, when he had backed the chestnut, ridden by Sam Roscoe.

Dinner that evening took the form of a celebration, to

which both David and Fred Higgins were invited.

Fred was very diffident at the idea of dining at 'the gaffer's table', but Keegan swept aside his protests.

David, though equally shy, was completely won over by Keegan's statement that he did not intend to institute proceedings against Ronny's Uncle Louie.

'He was completely dominated by Nick Mortimer, and I intend to see that that gentleman gets all he deserves,' Keegan said grimly.

'Mr Leroy is going to buy Dutch's Dyke and leave old Louie in as manager,' David told Jancis over coffee in the drawing room.

She glanced across the room, to where Keegan was deep in conversation with his cousin. Alyson was looking up into his face with the sweet vivacity which she turned on only for him. Jealousy racked Jancis, a green-eyed, primeval monster, a sensation that shocked and shamed her by its intensity, while it stabbed her, sharp as a thorn.

She was filled with a sense of the unfairness of life. She had taken a considerable risk yesterday . . . mainly on David's behalf, she had to admit, but her act had also redounded to Keegan's benefit. Yet it was Alyson, not she, who was receiving his undivided attention.

'Don't you think Mr Leroy's the greatest?' David was still talking eagerly. 'It'll be the saving of old Louie . . . and Mr Leroy's going to do up those two cottages that adjoin Dutch's Dyke. He says Ronny and I can live there, rent free, until my earnings increase. So we can get married right away.'

'Oh, David, that's wonderful! I'm truly pleased for you.' Jancis dragged herself away from her unhappy contemplation of Keegan and Alyson to congratulate the young jockey.

If only *her* problems could be so easily resolved. It was incredible to think that only five months had elapsed since that fateful day when Keegan had first come to The Kingdom. She would not have believed it if anyone had told her that her opinion of him could change so radically in so short a time. From looking upon him as an opportunist, a ruthless entrepreneur and the agent of her father's failure, she had been forced to admit that he was the saviour, not only of The Kingdom, but probably of her mother's health and peace of mind.

As for the difference he had made in her own life, from implacable hatred, she had progressed . . . albeit grudgingly . . . to respect, genuine admiration, and now . . .

Nerves quivered sensitively deep inside her, as she considered the extent of her changed feelings towards Keegan Leroy . . . feelings which had created a painful, aching void within her, as she realised the impossibility of him returning her love.

It suddenly dawned on her that she had been staring fixedly for some time and that Keegan had become aware of her scrutiny. He was returning her regard, a peculiarly arrested look upon his face, and for an instant it seemed to her that something intangible passed between them, before he turned away and said something to Alyson which made her laugh aloud, a high, tinkling, infuriating sound.

Shamed heat burnt along Jancis' skin. Had that comment been about herself? Had her face been so revealing? Had Keegan interpreted her intense stare correctly and shared his discovery with his cousin?

'Jancis! You're not listening,' David complained.

'I . . . I'm sorry.' She blinked back the betraying moisture from her lashes. 'What . . . what did you say?'

'I said Ronny would like you to be her bridesmaid. Will you? You . . . you don't think it's awful cheek, us asking you?'

With wry amusement Jancis realised that David still considered her status to be superior to his. Whereas she knew that, for all Keegan's efforts to make mother and daughter feel at home, she was just as much an employee as David himself.

'I'd love to be Ronny's bridesmaid,' she said warmly. 'I liked her very much, and I'm looking forward to getting to know her better.'

David's delighted thanks were interrupted, as Keegan circled the room, handing everyone a well-filled glass.

'I'd like you all to join me in a toast,' he said, 'to a very special girl.'

Terror coursed through Jancis' veins. She could not, would not remain to hear his next words. With a numbing certainty, she knew what he was about to say . . . it couldn't be anything else, after his obvious absorption in his cousin. He was about to announce his engagement to Alyson, and Jancis knew that once she had heard the words pass his lips, all lingering hope would finally die, that she would be unable to conceal her pain and misery. She half rose from her seat.

'No false modesty now, Jancis,' Keegan said.

Bewildered, she looked at him; his tone was teasing, lightly affectionate.

He looked around the assembled company, then lifted his glass.

'To a stubborn, impulsive little idiot, whose loyalty and courage outweigh her size. To Jancis!'

'To Jancis!' they all echoed.

As she looked around the room, seeing the varying expressions of affection and admiration on every face but one, a lump rose in her throat. This public demonstration, coupled with the relief of being spared ... for a time at least ... the announcement she had feared, was the overthrow of the courage Keegan had praised. With something between a laugh and a sob, she set down her glass and fled, ignoring their protesting cries.

'I thought I'd find you here.'

At the sound of Keegan's voice, Jancis lifted her face from The Linnet's silky neck ... The Linnet now restored to her rightful stall. Why, oh, why, she wondered resentfully, couldn't he leave her to indulge in her misery? A few bitter tears would have been a healing relief, enabling her to face the future with more resignation. That little speech of his, though it had been meant kindly, had finally cracked her hard-won self-control and hearing the lazy, comradely affection in his voice, it had been so easy to imagine how it would be if that affection were of a deeper, more abiding nature.

'I'm just saying goodbye to The Linnet,' she said gruffly, in a brave attempt to pass off her damp cheeks and brimming eyes. 'You won't want Nick's animals here now.'

'You forget,' said Keegan, 'The Linnet never belonged to Nick Mortimer. She and her twin are Louie Dutch's property ... or they were.'

'But they aren't now?' Jancis looked up at him questioningly. Keegan now owned Dutch's Dyke and, presumably, its livestock. 'You mean they belong to you now?'

Keegan shook his head.

'I sold The Skylark for what I could get.'

'And . . . and The Linnet?'

'She belongs to you.'

'To . . . to me? echoed Jancis. 'But . . .'

'I gave Louie a fair price for her, but she's yours . . . to run or not, just as you please.'

'Oh, Keegan,' she muttered brokenly, turning her head aside, 'I don't deserve you to be so kind to me, after all I've . . .'

'Rubbish!' It was not said emphatically, scoldingly, but in a disarmingly gentle tone of voice. 'I won't deny we've had our misunderstandings, you and I, but they're resolved now.'

If only they were, Jancis thought bleakly. The greatest, most insurmountable stumbling block to their friendship still remained: Alyson. Jancis loved Keegan too much for a lesser relationship to suffice.

He placed one hand upon her shoulder . . . a shiveringly familiar touch.

'Jancis,' his deep voice was troubled, 'what is it? Something is still bothering you?'

She forced herself to look up at him, a brittle laugh escaping from between her lips.

'Bothering me? Why should anything be bothering me? As you said, all my problems should be resolved now.'

'But they aren't,' he mused. His face darkened, and he clicked the fingers of his free hand impatiently. 'Of course! Fool that I am, I should have realised. Mortimer . . . It can't be pleasant to find that the man you love is a rogue.'

Inwardly, she contradicted him . . . to find that the man you thought to be a rogue is the man you love.

'You'll forget about him in time.' He sounded impatient now, angry almost. 'There'll be someone else. He's not worth moping over.'

Someone else. There is someone else. She wanted to scream the words at him. Was he blind? Yes, perhaps in a sense he was. Just as well, for the sake of her pride, she thought, that Alyson's image had veiled his eyes to her own tortured longing for him, which she felt must be delineated in every feature of her face.

As she did not answer him, he pulled her against the comforting breadth of his chest.

'Poor kid,' he muttered. 'Life hasn't been easy for you lately, one way and another.'

Somewhere, an instinct of self-preservation warned her to move away, to reject his comforting embrace, but with his vibrant nearness, every faculty but sensation surrendered helplessly to him.

'It's a fallacy, you know,' Keegan murmured against her bright hair, 'that there's only one soulmate in this world for each of us. Believe me.'

Jancis wanted to deny his words. For there *was* only one man for her, and without him, she felt that her heart would wither away and die, like a plant denied nourishment.

He tipped up her chin, the better to read her expression, and she closed her eyes, so that he might not see and recognise their longing . . . a longing tinged with desperation. He kissed her gently, coaxingly, then lifted his head as if to observe her reaction.

'There, that wasn't so bad, was it? You don't find *my* kisses distasteful?'

Nothing could be more *to her taste*, she thought but it was torture, nonetheless . . . a taste of unattainable paradise.

'Jancis?' His voice throbbed strangely, almost, she thought dreamily, as if their kiss had disturbed him too.

Her longing for him shuddered through her, and sensing her undisguised physical response, he slid his hands the length of her and for a moment of suspended time, she allowed her need of him to transcend all other considerations, blindly lifting her face, inviting his kiss. She heard his sharp intake of breath and felt his body harden as he pulled her closer. She thrilled to the realisation that he too was moved by their proximity.

His kiss was a tormenting invasion to which she submitted, totally submerged in him, aching for his possession. She knew that the treacherous weakness of her body was betraying her, but she was lost to all shame . . .

forgetting that only a moment ago she had determined not to reveal her feelings to him.

As his kisses increased in urgency, his hands moved to the twin peaks of her small breasts, causing them to swell and strain against the sweet pressure. Every movement of his lean fingers caused her to quiver, as if he were in truth making the passionate love to her that she desired.

His caresses were becoming less gentle and she knew with a surge of triumph that his need for fulfilment was as great as her own. Every curve of her soft body seemed moulded into every lean hard angle of his, as desire accelerated between them. His chest rose and fell unsteadily in agonised gasps, and she knew that if he attempted to make love to her, here and now, she would be unable to deny his demands, so strong was her own need of him. She could feel the violent trembling that shook his muscular frame. Soon, very soon, it would be too late to draw back, even if she had wanted to.

The loosebox next to The Linnet's was large, empty ... the straw freshly laid and inviting. Unresistingly, she allowed him to pull her down ... down ...

'Keegan! Keegan! Where are you? It's Alyson ... she's not well!'

It was Mary King's voice, high with anxiety, and in immediate response Keegan rolled away from Jancis, coming to his feet in one lithe movement.

'Stay there,' he murmured, as he moved towards the doorway, hastily smoothing his ruffled hair and brushing the straw from his trousers.

Stay there! Stay there, so that he could return when it suited him ... return to her straight from his cousin. It didn't occur to Jancis that Keegan's concern was for her, that her mother should not see her dishevelled condition and draw her own conclusions.

Jancis felt debased, as she realised how close she had come to submission ... submission to a man who would never be hers. How nearly she had given him that precious gift which, once bestowed, could never be retracted.

She dwelt broodingly upon Alyson's sudden indisposition. Had the other girl guessed that Keegan had followed Jancis? While her pride gave thanks that she had been saved from the final degradation ... that of giving herself to Keegan, who only sought to prove that she could be stirred by more than just one man . . . her tingling flesh cried out in protest against the abrupt withdrawal of his caresses, of his presence.

As soon as the sound of voices and footsteps had receded, Jancis left the loosebox and made her way, unseen, to the house and the security of her own room.

Now that common sense had asserted itself, now that her head was once more in charge of her unruly body, she knew that she had been weak. Twice before, she had decided she must leave The Kingdom, and twice she had faltered in her resolution. This time there must be no weakening. She must and would remove herself from the soul-destroying proximity of Keegan Leroy.

Never mind that she had no job to go to. She would throw herself upon the mercy of one of her former colleagues. Any one of them would be glad to give her a room, while she looked around for a situation. Anything would do . . . anything that would make her independent of Keegan.

Jancis began to pack.

CHAPTER ELEVEN

'ARE YOU going away?'

Jancis looked up from her packing, to see the slight figure of Alyson, standing in the doorway, her prominent blue eyes alight with eager curiosity.

'I didn't hear you knock,' Jancis pointed out resentfully, then, remembering, 'I thought you were supposed to be ill. You certainly made a quick recovery.'

Her suspicion, that Alyson had feigned illness, in order to recall Keegan to her side . . . and away from Jancis . . . became certainty, as the other girl smiled, a sly smile of self-satisfaction, and moved farther into the room, closing the door behind her.

'Keegan always knows how to make me feel better . . . and I don't see why I should have to knock on doors in my own house.'

'*Your* house?' Jancis stared at Alyson, unconsciously clenching her fists as she anticipated the younger girl's reply.

'As good as. It will be, anyway, when I marry Keegan.'

Alyson began to move around the room, inspecting its furnishings with an insolent assurance that made Jancis seethe. Nothing escaped her attention, and the collection of horses, Jancis' especial treasures, elicited a scornful smile.

'Collecting is for kids.'

Gritting her teeth, Jancis continued her packing, not caring about the order in which she crammed things into her suitcase. 'When I marry Keegan'. Alyson's words echoed and re-echoed in her mind. Surely the girl would not speak in that way unless she was totally sure of herself. There had been no announcement of an engagement, but perhaps Keegan and his cousin had an understanding.

Alyson repeated her earlier question.

'Are you going away?'

'Yes,' Jancis said shortly.

'For good?' Alyson's peaky little face was a study in avidity.

'Yes,' Jancis said again.

The expression on the pinched, narrow face became one of unutterable smugness.

'That's very sensible of you, Jancis, since there's nothing here for you. I mean, it isn't your home any more.' She paused, then, 'Is your mother going too?'

'No . . . that is . . . I don't know.'

Belatedly Jancis wondered what effect, if any, her departure would have upon Mary King's position at The Kingdom. She couldn't really see Keegan turning her mother out . . . not after all this time. He had always seemed genuinely fond of the older woman and she certainly ran his house efficiently. But of course, once Alyson was mistress of The Kingdom, things might be different.

'I think it would be a good idea if your mother left too,' Alyson stated. 'After all, it would be a bit embarrassing for you, visiting her here.'

Jancis bit her lip, clenching her fists until the nails gouged into her palms. She had a wild desire to rend the flesh of that smug little face, to slap the self-satisfied smile from the thin lips. When she had planned her flight, she had not taken her mother's future into her reckoning, so certain had she been that Keegan would not take out his certain annoyance on Mary King. But Alyson was a different kettle of fish ... and after all Mary King had done for Alyson ... the ungrateful little cat!

Keegan was almost certain to consult her wishes, once they were married.

Again, Jancis fought back the primitive urge to fall physically upon the other girl, to pull her hair, to banish the self-assurance from her pale face. Alyson, despite her hateful, sneaky ways, her exaggerated frailty, was genuinely not strong. To strike her, however great the provocation, would be unforgivable.

Besides, it was only the anger and frustration meant for Keegan that she would be venting upon the other girl.

'I'll say goodbye, then.' The object of her visit achieved, Alyson drifted towards the door. 'You *are* going immediately?' There was a trace of anxiety in her light, high voice.

Jancis nodded. She could not trust her voice. Only after Alyson has left the room did she allow the hot tears to slide down her cheeks. She was leaving behind everything, everyone that she loved ... home, her mother, The Linnet. Perhaps Keegan would sell the filly. She certainly couldn't give the animal a home now ... and worst of all, she was leaving Keegan, determined, whatever it cost her in terms of misery, never to see him again.

Jancis looked out of the window, upon the scene she had never expected to see again ... the lawns and tennis courts of Seafield College of Commercial Studies.

An impulsive visit to the Principal had elicited the fact that a temporary replacement was needed for a member of staff away on sick leave for an indefinite period, and the Principal had been only too pleased and relieved to let Jancis ... an experienced lecturer ... fill the vacancy.

That had been over a week ago, and Jancis now felt as if she had never been away, as if the interlude at The Kingdom had been some nightmarish delusion.

She had soon realised why Alyson was so anxious for her to leave immediately after their conversation. Keegan, she learnt, had been called out to deal with a problem which had arisen in connection with his new property, Dutch's Dyke. Obviously, Alyson had feared that if Keegan were present, he might intervene, forbid Jancis to leave. Jancis supposed she should have been grateful to have avoided such an encounter, but nevertheless, resentment against Alyson still smouldered within her.

Since her sudden departure she had received no news from home. She winced; she must stop thinking of The Kingdom as home. It was Keegan's home and soon it would be Alyson's.

Even her mother had made no attempt to contact her, though by now Mary King must have received the letter telling her where Jancis was staying. Mary had pleaded, then protested vigorously, when Jancis informed her of her sudden decision, but Jancis, her emotions still painfully raw, was not to be swayed, and, on Mary's side at least, mother and daughter had parted in anger.

Jancis had slipped back easily into the day-to-day routine of the college and was immensely popular with her students, but the college life no longer held its old fascination. She remembered wonderingly how reluctant she had been to give up her teaching post to go and work for Keegan Leroy. Now it was the memory of their hours together in the little office attached to the house which tugged at her heart.

What had Keegan's reactions been, what had he said, she wondered, when he'd learned that she was gone? She would have given anything to know.

Had he been angry, sorry . . . or relieved? He might well have been relieved, she thought, especially if he had regretted that incident in the stable . . . feared that he might have raised false expectations. Yes, perhaps he was glad to be rid of her.

At first intentionally, then unintentionally, she had proved to be a thorn in his side, not only through her bitter resentment over his ownership of the stables, but in her wilful disobedience of his edicts; and yet latterly she could have sworn that he did not altogether dislike her.

Certainly their physical attraction had seemed to be mutual, but then he was all male . . . and men, she had learned, could be aroused physically, without necessarily having any mental or spiritual commitment to the object of their desire. She had no doubt that Keegan had desired her ... both his words and his physical condition had attested to that ... but she was equally certain that it did not equate with love ... love as she defined it.

No, if he had been in love with her, he would not have allowed her absence to go unremarked. If, for any reason, he had objected to her leaving, she would have heard from him by now, in one way or another.

She must remodel her life, begin to forget about Keegan Leroy. Perhaps after all, she thought wistfully, he had been right in his sweeping assertion ... perhaps you *could* fall in love more than once. Maybe some day she *would* find someone else. But meantime, it hurt that he had not seen fit to contact her, even to send a message, commenting either favourably or otherwise upon her precipitate flight. It would be nice even, to know that she had his good wishes for her future success ... and happiness. Happiness! Without *him*?

Firmly, she began the well-nigh impossible task of banishing Keegan from her thoughts.

It was Open Day at the College and Jancis had taken the opportunity of a free period to escape from the endless stream of school leavers and their parents or teachers, being conducted around the building. She had been sitting at the window for almost half an hour, watching the constant flow of traffic up and down the drive, her eyes on the mini-buses and cars of varying degrees of opulence, her thoughts elsewhere ... with Keegan Leroy and his Kingdom.

In the past ten days, despite the demands of teaching, she had found her thoughts not wholly with her students. A career which had once been eminently satisfying, filling her days with contentment, a sense of achievement, no longer seemed important or worthwhile. The time she had worked for Keegan, though so brief in relation to her years at the college, loomed infinitely larger. The day-to-day life of the stable, her hours alone with Keegan, fraught though they had been with conflict, seemed infinitely richer than those spent in the classroom, or in the company of her colleagues.

But soon she would have to return to the classroom and banish personal problems in favour of her students' struggles with shorthand and typing.

It was fortunate, she mused, that teaching required almost her total concentration, giving her tortured brain a rest from the eternal merry-go-round of question and answer, decision and counter-decision. Had she done right in running away, or should she have stayed, fought for what she desired? Was the slender chance of success, the faint possibility of winning Keegan for herself, worth the ignominy of defeat? She thought not ... and yet nothing ventured, nothing gained. There she went again.

Go back to your classroom this minute, she told herself, and stop behaving like an indecisive teenager. You made up your mind once and for all, so you said, when you left The Kingdom. So now stick to it. You're a big girl now, Jancis King. Get a grip on yourself, your emotions. Put the past behind you and begin to live again, instead of dwelling in this half limbo of painful memories.

About to rise from the window seat, she stiffened, her hitherto casual regard focusing now intently upon the car at present circling the gravelled sweep below.

Surely she knew that car?

All doubt was swept aside as, the car parked neatly at the foot of the entrance steps, the tall, familiar figure emerged, then straightened, the keen eyes in those dark, hawk-like features surveying his surroundings.

Why was he here? How was she to face him, her recent thoughts still too near the surface, with their nostalgia for home, the stables ... but more especially for him? Seeing Keegan here, in surroundings which had once meant so much to her, only emphasised the contrast between her conviction of a few months ago ... that this was her true environment ... and her present feelings, that the whole world of commerce, of education, would be well lost for just a small part of his.

Instinctively she shrank away from the window, as if his eyes must instantly discover her. For that it was her he sought, she had no doubt. Was it only a moment ago that she had been regretting ... no, resenting ... his apparent lack of interest? Now, her first impulse was to avoid him ... but how?

It was too late to take the evasive action she contemplated, for already she could hear footsteps on the stairs and a high, girlish voice, explaining that Miss King would be in the staff room at this time of day. She heard the lower cadences of his reply . . . that deep voice, whose familiar note sent shivers of apprehension—half fear, half longing—down her spine. Until recently that voice had been a familiar ingredient of every day and, whether placatory or raised in anger, she knew her life had been emptier for the lack of it.

Behind her, the door opened and closed. Stubbornly, Jancis continued to stare through the window, refusing to give him the satisfaction of acknowledging her awareness of him. Even if she had not witnessed his arrival, she thought, some sixth sense must have warned her of his proximity, so strong was the effect upon her of his physical presence. She was determined to let him speak first, make the first approach. Besides, just for the moment, she could not trust her voice.

'Don't I even warrant a "good morning?" ' he asked.

Slowly, reluctantly, she turned round to face him, glad that her back was to the strong light, so that her too expressive face was in shadow.

'Good morning,' she said obediently, then, something of her usual spirit asserting itself, 'Perhaps you would like me to curtsey too, for good measure?'

She would let him see that she was now independent, mistress of her own destiny, assured, immune to him.

A short bark of laughter was all the reply she received in response to this sally, as Keegan closed the distance between them in three leisurely strides.

He towered above her, scrutinising her, and she felt sure he must see the new hollows in her cheeks, the shadows of unhappiness beneath her eyes, painted there by sleepless nights, yearning for all that she had left behind and for which Seafield College could never be a substitute.

'You haven't changed. Still the same Jancis, impulsive in speech and action.'

So he hadn't noticed.

'No, one doesn't change much in two weeks,' she said lightly. She could have added . . . two weeks that had seemed more like a lifetime.

He hadn't changed either, she thought, hungrily studying the well-known features, which she had thought never to see again, with their harsh lines, which could soften into amusement or tenderness. There was no change, unless . . . unless that was a faint sprinkling of grey at the temples, which she did not remember having seen before.

The warmth of an absurd tenderness ran through her, a longing to reach up and touch those little evidences of stress. Absurd, because it was obvious he would not welcome such a gesture on her part.

At present, his face showed nothing but irritation. There was no doubt about it, she was in for an uncomfortable interview.

'Won't you sit down?' she invited. She consulted her wristwatch. 'I have another ten minutes to spare, before I'm needed. Coffee?'

'Stop playing the gracious hostess.' Keegan too consulted his watch. 'I'll give you ten minutes to pack.'

'To . . . to pack?' She almost laughed. Did he honestly think he could come here and order her back home, like a recalcitrant, runaway child?

'You don't really think I would allow you to walk out on me like that, do you? Once I discovered your where-abouts . . .'

'You mean you've only just . . .?'

'Yes. From some sense of misguided loyalty, neither Alyson nor your mother told me that you'd left. I only found out this morning, when I got back from Scotland.'

Again Jancis stifled a laugh . . . this time of cynical disbelief. Loyalty on her mother's part, she could believe, though it was more likely to have been Mary's fear of Keegan's reaction to the news that Jancis had departed, but Alyson! Loyalty? Still, at least she'd been wrong about one thing. Keegan hadn't known that she'd left and ignored it. A glow of pleasure suffused her being at the thought that he'd come after her, the moment he'd found out . . . even if it was for entirely the wrong reasons.

'Well, what are you waiting for?' he demanded. 'Get your things.'

The glow faded and died.

'I'm not coming back,' she said flatly.

Secure in his own arrogant certainty, he leant back in the chair, arms folded, with every evidence of becoming a permanent fixture there, until she complied with his wishes.

'Oh yes, you are!'

'I can't,' Jancis told him desperately. 'Even if I wanted to ... which I don't ... I have a class in five minutes. I can't just walk out and leave the college at a moment's notice.'

'I telephoned your Principal before I came,' he said with maddening assurance. 'I understand that the member of staff whom you're replacing returns tomorrow. The Principal was very understanding and quite willing for you to leave today.'

Quite understanding ... the Principal? I bet she was, Jancis thought. The Principal was a woman, unlikely to be immune to the charm Keegan must have exercised.

'Understanding about what?' She stared at him, appalled by such high-handed behaviour. She couldn't believe this was happening.

'About your leaving, now, today.'

'How dare you ... how dare you?' she whispered, ashen-faced.

'Had you another job to go to, after tomorrow?' he demanded.

'No, but ... I'll find something. I ...'

'You won't ... you know as well as I do what the employment situation is like at present. Do you really think I'd allow you to starve in some garret, when you have a job and a good home waiting for you?'

'I wouldn't be in a garret ... it isn't *my* home ... you know what you can do with your job!' Normally soft brown eyes were hard with anger.

'So it still rankles. Damn it, Jancis, I thought you'd finally come to terms with my ownership of The Kingdom? Do you intend to go on bearing this grudge for the rest of our lives?'

If only she could tell him that she didn't bear a grudge, could tell him that it was no longer *his* presence she resented, but Alyson's that she *feared*. That, on the contrary, she would welcome his ownership, his presence at The Kingdom, if *she* could be the one destined to share it with him. She remained silent.

'Well, you'll have to put your own feelings second for once,' Keegan informed her brusquely, 'and consider your mother instead. That's really why I'm here.'

'Because of Mummy? Is she . . .? Mummy's not well?'

Her brown eyes, enlarged by sudden fear, were enormous in her small, piquant face.

He avoided her gaze, staring out of the window.

'She's not been herself since you left. I said I'd bring you home.'

Though thoroughly alarmed to learn that her mother had not been well, Jancis could not help a stab of disappointment that he had not come on his own behalf.

'Of course I'll come,' she said. 'I have no choice, have I?'

'None,' he agreed with an irritating air of complacency.

He might show a little more concern, she thought, for her feelings, for her mother's state of health. True, he had come to bring her home, as soon as he had learnt of the state of affairs at The Kingdom. But there was more of an air of triumph than relief in his manner.

If Mary King had been ill, why on earth hadn't she sent a message? Even if she was too ill herself, Alyson could have telephoned. Or had Alyson deliberately kept her in ignorance? If that was the case, if she found out that Alyson . . . Jancis ground her nails into the palms of her hands.

Ten minutes later, for the second time in her career, she was leaving Seafield College, seated beside Keegan this time, in the luxury of a powerful car, which made nothing of the distance they had to travel.

They spoke little. Jancis was too concerned over what she would find at home. Keegan was irritatingly vague about the nature of her mother's illness.

'Damn him! Damn him! The lying so-and-so! He has the nerve of the devil!' Cheeks flaming, Jancis stormed angrily around her mother's room. 'He's bossy, interfering, and what's more, he's a barefaced liar! He told me you were ill.'

Mary King looked shocked.

'Oh no, dear, there must be some mistake. I can't believe Keegan would tell a deliberate lie. You must have misunderstood him.'

'Like hell I did!'

Jancis taxed her brain, in an effort to remember Keegan's exact words.

'He made darn sure I misunderstood him, the rat!' she

snapped at last. 'He said you hadn't been yourself ever since I left. How was I *supposed to* interpret that?' She drew in a harsh breath. 'Idiot that I am, I should have suspected. How could he know you'd been ill ever since . . . he wasn't even here . . .'

'Well,' Mary admitted, 'it *was* true in one way. I *haven't* been myself. I've been very worried about you . . . and unhappy. We didn't exactly part friends, did we?'

'That could have been put right by a phone call,' Jancis said. 'After all, you knew where I was . . . I wrote to you . . .'

'I did think of phoning,' Mary admitted, 'but I thought that might only make you more determined to stay away, and after all,' she sighed, 'though I do tend to forget it, you *are* an adult now, I've no right to ask you to come back . . . and then it just seemed best to wait for Keegan. I knew he'd know what to do, that he'd be able to persuade you better than I could.'

'Persuade me?' Jancis' voice was unnaturally high. 'Blackmail me . . . delude me into coming back!'

'Yes . . . well, anyway, dear, you're here now,' Mary said comfortably, 'and that's all that really matters.'

'It isn't all that matters,' Jancis argued. 'I don't *want* to live here any more. I want to be independent of The Kingdom. I was going to look for a job . . .'

'But you have a good job here, dear.' Mrs King seemed to be wilfully misunderstanding.

Jancis sighed. If only her mother weren't so besotted with Keegan, she could have confided in her, told her the true reason for her flight, her need to get away from The Kingdom. But her mother was just foolish enough to pass on her daughter's confidences, convinced that there was nothing the great Keegan Leroy could not put to rights.

He's done a lot to ensure my mother's happiness, she thought with grim humour, but I don't think even his good nature would run to marrying me just to please her.

'I still don't intend to stay,' she told Mary firmly. 'Now that I know you're O.K., I can start looking round for another job . . . so you can just look upon this as a visit . . . and Keegan needn't think I'm going to work for him while I'm here!'

Jancis held an almost identical conversation with Keegan, in the office, half an hour later.

'You deliberately misled me,' she accused, 'got me back here under false pretences.'

He gave a lopsided grimace, accompanied by that infuriating lift of his eyebrow.

'Well, at least it got you back here willingly. It might have caused raised brows if you'd left Seafield College slung over my shoulder.'

In spite of her indignation, she could not suppress the smile this picture evoked, and he took the relaxation of her features for a softening of her mood.

'Now that you *are* here, why not stay?' he coaxed. He rose and came round the desk to face her, and she felt that swift tensing of her stomach muscles, which always signalled her reaction to his nearness.

'I . . . I don't want to.'

Helplessly, she stared up into those dark features, his eyes and smiling mouth cajoling her. She had neither the will nor the desire to fight him further. Nevertheless, she backed away out of his reach, certain that, should he touch her, it would prove her undoing.

'Are you afraid of me?' he asked softly.

'No . . . no, why should I be?'

'You always seem to be in retreat. Come here, damn you.'

'I won't . . . why should I? she challenged.

'I seem to recall certain unfinished business between us.'

'Really?' Wilfully misunderstanding, she looked across at her impeccably tidy desk. 'I thought I'd left everything straight.'

'I don't mean that,' he said impatiently, 'and you know it.'

The line of his mouth was grim now, as he moved relentlessly towards her, until he had her trapped between the wall and the immovable bulk of his body.

'D-don't . . .'

She was immobilised, helpless, hypnotised by the gleaming intent in his eyes. He did not have to touch her. As he bent his head, the warm touch of his lips against her was enough to hold her captive; the heat of desire emanating from him was a tangible thing, an indefinable aura of sexual excitement.

But her passivity was not enough for him; he moved

closer, forcing his body against hers, his mouth moving hypnotically upon hers, practised fingers now initiating the caresses he had at first withheld.

Jancis ceased to resist. Instead, there was a wild compulsion now in her response, as her own submerged needs, denied and beaten back for so long, escaped ·the bonds that pride had imposed upon them. Weak, shaken, she pressed against him, her entire being suffused in a sensuous warmth, utterly pliant in her rapturous acceptance of his lovemaking. His kisses deepened, consumed, demanded with hungry insistence, denying even her right to breathe.

But at last, small fists clenched, she beat him off, sobbing for air, fighting for self-control, as reluctantly he released her lips from his suffocating possession.

'Let me go! Please!' She could barely articulate the words, so dry was her throat.

Keegan shook his head. His arms still confined her, his thighs still inflicted their intimate pressure, and she could not but be aware of his desire. She had forgotten just how compelling he could be at close quarters, how he always made blatant use of his sheer virility to overcome all her opposition to his will.

It was ironic to comtemplate how very different her sensations would be if she were in Alyson's happy situation, supremely confident of this man's love; but to continue to submit to this assault upon her deepest, most intimate feelings was to profane all that she held most sacred ... her belief that, while inextricably bound up with its physical expression, love should also be an ennobling, a sanctifying emotion.

Again she resisted him, her body's desires warring with the necessity of rejecting him.

'Damn you! *Will* you let me go!'

'Why?' Lazily, his passion-darkened eyes surveyed her, roaming over her flushed cheeks, dishevelled hair ... her soft, bruised lips.

He bent his head again and she evaded that persistent, seeking mouth to shout the words at him.

'Don't you know why? You should know better than anyone. All right, so you've got me back here ... for the time being. But you're not chaining me to this office. You've no right to demand that I work for you, no right to demand my time . . . and you certainly have no right to demand . . . other things! Do you understand?'

There was an ominous stillness in him, as his lean body went rigid with sudden hostility.

Fearfully, Jancis looked up, to encounter the dangerous glitter of anger in black eyes. Every instinct bade her take back the blistering words, to give herself to him, blindly, unquestioningly. But she fought back the traitorous impulse, steadfastly forcing an image of Alyson to superimpose itself upon his taut features.

'You never give in, do you?' Keegan said huskily. The twist of his lips might almost have been mistaken for anguish, had she not attributed it to his outraged masculine pride.

'Very well, Jancis, from here on in, we'll play it your way. You'll have to ask me . . . beg me to do so, before I will ever lay so much as a finger on you again.'

She forced a glittering smile to her bruised, trembling lips.

'Thank you, kind sir. How magnanimous. That will ensure me a lifetime's immunity!'

The wooden panels of the office reverberated to the violence of his departure, and Jancis was left with the doubtful satisfaction of knowing that she had finally discouraged Keegan's amorous intentions.

CHAPTER TWELVE

'ONLY the two of us for breakfast?' Jancis asked, as she slipped into the seat opposite her mother's one morning a few days later.

Mary King had looked a little depressed during the past week, her daughter thought. Feeling rather low in spirits herself, Jancis had recognised the signs, but now Mary seemed unusually cheerful.

In spite of her enquiry, Jancis was not displeased to find herself alone with her mother for once. Her last meal at this table, dinner the previous evening, had been particularly uncomfortable, ruined by the presence of two hostile witnesses. Only Mary had chatted normally, either not noticing or ignoring the signs of constraint; Alyson had been openly sulking and Keegan had only spoken when good manners demanded it.

Since her outburst in his office, he had not addressed Jancis directly, and Alyson had made no attempt to hide her surprise and resentment at Jancis' unlooked-for return.

'What have you come back for?' she had asked, the instant Keegan and Jancis crossed the threshold.

The younger girl was not usually so blunt in her cousin's presence, taking care normally to show the sweeter side of her nature to Keegan, but for once the careful mask had slipped, showing Alyson in her true light.

Jancis had detected a swift, sideways glance from Keegan, but he had made no comment. Bitterly she thought that, had the positions been reversed, with Alyson on the receiving end of a remark from her, he would have been swift to condemn.

It hadn't taken Jancis many hours to realise that the atmosphere at The Kingdom had changed while she had been away, imperceptibly it was true, but nevertheless there was a subtle difference. Before her departure, she had sometimes felt that she was on one side, Keegan, Alyson and Mary King all ranged against her ... Keegan and Alyson in hostility, Mary in reproachful support of her employer.

Now only Alyson seemed to be actively against her, and for the first time Mary King seemed to recognise Alyson's deliberate sniping at her daughter; while Keegan, apparently, was quietly neutral.

Jancis repeated her opening remark.

'Why only the two of us ... where is everyone?'

'Keegan has gone away for a few days.'

'And Alyson?'

'Alyson went with him.'

Mary King's face broke into a sudden smile, the first Jancis had seen since she came home.

She's pleased, Jancis thought ... pleased that they've gone off together, that the romance between Keegan and Alyson is progressing. My own mother!

Then she reproached herself for unfairness. Mary didn't know how she felt about Keegan ... how could she? Jancis had never dared to confide in her, and now she was glad she hadn't. She couldn't have borne it ... to be the object of her mother's pity. Her mother would mean well, of course, but she would be for ever sighing and looking at Jancis anxiously, continually expressing her sympathy ... and Jancis would never be able to forget, to grow away from her sense of loss and deprivation.

'Where have they gone?' Jancis asked. It cost her a supreme effort to appear casual ... only mildly interested.

'London, I believe,' Mary said vaguely.

'Do you think Alyson will be able to stand the pace?' Jancis asked in surprise.

'Oh, I'm sure Keegan will see to it that she has every comfort,' Mary assured her.

Jancis was sure of it too. She pictured Keegan and Alyson in London, sightseeing, shopping, Keegan solicitously handing his cousin in and out of taxis.

She wondered whereabouts in London they were staying ... and with the thought came another question. Could this be a wedding trip? Were they going to get married while they were away? She fought back the rising panic. Even though she knew it must happen eventually, every day that was not Keegan's wedding day was a reprieve of sorts.

Common sense came to her aid. Surely Keegan would not proceed in such a hole-and-corner fashion. When he got married it would be in splendid style ... a style he would want the world to witness, the seal of happiness being set upon his success.

'Did ... did they say how long they'd be away?' she asked.

Mary gave an exaggerated start.

'Goodness, is that the time? I must get on.'

It seemed that, for some reason, Mary did not want her daughter to enquire too closely into Keegan's activities ... this was so obviously an excuse. There was no reason why her mother should be pressed for time today, Jancis thought. With Keegan away they could all afford to relax.

'Can I help with anything?'

'No ... no, dear, I can manage. Why don't you ...' Mary seemed struck by a sudden inspiration. 'Why don't you go and see that nice little filly Keegan gave you? You haven't been down to the stables much since you got home. That isn't like you. Why, I remember, when you were a little girl, and even since then . . .'

Mary rambled on, as she hastily cleared the table. She seemed unduly anxious to be rid of Jancis, not giving her a chance to interpose a word, let alone to ask a question.

Jancis left her mother and, still thoughtful, wandered down to the yard. She might as well follow her mother's suggestion. Since she had refused to work in the office, she had nothing else to do. For the last week she had been guiltily aware of Keegan trying to catch up on his paperwork and teach the routine to the temporary secretary hired from an agency. She wondered that he had not advertised the post . . . a permanent secretary would be far more satisfactory. She hoped he wasn't still thinking that she could be persuaded to remain.

Suddenly she was eager to see The Linnet, to chat to Fred and the other lads, to hear David's latest news . . . his plans for the wedding which would take place soon.

'Miss Jancey! I was beginning to wonder where you'd got to.'

The sight of Fred's familiar, homely features brought a lump to Jancis' throat.

'It's nice to have you home again, miss.'

'Only for a while,' she told him.

His face fell.

'Thought you'd be home for good this time. Specially as the gaffer . . .' He stopped.

'As the gaffer what? What about Keegan?'

'Oh, nothing . . . just a thought,' he mumbled. 'Suppose you've come back to look at that filly of yours.'

Just like her mother, Fred was changing the subject.

'Yes . . . yes,' she said impatiently, 'in a minute . . . but what were you saying about Keegan?'

He scratched his head, his faded blue eyes avoiding hers.

'Can't rightly remember . . . gone, it has, all of a sudden. Still, p'raps it'll come back to me.'

And perhaps it wouldn't, she thought in exasperation. What *was* going on? First her mother, and now Fred. Why were they acting so mysteriously? It had to be something to do with this trip to London . . . with Keegan, and Alyson.

She felt as if she would go mad with frustrated curiosity if someone didn't enlighten her.

She resolved to take David on one side later.

The Linnet had not forgotten Jancis and shuffled happily, nosing her for the expected titbit. Jancis did not disappoint her, and soon the filly was crunching the chocolate she loved so much.

'She'll be getting fat,' Fred said disparagingly.

'Nonsense, a bit of chocolate won't do her any harm. She's in marvellous condition, Fred.'

'Wasn't referring to the chocolate,' said Fred. 'What I'm saying is, it's about time she did some work.'

Jancis was shocked.

'Do you mean nobody's been exercising her? Oh, Fred, that's not like you!'

'No, no . . .' He shook his grizzled head in denial. 'She's been out with the string, same as usual every morning, 'course she has. I'm talking about races. Gaffer's not declared her for anything. Says she's yours now and that the decision's yours too.'

Jancis looked at him, a worried frown marring her normally smooth brow.

'I can't take the responsibility, Fred. I love The Linnet dearly, you know that, and I was thrilled when Keegan said she was mine . . . but I'm not going to be here much longer, and I certainly can't take her with me.'

Fred regarded her thoughtfully.

'How long you here for then?'

'I . . . I don't know. I have to find another job.'

'What's wrong with the one you've got? That female he's got up there now is neither use nor ornament.'

The faded blue eyes were shrewd and Jancis shifted uneasily from foot to foot. She had never been able to deceive Fred; he could read her through and through. Still, she must try.

'I don't like working for Keegan,' she said firmly, when the silence had grown unbearable. 'I . . . I don't like him.'

'And that's a fib, for a start,' Fred commented.

He opened the half door of The Linnet's stall and led her out, whistling between his teeth as he began to put on the saddle and bridle ready to hand.

'I don't,' Jancis repeated emphatically.

He shot her a quizzical glance.

'You'll have to think of a better one than that . . . you're in love with him,' he said, his tone so prosaic that Jancis could have laughed, if she'd felt able to. 'And don't try to deny it to me my girl. The evidence is written all over you, when he's about.'

Jancis gave a shaky smile.

'Dear, knowing old Fred! I never could fool you, could I? You're right, of course . . . only that's just between you and me, remember. I only hope it isn't as obvious to anyone else . . . to him. I couldn't bear that.'

'Nope,' said Fred, adjusting The Linnet's stirrups. 'He hasn't a clue. Because,' he added somewhat cryptically, 'he's as blind as you are.'

Blind! Jancis thought. She would scarcely have called Keegan blind. Sometimes those dark penetrating eyes saw too much. She supposed Fred must mean that Keegan was blind to Alyson's faults.

'Now,' Fred went on, as he gave a final check to the girths, 'there you are, Miss Jancey. You just get up aloft and get out on to the downs . . . blow some of that cobwebby nonsense out of your head. Nothing like a bit of fresh air for making you see straight.'

Jancis looked down at him from the saddle. The filly, scenting exercise, was restless and eager to be off.

'What are you trying to say, Fred?'

'Ah!' He shook his head. 'That'd be telling . . . and now isn't the time or the place. All I'm saying is there's none so blind as those that don't want to see. Off you go now—I've got work to do.'

He was as bad as her mother, Jancis thought as she turned the filly's head towards the gallops . . . only worse, because he had said far more . . . only, infuriatingly, none of it made sense.

She could understand Fred wanting her to stay here . . . she supposed it would have appealed to his sense of the rightness of things, if she had married Keegan, been mistress of The Kingdom as her mother before had been. That would have pleased the elderly man, her friend since childhood. Well, it would have pleased her too . . . what a totally inadequate word 'pleased' was! But it was no use dwelling on it. Neither she nor Fred would get their wish.

It was a perfect day for a ride ... a mild, gilded autumn day; the gentle, slanting morning light held just enough warmth to draw a gentle, steaming mist from the earth, bringing to her nostrils the sweet, pervading scent of damp grass, which blended deliciously with that of leather and saddle soap.

This really was her element ... away from here, she was only half alive. The realisation came to her suddenly. Even before she'd met Keegan, fallen in love with him, when she had thought she was enjoying her career, she had missed all this, had looked forward with eager anticipation to the long school holidays.

How could she ever bear to go away again, to be cooped up in a classroom or an office, now that this place held more ... so much more. To her love of the rolling countryside, of her gracious old home, of the beautiful horseflesh which filled the stables, had been added another obsession, more potent than any of the rest, to draw her back to The Kingdom ... dearer to her heart than any of the loved familiar sights, sounds and scents.

A mood of reckless desperation possessed her and she clapped her heels to The Linnet's sides, giving the filly full rein, as she responded to this sudden demand. Horse and rider seemed to be flying an inch above the ground, the speed of their going startling into flight small birds and scuttling rabbits. Over the springy, resilient surface of the downs they blazed, light and swift as fire ... a blur of speed that flashed the downlands unfocused past Jancis' eyes.

She leant lower and lower over The Linnet's neck, exulting in the sensation of movement. All it needed, she thought, was other horses ... opposition to outstrip ... a race.

'Whoa, Linnet, whoa ... steady, steady!'

She pulled The Linnet into a wide circle, gradually slowing to a canter, then to a jagged trot and at last to a walk.

A race? Why not? The filly was hers now, for a while at any rate ... for as long as she chose to remain. Keegan couldn't raise any objection, if she entered The Linnet in an event, and rode the filly herself; and even if he did have any objection, groundless or otherwise, he wasn't here to prevent her.

Filled with determination and a new sense of purpose, she turned the filly for home, anxious to consult Fred, to see how soon a suitable race could be obtained.

To her surprise, Fred made no demur. She had expected to have to coax him into letting her ride. Instead, he seemed enthusiastic at the idea.

'Why not, it'd do you good. Give you something better to think about than the silly notions you've had in your head lately,' he grunted.

Silly ideas! Jancis supposed he meant her being in love with Keegan. It didn't seem silly to her ... just useless. Still, Fred must know as well as she that Keegan's sights were set on Alyson, so maybe he was right. She did need a new interest, and this would do very well for the time being, until Keegan chose to return.

Then she would move on. She would ask him to take the filly back. He surely wouldn't refuse. The Linnet was a splendid little animal and by that time might have a couple more wins to her credit.

Fred's only stipulation, his sole condition for help-ing her, was that she did not reveal her plans to her mother.

'No point in worrying your ma,' he said. 'Stands to reason she'd worry, if she knew you were riding yourself.'

'Now, remember,' Fred said for the umpteenth time, as they loaded The Linnet into her travelling box, 'this isn't an important race in terms of money.'

'No, Fred,' Jancis repeated obediently ... also for the umpteenth time.

'It's more of a comeback for The Linnet, and a little test for you.'

'Yes, Fred.' He had also made this remark before.

'And remember, this filly is a stayer. She likes to get out in front and stay there.'

'I'll remember.'

'You don't *have* to win. I'll be happy just to see you finish the course. Of course, if you *can* get her name in the frame . . .'

'Fred!' Jancis protested. 'I'm going to win. I am *not* going to be "in the frame" . . . second or third isn't good enough for The Linnet. She's going to be first.'

She watched the filly enter the box, quietly confident in her handlers, latent power in every stride of those gleaming quarters.

Four days earlier they had declared The Linnet, as statute demanded, and for those four days Jancis had been in a fever of excitement and anxiety . . . anxiety lest Keegan should return too soon and put some obstacle in the way of her plans. But now race day was here and her anxiety had given way to nervous excitement.

'Looks like rain,' Fred grunted, as the Range Rover towing its load turned on to the main road.

Jancis scanned the sky heavy with clouds . . . grey phantoms, pregnant with rain.

'Not to worry,' Fred told her. 'The Linnet doesn't mind if the going's a bit soft.'

The rain was still holding off, when they reached the course, much to Jancis' relief. This particular racecourse was a bleak place at the best of times, wide open to the four winds, and there was still a slight chill in the air . . . the chill which heralded the onset of autumn.

The stadium was already thronging with boisterous, enthusiastic punters, as they unboxed the filly.

Jancis made her way towards the weighing-in room, presided over by the Clerk of the Scales, carrying her saddle and martingale. There were no problems and, the weigh-in satisfactorily concluded, technically, she knew she was supposed to relax, while Fred prepared her mount. But to her this seemed the tensest moment of the day, with nothing to do except imagine what might go wrong in the race ahead of her. There was a slight feeling of sickness in her stomach as she experienced a faint presage of ill luck, the sweat breaking out on her forehead, as her limbs trembled uncontrollably.

It was a lonely feeling . . . the knowledge that once the race had started, she would be out there, to all intents and purposes, alone. Nobody else could help her.

Irresistibly, her thoughts turned to Keegan. Where was

he? What was he doing at this moment? Presumably enjoying himself somewhere with Alyson, little knowing what his erstwhile secretary was up to. Jancis shivered again, as she remembered his wrath after some of her earlier escapades. Still . . . she lifted her chin, unconsciously straightening her back . . . The Linnet was her horse, and she was no longer in Keegan's employ. She was free of him . . . as free as she ever would be, she qualified the thought.

By now the runners and riders had been announced over the public address system. It was time to make her way to the parade ring, where already the veterinary surgeon was checking each horse, paying particular attention to shoes and the way the bit had been fitted.

'All right, Miss Jancey?' Fred asked.

Jancis nodded wordlessly. Now that the race was almost upon her, she felt far from all right.

Fred, with years of experience of jockeys, of race-day nerves, patted her shoulder encouragingly.

'You'll be all right, love. Just remember everything I've taught you. Up you go now!'

Jancis was glad that it was Fred's hand on the leading rein as they circled the parade ring, and she began to glance around her, studying the mood of the other horses, assessing the competition.

She drew a sharp breath as she recognised Sam Roscoe, riding the showy chestnut he had ridden at Newcastle. Surely he wasn't still riding for Dutch's Dyke, now that the stables belonged to Keegan. She leant down to question Fred.

'No, he's not with Louie Dutch any more . . . but that chestnut belongs to Roscoe himself. I've no idea who he rides for these days.'

'He wasn't warned off, then,' said Jancis, 'after the business with The Linnet?'

Fred shrugged. 'Apparently there wasn't sufficient evidence against him. Mortimer was the one who copped it.'

'Tell me something, Fred. It's puzzled me ever since. Why should a well-to-do man like Nick Mortimer take a risk like that? It doesn't make sense . . . he couldn't have needed the money?'

'Seems he did,' said Fred. 'All came out when the police

tackled him. Mortimer Plastics had been on the downward slide for some time.'

'Poor Nick,' Jancis said involuntarily. She couldn't forget that they'd once been friends.

'Poor Nick, nothing,' Fred retorted. 'You want to watch out for him . . . and Roscoe. They're still mates, and Sam's not above a bit of bumping and boring . . . bear you a grudge for a long time, he will.'

'That chestnut he's riding is the same one that beat The Skylark at Newcastle,' Jancis commented.

'Well, that was The Skylark . . . she won't beat The Linnet,' Fred said confidently. 'Too long and low, and heavy on the shoulder.' He checked girths and elastic breast girth, then slipped the leading rein. 'Good luck, Miss Jancey.'

As she returned Fred's grin, Jancis was aware of a sudden flurry, as colourful umbrellas began to mushroom. Somehow the bookies always anticipated the actual moment when the first drops of rain would fall. It looked as if she was in for a wet ride.

The horses filed out of the parade ring and as Jancis awaited her turn to pass through the gap in the rails, she caught sight of a familiar face in the crowd pressing against the barrier.

'Keegan!' she breathed, as her appalled gaze met that of the dark eyes in a taut, set face. He was so near that if she had reached out with her whip, she could have touched him.

'What the hell do you think you're doing?'

She could not hear the words above the tumultuous noise of the crowd, but it was all too easy to make out the words formed by his lips.

It was a relief when she had passed him. Just for a moment, she had experienced a wild, illogical fear that he would leap the barrier and physically restrain her from going down to the post.

What on earth was he doing here? He was supposed to be in London, with Alyson. Was their holiday over already? And why, out of all the racecourses in England, had he chosen to come here? As if she wasn't nervous enough, she had to ride with the knowledge of those dark disapproving eyes upon her performance.

Though Keegan had been forced to admit that she rode well, and had allowed her to exercise with his string, he had never extended this amnesty to any other girl ... and many had applied to him for a job in the past months. He still held fast to his distaste for women in a stable, and despite his concession to her, Jancis knew he certainly would not approve of her riding in an actual race. He not only disliked female stablehands, but also disapproved of women jockeys.

'Well, like it or not, there was nothing he could do about it, she thought triumphantly.

The Linnet's behaviour going down to the post was impeccable, her stride sweeping, majestic, and Jancis thought back with self-contempt to the last race in which she had ridden. How could she possibly have mistaken The Skylark for The Linnet? There was no comparison.

The moments before they came under starter's orders seemed some of the longest in Jancis' life ... and the loneliest. Here they were, she thought, congregating for a race ... something that ought to be a social occasion, an opportunity for exchanging conversation, a joke perhaps ... confiding their nervous fears. Instead, each jockey seemed lost in a world of his own, silent and withdrawn, preoccupied in the nervous introspection, which, she knew, affected many participants just before a sporting event.

As if attuned to the mood of their riders, horses frisked rebelliously, one actually unseating its jockey and running loose. There was the inevitable delay while the animal was recaptured and its rider reinstated in the saddle.

The starter called the roll, and Jancis noticed that Roscoe's mount was giving trouble ... either that or he was indulging in a bit of gamesmanship, sidling into and jostling other runners. Finally, a steward came forward to lead the chestnut, keeping such a tight hold on her head that she had no choice but to move crabwise to the stalls.

Jancis had intercepted a few glowering looks from Sam Roscoe, and this increased her already nervous tension. She was glad to see that he had been drawn well away from her, and vowed she would maintain that distance at all costs.

The Linnet had been drawn in the inside position, on the rails, and at the signal, the field surged away in a tightly packed formation, The Linnet going so strongly that Jancis had difficulty in restraining her until a gap appeared, and as soon as the filly saw daylight, she took command.

Soon the field began to spread out and the battle was on in earnest. There were six horses still ahead of Jancis, and one by one The Linnet began to pick them off. The camber of the bends was perfect for maintaining an even stride and the filly was pulling hard for her head, eager to overtake the remaining opposition. She powered her way into second place, with only the chestnut ridden by Sam Roscoe to overtake.

When asked for the final effort, the filly gave it unstintingly. As they began to draw level, Jancis saw Sam look back over his shoulder, and below the goggles, his face contorted in a furious grimace.

She knew what he was going to do before he jerked viciously on the left-hand rein, causing the chestnut to veer in front of her. It was a flagrant bit of crossing, and on the run in too ... right in front of the stands.

There was no time really, or space, to take evasive action, but instinctively Jancis tried, as she saw the whites of the chestnut's eyes rolling back, in a prelude to a hefty kick.

The Linnet, for once startled out of her stride, almost stopped dead, and Jancis lost an iron as she was jerked forward. She tried desperately to kick free of the other stirrup, as the filly went down, but with a thrill of horror she felt her boot go through the stirrup iron, twisting round, as The Linnet thrashed about on the ground and the rest of the field swept by.

Then The Linnet was struggling to her feet, and in a split second of terror, before she lost consciousness, Jancis knew that if the filly set off to follow the other runners, she would be pulled under the animal's hoofs, kicked and cut about by the steel racing plates.

Jancis regained consciousness in the clinical whiteness of a hospital room. It took her a while to realise where she was, to recall how she must have come to be there. Experimentally, she moved first one arm, then the other. She tried her legs. Miraculously she seemed to be intact ... nothing broken. She lifted her head from the pillow, then winced and fell back hastily as the room spun round, a kaleidoscope in shades of whirling white, as her head throbbed unmercifully.

She put up her hand to feel the swathe of bandages . . . she must have sustained a severe blow to the head.

The door opened and a white-capped head came round it. The young nurse smiled cheerfully.

'Back in the land of the living, Miss King? I'll tell the doctor you're awake.' She turned and spoke over her shoulder to someone Jancis could not see. 'You can come in now, sir, but remember . . . only five minutes.'

Expecting, for some reason, to see Keegan, Jancis was flooded with disappointment when Fred's gnarled little figure entered the room, cloth cap clutched tightly in his hands.

The nurse placed a chair at the bedside and withdrew, repeating her remark that the doctor would be along presently. Fred sat on the extreme edge of the chair.

'Rare fright you gave us, Miss Jancey,' he told her.

'I scared myself a bit, too,' she said ruefully. 'What happened? I expected to be kicked to pieces.'

'Ah, and you can thank the gaffer you're not.'

'Keegan?'

'Mmmm . . . real quick thinking on his part that saved you. Right on the rails in front of the stands, he was. Seems he anticipated foul play on Roscoe's part. The minute that chestnut began to veer, he was over the rails . . . no holding him . . . and by the time the rest of the field was past, he was at The Linnet's head. Good little beast hadn't bolted straight off. It was those few seconds when she stood that saved your bacon, I reckon.'

Jancis' eyes filled with weak tears.

'The Linnet . . . is . . . is she all right?'

'Not a scratch on her,' Fred said cheerfully. 'So don't you fret about her, Miss Jancey.'

'What . . . what did Keegan say?' she asked fearfully. 'Was he furious?'

'With that Sam Roscoe, he was. I think if the stewards hadn't intervened, he'd have knocked the living daylights out of him there and then.'

'Where is Keegan now?'

He might have come to the hospital himself, she thought.

She felt in need right now of his strength.

'Stewards' enquiry,' Fred said laconically. 'Technically The Linnet is still his responsibility, as her trainer.'

At this moment the nurse returned, followed by a doctor, and Fred got up to leave.

'Fred . . .' Jancis held out a detaining hand, 'where are you going?'

'Home, lass. D'you know what time it is? You've been out cold for nearly four hours . . . it's eight o'clock. It'll be ten by the time I get back. I need my beauty sleep if I'm to be up for morning stables.'

Jancis turned to the doctor. 'Can I go home with Mr Higgins?' she pleaded.

'You're a very brave young lady, I understand, but you have had a severe blow to the head. I think we must at least keep you in overnight. Then we'll see.'

'Doctor says you can go home today.' It was a different nurse who brought Jancis the good news. 'We're sending you in an ambulance, just to be on the safe side, and when you get home you're to go straight to bed.'

Jancis was amazed at how wobbly her legs felt, as the nurse helped her into a wheelchair, and she was very glad not to have to walk the miles of corridor that led to the ambulance bay.

Although she was lying down, the ride was not as comfortable as Jancis could have wished, and she thought wistfully that she would have felt better riding in Keegan's well-sprung car. Still, she supposed it was too much to expect him to come all this way to pick her up. He was probably thinking that all this discomfort served her right, for her reckless behaviour.

Only it *hadn't* been reckless, she thought somewhat resentfully. There were plenty of women jockeys these days, and she rode as well as any of them. In fact, if it hadn't been for Sam Roscoe's villainy, she would have won that race. She was sure of it.

It was pleasant to be in bed, in her own room, with her mother fussing over her. Almost like old times, when she had been confined with some childish ailment. She could almost imagine that at any moment her father's head would pop round the door, with a cheery, 'How's my girl, then?'

The head that did appear round her door later that evening was Keegan's.

Jancis had been sitting up, attempting to read, although her head tended to throb a little. The bandages had been removed and she was very conscious of the ugly purple bruises only a fraction away from her temple. She was lucky to be alive, she knew . . . only she didn't *feel* lucky. She supposed it was delayed shock, but she felt depressed, with a distressing desire to burst into tears every time she thought about the future, when she would have to leave The Kingdom again.

'How's our little jockey, then?'

The tone if not the exact words was so like her father's would have been that Jancis felt the tears begin to brim over.

'Hey, that's enough of that! I'm not supposed to upset you.' Keegan came to sit on the edge of her bed, looking at her with real concern upon his rugged face.

Not supposed to upset her! Didn't he realise that he had upset the rest of her life? She regarded him mistily.

'Wh-what are you doing here?'

'Visiting the sick,' he said gravely. 'Your mother had to go out, so I said I'd look in to see if you were all right.'

Mary King out . . . that was an innovation. Jancis couldn't remember the last time her mother had gone out in the evening, unless it had been with her father to a social function. She realised, with some apprehension, that she was alone with Keegan . . . no, not quite alone, of course, Alyson would be around somewhere. Strangely, this thought was disappointing rather than reassuring.

'Is there anything you want . . . need?' Keegan asked.

She stared at him, brown eyes still moistly luminous. If only she could tell him what she really wanted . . . really needed. She sought frantically for a safe topic of conversation.

'Did . . . did you and Alyson enjoy your holiday?'

'It wasn't exactly a holiday,' he told her, 'but never mind that for the moment. I have a few words to say to you, young lady.'

Not exactly a holiday . . . then it *had* been a special trip of some kind. Jancis felt her tongue cleave to the roof of a

suddenly dry mouth . . . and to top it all, Keegan was about
to lecture her, and she didn't think she could bear it.

'That was some race you rode!' Keegan told her. 'Pity that
. . . that Roscoe fellow ruined it for you. I really believe you
would have won.'

She stared at him, disbelief in her expression. He wasn't
angry. He was actually praising her.

'How's the head?' he added.

Remembering the unsightly bruise, she put up a hand to
hide it.

'Sore,' she said feelingly.

He leant forward, a swift movement which took her by
surprise, and removing the sheltering hand, brushed his lips
over the bruised skin.

Still in a highly charged state of emotion, she flinched
away from him.

'Don't,' she gasped. 'Don't do that!'

He frowned. 'I thought I'd been very gentle.'

'You were . . . oh, you were, but I . . .'

'Don't like me to touch you.'

His brows drew together in a scowl. Now he *was* going to
be angry. Jancis lay back against her pillows, her face pale
with fear.

Keegan stood up and began to pace restlessly. He moved
around the room, much as Alyson had once done, inspecting
the furnishings. When he came to the collection of horses, he
picked one up, lightly tracing its shape with an appreciative
finger.

'Lovely,' he murmured. He put the horse down abruptly
and turned towards Jancis. 'We have so much in common.
Why don't we get on?' His tone was terse.

Jancis pleated and re-pleated the edge of her quilt, her
eyes as intent upon her fingers as if they had been
performing an important task.

'I . . . I don't know.'

She did know. It was because she was so wildly attracted
to him, because she mustn't show it, so that she was forced
to appear antagonistic . . . rejecting any overtures of
friendship from him.

'I'm sure we could get on . . . very well.'

His voice was coaxing, as he returned to the bedside. He

took one of her hands, spreading the slender fingers, caressing each one in turn. 'Couldn't we try . . . see how we get on?'

'There's no point.' She hoped the trembling of her body beneath the covers was not apparent. 'I shan't be here much longer.'

'But why?' The cry was almost agonised, almost as if it mattered to him. 'Have I ever made you feel unwanted, tried to drive you away?'

'No,' she admitted, her voice low and husky, her eyes still lowered before his probing gaze. She was driving herself away, running scared, afraid for her own self-respect.

Keegan sat down again, reaching for her.

'Look at me, Jancis,' he ordered. He forced her chin up. 'Look at me and tell me the truth for once. I always feel that you're evading me, that I can't reach you . . . the real you, that is. You . . . you seem to erect a barrier around yourself that I can't penetrate. Damn it, Jancis, be yourself just for once! Let me be near you.'

She dared not let him near her, either mentally or physically, though the latter was the most dangerous. Verbally, she was capable of fencing with him, but physically he could overwhelm her . . . and he was reaching out for her now and they were quite alone and she was still weak from the effects of concussion.

'Don't,' she moaned. 'Keegan, I . . .'

Her words were stifled by his mouth, as he began to kiss her, one hand held her firmly against his broad chest, while the free hand began to caress her in places that she had never dreamt could be so sensitive . . . so responsive, sending ripples of ecstasy through her.

A groan of desire escaped her, as gently he pressed her down against the pillows, imprisoning her with his own weight, making her aware of the urgent demands of his body. She shifted against him, wanting, needing to be closer, and she felt his hand begin to remove the lightweight quilt that covered her. It was then that she realised just what she was doing. She was allowing him to make love to her, and soon it would be too late to stop him.

With a strength she did not know she possessed, she thrust him from her and gripping the quilt with both hands, she pulled it high about her shoulders, staring at him over the top with eyes made larger and brighter with fear.

'Now what?' he shouted furiously. 'What *is* it with you, Jancis? Do you hate me . . . is that what it is? Because . . .'

'No!' She cried the word aloud, tortured because she could not tell him that her feelings were the very reverse of hatred.

'Then what *is* it? I've always thought of you as being such a straightforward, honest girl. In the past you never scrupled to tell me your feelings.'

She racked her brain for a reason . . . an excuse which would sound acceptable to him. The truth he demanded was too damaging to her pride . . . that she had to go away, because she loved him and he didn't love her, he loved Alyson. Alyson! That was it. It wasn't a watertight excuse, but it would have to do.

'Why won't you stay?' he reiterated.

'I know she's your cousin, Keegan, but I just couldn't live happily in the same house as Alyson. We . . . we don't get on.'

And I couldn't bear to see her as your wife, she thought, to know that she was there with you . . . in your bed . . .

The moody expression disappeared from his tanned face.

'Then there's no problem. Alyson isn't here any more.'

'Not . . . not here?' She stared at him. 'You mean she's still on holiday? But she'll be back.'

'No, she's not coming back.'

'Not . . .'

'By now Alyson is in Australia.'

'Australia? But I thought you . . . she . . .'

'So apparently did Alyson.' Keegan smiled grimly. 'I must have been blind to what was going on in her mind. But I swear to you, I didn't realise her plans for me until just recently. Then I knew I had to act . . . fast. But I had to be careful. I didn't want to hurt the poor kid . . . she really isn't very robust.'

'But how did you . . .?'

'I telephoned Australia.'

Just like that, she thought, as if it were the most ordinary, mundane thing in the world.

'And I asked our relations there to invite her over.'

Keegan smiled. 'They have some very attractive sons, nearer Alyson's age. I'll hazard a guess it won't be long before she's forgotten all about Keegan Leroy.'

As if any woman who had ever seen Keegan could forget him, Jancis thought wistfully. Aloud, she asked:

'But what did you tell Alyson . . . didn't she object?'

'Vociferously,' he grinned. Then his eyes softened. 'Poor kid!'

'Hardly that, with all her money!'

'All that she has left of her family,' he reminded her gently. 'Better surely to have living parents than just their worldly goods. Riches don't make you any the less lonely.'

'No, but they can be very useful, in businesses such as this.'

'Meaning what?' Keegan asked, a dangerous glitter in his eyes. 'Are you still harking back to that old resentment, that I bought The Kingdom . . .?'

'No . . . no,' Jancis assured him hastily. 'I was referring to Alyson's money. It would have been very useful to you, if you . . . if she . . .'

His eyes narrowed. 'You really think I would marry a girl for her money?'

'No . . . yes . . . that is, I thought you probably loved her too.'

'Oh, thank you,' Keegan said sarcastically. 'At least you didn't consider me utterly mercenary!'

It was time to change the subject, before they began covering the old familiar hostile ground.

'How did you persuade Alyson to go?' Jancis asked.

'I told her I was going to marry you.'

'*What?*'

Her startled cry brought him back to her bedside in two strides.

'It's no use, Jancis. Oh, don't worry, I'm not going to touch you . . . but I can't hide it from you any longer. I've always wanted to marry you, right from the start . . . ever since that ridiculous incident at Doncaster, when your horse nearly flattened me. I . . . I told your father, when . . .'

'You did?' she breathed.

It was unbelievable. Keegan was standing in front of her, his hawk-like features contorted in an agony of loving and longing mingled with despair, telling her that he wanted to marry her . . . Her! Jancis!

'I told him, when he came to me that time . . . that's why I had to blackmail you to stay here. I wanted a chance to get to know you, to give you a chance to get to know me, to realise that I wasn't as black as your imagination had painted me. I thought, if we were under the same roof long enough, saw each other every day . . .' He shrugged helplessly. 'But instead, I seemed to do everything wrong . . . put your back up still further. When you teamed up with Mortimer I was so jealous . . .' He smote the palm of his hand with the fist of the other. 'God, it was agony! And then those foolish risks you took. I thought you'd kill yourself before I had a chance to make you love me.'

He laughed. It was a bitter sound.

'I might as well have spared myself all the agony. It did no good, did it? You . . .'

'Keegan! Shut up a minute!'

His impassioned flow of words peremptorily interrupted, he stared at her.

'Shut up and let me get a word in. We must be the biggest pair of fools alive today. Now I know what Fred meant about "blindness!" Just tell me one thing . . . no, two. Did my mother know you wanted to marry me? And did she and Fred know where you were this last week, what you were doing?'

'Yes to both questions . . . but I don't see . . .'

Jancis held out her hands towards him with a pretty, inviting gesture.

'Keegan!' His name was a caress on her lips, an expression of all her pent-up longing.

Like a man in a dream, he moved towards her, sinking on to the bed, as if his legs had suddenly refused to hold him.

'Jancis? You mean? You . . . you *love* me?'

Wordlessly, she nodded.

He shook his head disbelievingly.

'I want to hear you say it . . . actually say the words,' he whispered.

She leant forward, encircling his neck with her arms, feathering his cheek with her lips, punctuating her words with kisses.

'Keegan . . . my darling, darling, Keegan. I love you. I've

loved you for ages, and . . .' her voice faltered. 'I want you so much that it hurts!'

He drew back a little, taking her face between his hands, regarding her intently and his desire was in his eyes, leaping, flickering, yet held in check.

'We'll be married?'

She nodded.

'Soon?'

'Very soon,' she whispered. 'Please!'

Keegan was quite still.

'You know we're alone here? Your mother really *is* out.' Jancis' voice was shaky.

'Will she be long?'

'Ages!'

His eyes were questioning, but he was holding back, waiting for her assent.

Slowly, gently, she drew his head down to her breast, where a scanty nightdress revealed the valley between her small but perfect breasts. Tremulously she guided his mouth to one nipple, taut, erect, responsive.

Keegan gave a great shuddering sigh and his eagerness tempered by gentleness, he drew back the quilt. This time she made no effort to prevent him.

As tangible as the touch of his hand, his eyes were a warm caress on the softness of her breasts, moving downwards to the curve of a slim waist, the swell of a thigh. Dark eyes looked lingeringly into soft brown. He kissed her, softly, experimentally at first, then inflamed by her fierce response, his hand swept the length of her back, caressing the sensitive area at the base of her spine, moulding the soft firm buttocks, pulling her tightly against him.

The soft willingness of her compliance aroused him still further and he swore impatiently, as he struggled with the waistband of his trousers.

With a little thrill of amazement at her own temerity, Jancis helped him to shed his garments, welcoming him back into her arms with eager impatience. His hands moved once more over the silky skin of her breasts, gently finding the most sensitive parts of her body, controlling his own rising desire, as he brought her to a fever pitch of almost unbearable longing.

Endearments, murmurs of pleasure mingled on their lips, as their mutual need became exquisitely intolerable, racking their closely pressed bodies with more and more violent shudders.

Sensation mounted ... climaxed ... subsided. Jancis cried out, then whispered her delight against his lips. They rested closely together, unwilling to end this first perfect moment of physical intimacy.

Dimly, through a haze of sensual well-being, Jancis heard Keegan's murmured words.

'Jancis, my very own darling, you ... you are Keegan's Kingdom.'

"THE MOSTEST HORSE THAT EVER WAS"

In 1919, at a New England racetrack, a stable jockey named Johnny Loftus was given a two-year-old racehorse called Man o' War to ride. After Loftus mounted, the horse reared up on his hind legs, took three great bounds and galloped half a mile down the track in forty-seven seconds. Johnny, an experienced horseman, dismounted pale and wide-eyed. Never had he ridden such a horse. But then, never had there been such a horse as Man o' War!

Man o' War was bred by a Kentucky horse racer from a stallion named Fair Play and a mare named Mahubah. Both came from a long line of champions.

As a colt, Man o' War was sold to Samuel Riddle, a Pennsylvania manufacturer. The horse was tall and gangly, and Riddle thought he might make a good hunter. Because Man o' War had rich chestnut-colored hair, the stable boys began calling him "Big Red," a nickname that soon became widely popular.

And big he was! His groom called him "the mostest horse that ever was." But not just because of his size. Man o' War was the strongest and fastest racehorse of his day, a true champion. In his two-year career, this giant Thoroughbred broke seven track records, winning hundreds of thousands of dollars and losing only one race.

Man o' War sired many well-known racehorses, but none quite as unforgettable as he was. People who know horses say that racing legends are born not only of beauty and speed but of personality and courage. The great Man o' War had them all.

HARLEQUIN
PREMIERE AUTHOR EDITIONS

6 top Harlequin authors—6 of their best books!

1. JANET DAILEY Giant of Mesabi
2. CHARLOTTE LAMB Dark Master
3. ROBERTA LEIGH Heart of the Lion
4. ANNE MATHER Legacy of the Past
5. ANNE WEALE Stowaway
6. VIOLET WINSPEAR The Burning Sands

Harlequin is proud to offer these 6 exciting romance novels by 6 of our most popular authors. In brand-new beautifully designed covers, each Harlequin Premiere Author Edition is a bestselling love story—a contemporary, compelling and passionate read to remember!

Available in September wherever paperback books are sold, or through Harlequin Reader Service. Simply complete and mail the coupon below.

Harlequin Reader Service

In the U.S.
P.O. Box 52040
Phoenix, Ariz., 85072-9988

In Canada
649 Ontario Street
Stratford, Ontario N5A 6W2

Please send me the following editions of **Harlequin Premiere Author Editions.** I am enclosing my check or money order for $1.95 for each copy ordered, plus 75¢ to cover postage and handling.

☐ 1 ☐ 2 ☐ 3 ☐ 4 ☐ 5 ☐ 6

Number of books checked _____ @ $1.95 each = $ _____

N.Y. state and Ariz. residents add appropriate sales tax $ _____

Postage and handling $ _____.75

I enclose $ _____ TOTAL $ _____

(Please send check or money order. We cannot be responsible for cash sent through the mail.) Price subject to change without notice.

NAME _____
(Please Print)

ADDRESS _____ APT. NO. _____

CITY _____

STATE/PROV. _____ ZIP/POSTAL CODE _____

PA-S

Offer expires January 31, 1984 30756000000

4 FREE
Harlequin Romances

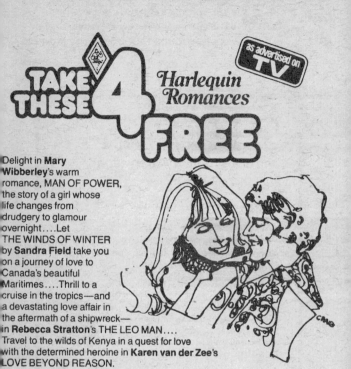